Even with his nose plugs in place, the reek from the lozenge-shaped container hit Peter hard. It was acrid, with overtones of putrefying sweetness. The odor sank deep into his lungs and then plummeted past them into his stomach. He stared with nauseated bewilderment at what the tank contained.

Floating in a particle-clouded but otherwise clear liquid was a chalky grayish green, marrow-shaped object. It was about five feet long and totally featureless. A circular alloy band was clamped around its narrower end, with wires leading from it to connections at the far end of the tank. More wires and flexible tubes projected from it at various points, fanning out to other connections around the tank's perimeter. The thing was passive, making no movement of any kind. As he watched, he realized that the clouding of the liquid was being caused by the slow disintegration of what was suspended in it.

"It is dead, as you can see," Corma said.

THE BIG LOSERS

Robert J. Tilley

Cover illustration by David Cherry

New Infinities Productions, Inc.
P.O. Box 657
Delavan WI 53115

THE BIG LOSERS

The New Infinities Productions logo is a trademark owned
by New Infinities Productions, Inc.

The name "Ace" and the "A" logo are trademarks belonging
to Charter Communications, Inc.

First Printing, June 1988

Printed in the United States of America

Distributed to the book trade by the Berkley Publishing
Group, 200 Madison Avenue, New York NY 10016

9 8 7 6 5 4 3 2 1

I S B N: 0-441-06091-9

New Infinities Productions, Inc.
P.O. Box 657
Delavan WI 53115

For Rachel and Steve

Some are born to sweet delight,
Some are born to endless night.
                              — William Blake

1

Stillness was their first line of defense.

*Without weapons or adequate protective casing and sur-
rounded by a remorselessly steady growth in predatory activity, an unkind biological matrix had made it necessary
for them to develop their own unique pattern for survival.
Normal mobility would have betrayed their true nature, and
since the alternative was linked in their racial consciousness
to the reproductive process, they viewed it as an ability that
was to be used for defensive purposes only in cases of extreme emergency.*

*Instead, they had taught themselves over a long evolu-
tionary period the techniques of withdrawal, blurring their
recognizable characteristics to near-anonymity. The proper-
ties that made them distinguishable to the visual and olfactory senses were gradually suppressed, and further dis-
guised by the mixture of small crustaceans and trailing
weeds that they permitted to accumulate around them, so
that to the eye and nose of the passing observer they were
now odorless and therefore, logically, tasteless environmen-
tal ingredients that belonged in the same neutral category
as a rock or some other inanimate feature of the seabed.*

*Their world was almost entirely internal now. The only
movements they normally made were when their ingestion
orifice opened to permit entry of the algae that permanently*

clouded the water in which they rested, and the occasional discreet excremental ejection that occurred at their bulkier end. Once a year each of them brought its distinctive ability into use, instantaneously relocating itself in shallower, less nutritious but thinly inhabited water where it reproduced by fission, precipitating miniatures of itself into the surrounding sea. Those that were fortunate enough to complete their natural life span similarly removed themselves to the barren neutrality of the sandbanks, where they could die and rot without witness.

Despite their reluctance to utilize their special ability as a second line of defense, its use was occasionally necessary when they attempted to evade the attention of some curious newcomer to the area that they normally inhabited. Eventually, their presence was detected by the biological sensors of a deep-space probe that had been circling the planet for several weeks and which had already registered the activity responsible for the generation and maintenance of their internal existence. The probe found these behavioral idiosyncrasies interesting enough for it to immobilize several specimens and extract them for later analysis.

2

On an evening in April 1920, Sidney Walsh sprawled amiably on the living-room sofa of a pleasant apartment in Cleveland, Ohio, not exactly drunk but not entirely sober, either.

Sidney Walsh was tall and had the kind of fair, slightly creased good looks that both sexes found attractive. He had grey-green eyes and a humorous mouth with a small scar just below the right corner that he liked to jokingly tell people had been caused by a fleck of shrapnel during his time in France, although he had actually only nicked a piece out of himself when somebody had jogged his shaving arm on the troopship on the way home. On this particular evening he was twenty-eight years, four months and six days old, and although he didn't know it for a cast-iron fact, he had what he saw as a very good reason for believing that he was on the threshold of a highly successful career in light engineering.

It had been a good day, Sidney thought. He let his mind wander contentedly over its events. A very good day. There had been no denying that he'd had his share of worries and frustration lately, but now that Meakin & Fox had made the decision, he'd be able to get on with the expansion program without any more fooling around.

Good times, Sidney told himself, are just around the

corner. Tum-tiddly-tum-tum. . . . "Tum, tum," he said aloud. He belched, lightly, and looked around the room. It was fairly large, with moderately expensive, carefully chosen furniture. It looked like the living room of somebody who wasn't doing at all badly; nothing really extravagant, no overt signs of what might have been called real prosperity, yet somehow hinting that it could be a preface to such possibilities.

To Sidney's presently self-satisfied eye, it looked very much like a promising beginning, a secure base on which it would now be safe to build.

"Darling, I'm going to bed," his wife said. "Mildred can cope with this stuff in the morning." She had come back into the room from the kitchen and was sweeping crumbs onto the last of the plates that they had eaten off. They usually ate in the dining room, but because of Sidney's good news about Meakin & Fox and because they hadn't really felt like going out they'd had a kind of celebratory picnic in the living room, using the low table that normally held an ashtray and magazines and such. She was kneeling on the floor to get at the crumbs, and her hair had fallen down one side of her face.

Sidney stared at her. He felt very good. He felt warm and contented, and suddenly very affectionate.

"Bed," he said. "Great idea." He winked and made an exaggerated clicking sound with his tongue. "Let's go."

Marianne Walsh laughed. "My, but you're subtle."

What followed a little later was generally satisfactory for both parties involved. But although Sidney had no possible means of knowing it, he wasn't simply making love with his wife because he was feeling good after a successful day's business.

That was only a small part of what was actually happening. What was much more important was that he was planting the seed that would eventually determine the future of a great many worlds, including his own.

3

A little more than eight hundred miles away from where Sidney and Marianne were celebrating, a girl in a thin print dress and high-heeled shoes that rubbed the backs of her ankles stood in the shadows of a dockside warehouse, arguing with a stocky man in a heavy work jacket.

"Ah, dammit," the man in the work jacket said. "You're a right fussy one, and that's the truth." He felt a warning jab of prudence and modified his voice. "You're right, though, you're right. Something as important as this . . ." He shook his head solemnly, and wished to God she'd get on with it.

The girl continued to fuss. He mustn't get the idea that she was used to this kind of thing, that she would let just anybody . . .

In the end it was done up against the wall at the rear of the warehouse, with a cold breeze coming in off the bay and the slow, heavy slapping of water against the quayside for lugubrious, out-of-tempo accompaniment. It was very quick, as well as being painful and messy, and a considerable disappointment to the girl, who genuinely had been a virgin when it all started and hadn't really known what to expect. In fact, she had got a great deal more than she had bargained for in her worst imaginings.

He fixed his clothes and glanced down at his wristwatch. "Ah, well," he said. He maneuvered onto his face what he hoped would pass in the dim light for a look of regret. "Till the next time, me beauty." He heaved a sigh. "Here, now, let me walk you to the bus. I have a little while before me ship goes. Would you like a fag, now? Me, I always—"

His monologue was interrupted at this point by a shrill response. The girl had had enough, and now she had heard enough. He swore, and hurried away from the sudden eruption of tears and abuse provoked by his tactlessness.

He noticed more yellow discharge when he used the urinal later that evening.

Ah, well, he thought. With a face like that on her, she didn't deserve no better. He winced, ground his teeth, and reluctantly made his way to the ship's doctor's quarters.

4

On the same April evening, on the northbound platform of the railway depot at Greenwood, Mississippi, John George Fuller and his wife Sarah sat on their two suitcases, waiting. Although they were both excited, they were scared, too, and they didn't talk very much.

The baby was asleep, occasionally making small sighing sounds. John George rocked him gently while he stared south, down the dwindling track, listening for the sounds that would tell them that the train was on its way. Although they had made up their minds to do it more than a month ago, he still couldn't really get used to the idea that they were actually going — leaving Greenwood for good. But it was all for the best, he supposed. After all, things had been bad for him and Sarah almost from the day that they had been married. The mill had closed very soon afterward, and in the year and a half since then all he had been able to find had been casual work: digging roads, washing dishes, a little gardening. Openings for full-time jobs were hard to come by since the closedown — and when they did occur, white applicants nearly always got preference anyway.

Then they had got the letter. It was from Sarah's cousin Martin Bush, who had gone north to New York while Sarah was still in school, and whom she remembered as a good-humored man, generous with candy and small change. The letter said that he had heard they were having a hard time and that he was able to offer John George a waitering job in his restaurant. The pay would be fifteen dollars a week and tips, and in a good week, the letter said, that could total around twenty-five, thirty dollars.

Thirty dollars a week was the kind of money that John George hadn't even dreamed of in his rare bouts of wishful thinking. The idea of going to New York scared him, but he had thought a lot about it and decided it was the only thing to do. They didn't only have themselves to think about now. The baby had to be brought up right, and not just in the sense of being taught to be honest and God-fearing.

They had to have money for good food and nice clothes as well. So they had written off to Martin Bush, saying yes, and he had sent them their rail fares, and now here they were.

Some distance away, a signal clanked. The few people on the platform began to stir, checking their belongings and drifting toward the platform edge.

"Well," John George said. He could hear the train now, the gradually growing sound of its approach. He swallowed hard. Lord bless us, he thought, and please try to find time to protect us in that big place. Amen. "Here she come." He stood up, feeling conspicuous in his wedding suit. He glanced down at Sarah, still fussing with her hair and turning her face back and forth in front of her compact mirror. "Honey, come on. Train's just about here."

"Not here yet," Sarah said. She looked at her image sideways, making some minute adjustment to where her hair curled just above her ear. She said fretfully, "Damn it, I can't get this right nohow."

John George wished she wouldn't swear. What would Cousin Martin think if he heard her? "Looks fine," he said. "Just fine."

"Oh, what would you know?" Sarah said.

5

In a bedroom in a small house in Ashcroft, Virginia, Dr. McCready took the stethoscope from Walter Hurley's chest and said, "Mmmm." He pulled the earpieces out of his ears and let the stethoscope dangle around his neck.

"Well, I don't know, young fellow. You seem in pretty fair shape to me, but I guess a day or two more in bed won't do you any harm." He put the stethoscope back into his bag. "You've been missing quite a bit of school just lately, haven't you, what with one thing and another?" He picked up the comic book from the bedside table and opened it. "How's the reading coming along? Still getting those headaches, are you?"

Dr. McCready was in his late thirties, but to Walter Hurley's already myopic eight-year-old eyes he just belonged somewhere in that broad area occupied by adults where actual age was a matter of no real concern. He might have been thirty or he might have been sixty, but whatever he was, he represented Walter's idea of what he wanted to be when he grew up. He was kind and amiable and unhurried, and he never gave the impression that his frequent visits constituted any kind of a chore. Walter often pictured him on his rounds, bandaging people up and sticking thermometers in their mouths and generally making them feel good again.

Walter said, blushing, "I can read pretty good, really." That wasn't strictly true, but he didn't want Dr. McCready to think he was stupid. He hesitated. "Not for long, though. The words get kind of . . ." He searched for the right word. "Kind of . . . fuzzy after a bit. That's when my head hurts."

"Mmm," Dr. McCready said, patently absorbed. He turned a page. "Well, you'll just have to take it easy until we can get your eyes tested again." He put the comic book back on the bedside table and got up off the bed. "You like vegetables any better these days?" he asked abruptly. Walter blushed again. "To tell you the truth," Dr. McCready said, "I was never too keen on them myself at your age. I'll let you have some more of that tonic. That ought to do it." He patted Walter's shoulder. "Don't rush things, and I'll see you in two or three days."

He went downstairs to where Mrs. Hurley was ironing in the kitchen. She was a round-shouldered, bitter-looking woman, her pinched tiredness making her seem a good deal older than she actually was.

"He's going to be just like his father," she said. "Same eyes, same chest."

She parked the iron at the end of the ironing board and began folding a shirt. She shook her head. "Poor George. Never harmed a fly, George didn't, and look how he ended up. There's no gratitude."

Dr. McCready had sadly arrived at that same conclusion very early in his professional life. He wrote a prescription, repeated his intention regarding his next visit, and left to continue his rounds.

6

"Darling," Marianne Walsh said. "Do you have a minute?"

Sidney Walsh silently mouthed a rapid calculation, jotted it in the margin of the document he was checking, and said, "Right with you." He made another calculation and lifted his eyebrows in pleased surprise. "Well, well. . . . Even better than I thought. I guess the Buffalo sale swung it. Did you know . . . ?" He saw the look on his wife's face and diplomatically checked himself. "Sweetie, I'm sorry. You wanted to tell me something."

She told him — and Sidney's cup, which was, metaphorically speaking, already pretty well filled to the brim, overflowed. He hugged her and babbled the kind of nonsense that fathers-to-be usually babble on such occasions.

"Well," he said, after his initial excitement had abated just a little. "Well, how about clever old us. Hey, do you think it was that time when we had supper on the floor and you were cleaning up after, and . . . ?"

Marianne Walsh confirmed that the date in question appeared to coincide pretty well with the duration of her present condition, so they cracked a bottle of real champagne that Sidney had sneaked back across the border on his last trip to Canada. They drank a toast to the baby and another one to Meakin & Fox, who they decided were sort of godparents by virtue of investment.

7

The girl had enough sense to know that she'd be kicked out of the house anyway, so she decided to spare herself that additional humiliation. She wrote a note that put forth the bald facts and said that she had somewhere definite to go — a lie — and that she'd write, and then left via the fire escape while her parents slept in the next room.

She struggled with her suitcase as far as the bus terminal and sat on a bench inside. It was a moonless night, with a little rain in the air. Every so often a bus would arrive or depart. People walked past her, some alone, some in pairs or threes or fours. A middle-aged woman who talked to herself sat on the far end of the bench for a while, and then got on a bus going to Ruskin.

Ruskin was about sixty miles upstate. It wasn't really very far, but the girl only had a little money, and she knew she'd have to increase the distance between herself and her parents by easy stages.

She bought a single ticket and got on the bus. After a few minutes it left the terminal and drifted out into the dark countryside, where the only lights apart from the bus's came from passing traffic and occasional houses.

She felt sick, and there was a slight ache that kept recurring in her groin. She couldn't really understand that. In the book it had said that the pain didn't start for quite a while yet, and it had only been a little more than three months since the evening when she had gone behind the warehouse with the man in the work jacket.

8

The land began to cool as the massive globe of the sun sank below the horizon and darkness drifted in from the east, shadowing the dusty ground and the cluster of cone-shaped hills.

Corma materialized the ship a short distance from the smallest of the hills. He checked the ship's alarm and shielding systems, opened the exterior vents in the lower chamber, then scanned the surrounding area. It was deserted, the would-be attackers already having taken refuge beneath the earth to escape the cold that came with the loss of light. Satisfied, he focused on the base of the hill.

There was a solitary guard near him that met the requirements. Corma drew him to the ship, and then inside. He put on breathing apparatus, broke out the items he needed, then went to the lower chamber where the guard was waiting. He directed the creature onto the central dais and studied it.

The guard was young; full-grown at eighteen inches or so tall, but its chitinous exterior still lacked the purplish cast that identified the more mature members of its species. Corma estimated the amount of serum he needed and inject-

ed the creature as he had been instructed. The guard remained motionless throughout, its faceted eyes fixed unwaveringly to the front.

"You are the chosen one," Corma told it. The guard could not hear him and would subsequently remember no break in its normal activities, but it amused Corma to impart this unacknowledgeable information. He drew the needle out for the last time. "Father of victory, I return you to your people." He reopened the hatch and dispatched the guard back to its post, watching the creature on the screen until it was safely there.

He returned to the control area, flushed out the lower chamber, and closed the vents again. As he reset the controls, he wondered how well the injections would work. The serum's composition and strength had been computed as accurately as possible on the basis of biological knowledge of the species, obtained from the dissection of several examples that had been taken at the time of the initial checkouts, and theoretically at least the chances of success were high. Bearing in mind the limitless fecundity of their bulbous queens, it should take little more than one of the planet's years for a new, larger, and significantly better-armed version of the creatures to have been produced in sufficient quantity to ensure their survival, at least in the necessary short term. Nothing could be done to shore up their dangerously crumbling world, but in the time that remained they would be able to deal adequately with the predators that ceaselessly circled their brittle fortresses during the hours of daylight.

Long enough, Corma thought. At least, it should be. It was a gamble that contained a fascinating number of possible pitfalls, but on balance the computations had been favorable.

He noted that there was a small loss of power from the number four unit. He must report that as soon as the run was over. It was possible that deterioration had set in after launch, but if this was so it was a clear indication that current precautionary measures were still inadequate. Pleem breeding techniques had been at such a consistently high level for so long that the recent incidence of occasional physical failure was a matter for some concern. In the realms of the psyche, thankfully, they remained apparently unchanged; an ally that continued to defy understanding but still responded to the stimulation that ensured their eager cooperation. But the lack of success in diagnosing the deterioration problem was something that must be looked at very carefully.

Later, the east/west guardian satellite passed over the same cluster of hills, but even if Corma's ship had not been shielded from their detectors, he would not have been in jeopardy. He had long since completed his mission to the four areas on the planet's surface where life still stubbornly refused to capitulate to the relentlessly growing power of the bloated sun.

9

John George and Sarah had found Harlem exciting at first. It was a noisy, busy place, a bit like a shabby Babylon; scary in some ways, but there was so much going on during their first few weeks there that they didn't really have time to think about things like that a lot.

Cousin Martin's restaurant wasn't at all like John George had expected. It was more of a club than a restaurant, with a band and cabaret acts in the evenings, which meant that he had to work pretty long hours. He didn't really mind that, though. The money was everything that had been promised, even more, and the customers were friendly enough for the most part, but they had a kind of city hardness about them that he couldn't really take to. Some of them, to John George's way of thinking, looked pretty mean and rough, and none more so than the ones he came to recognize as particular cronies of Cousin Martin.

He had somehow surmised that since Martin Bush was Sarah's cousin, he'd be the same basically God-fearing type as the rest of the Singleton family. But he hadn't turned out like that at all. He was genial and generous and made allowances for John George's frequent clumsiness while he was learning his way, but there was little doubt in John George's mind that Cousin Martin was a deep-dyed sinner who kept some pretty bad company a lot of the time.

But the money was good and they had an apartment with three rooms and a real bathroom, and Sarah liked New York, so he swallowed his feelings and concentrated on the job. He didn't like being away from Sarah and the baby until the early hours of the morning, but it was all part of the way things had to be, so he didn't fuss about it. It had been good of Cousin Martin to give him the job, and when he thought back to Greenwood and the way things had been there he decided to be grateful, even though there were aspects of his new life that he didn't like at all. He wondered, guiltily, how God felt about it, and made sure he still read his Bible three times a day, just like always.

10

On the evening of the two hundred sixteenth day after she had been with the man in the work jacket, the girl fell down some stairs. It wasn't much of a fall in distance, only a few steps, but it jarred into motion what was inside her.

The fall happened at the rear of the building where she had been employed as a cleaner for the past two months, a small department store in a midwestern town. The other cleaner found her, recognized the situation, and with the help of the assistant manager, who was still on the premises for the purpose of stocktaking, carried her into the women customers' bathroom, the nearest place where hot water was available.

Several minutes later, the baby emerged. The assistant manager was still trying to get through to the hospital when it happened, but the cleaner who had found her was an older woman who knew the rudiments of the necessary procedures. When the young intern who was all the hospital had been able to spare finally got there, the baby had been given a semblance of a wash and was wrapped in a sheet that the assistant manager had reluctantly appropriated from the bedding department.

The girl was only just conscious, overcome partly by the severe crack on the head that she had received when she slipped on the stairs, and partly from the pain inside her. She wanted to die, and she said so, repeatedly, in a barely intelligible whine.

"No, of course you don't," the intern said. He was very young, and all he knew about real pain and genuine despair was from watching it. The ambulance crew lifted the girl onto a stretcher. "You take it easy, now. Everything's going to be fine." He took the baby from the older woman, glanced down at it, and shuddered. "The baby's fine," he said to the mother. "Everything's just great."

After the ambulance men carried the girl out, the intern turned to the older woman and the assistant manager. "God . . . This sure is some ugly kid, isn't it?"

It was. It looked like a slightly imbecilic monkey. Its head was misshapen, the crown slewing distinctly from right to left, and its eyes, although squeezed shut at the moment, were noticeably close together.

It opened its mouth and howled.

"I guess you've got a right to squawk," the intern said. "Boy, they really shortchanged you, didn't they, handsome?" He began to massage the distorted crown gingerly.

11

Marianne Walsh had a pregnancy that was the envy of her married female acquaintances and friends — no complications, no discomfort to speak of. Eight months and twenty-four days after the celebratory alfresco supper that had preceded his conception, she went to the hospital and there gave birth to a boy. He weighed nine pounds, two ounces, was plainly bursting with health, had grey eyes — like hers — and fair wisps of hair plastered to his well-shaped scalp.

"Well," Sidney Walsh said on his first encounter with his son. "Hey, he really is something, isn't he? I thought babies were supposed to be pretty ugly right at first." This not altogether accurate generality certainly didn't apply in the case of Peter Franklin Walsh, whose name had been settled on during the third month of pregnancy. He was an exceptionally handsome child, with an alert and candid demeanor that Sidney found enormously fetching.

He stuck out his forefinger, invitingly, and had it taken in a soft, faintly moist but decidedly firm grip. "Hey, the little so-and-so wants to Indian wrestle!" He waggled the caught finger a little. "Think you can take your old man, do you?" He continued to waggle the finger, lightly brushing aside Marianne's not really serious protestations, filled with the unique pride of parenthood.

"He really is something, isn't he?" Sidney said again.

12

One of the hills was no longer cone-shaped. The whole of its southern flank had collapsed, and inside the exposed tiers of corridors there was frantic, scuttling activity as masses of cerise and purple bodies fought to effect repairs.

Corma idled his ship a short distance away and watched with interest. A straggling horde of predators, including one or two types he had not seen before, was advancing on the half-ruined fortress. As the creatures fanned out around their objective, figures emerged from the shadowed entrances to the broken hill. They were similar in shape to the guard that he had injected, but noticeably larger, and their exoskeletons looked hard and heavy.

They engaged the predators, some of them directly below him. Corma activated his cameras, drifted the ship above the ragged circle of struggling bodies, and observed the progress of the battle. Gradually, the predators broke away and attempted to escape, but the purple defenders pursued them and hacked them down. In a little while the only detectable movement among the mass of bodies that littered the ground was an occasional delayed muscular reflex, a ghostly echo of departed life.

The defenders returned to their posts, taking their few wounded with them. Corma watched them go, then switched off the cameras.

The serum had plainly done its work well. The steadily rising heat of the swollen sun and the now numerous ground tremors meant that the hills would collapse with ever-increasing frequency, but by this time their occupants were adequately equipped to defend themselves when it happened. It was a make-do existence, but it should suffice until the sun eventually exploded, a matter of some two decades from then if the computations had been accurate.

He took some readings and studied the results thoughtfully: a little higher than forecast, but not dangerously so. Even with our advantage, he thought, a situation of this kind inevitably contains a high degree of uncertainty, but on balance the odds were still comfortably in our favor.

He watched the rapid reconstruction of the hill, admiring the skill being demonstrated by the scurrying lines of workers and mildly entertained by this ultimately pointless endeavor.

13

When Peter Franklin Walsh was one year and eight months old, the Walshes moved to a house in the Cleveland suburbs, a pleasant building located on its own quarter-acre of attractively laid-out grounds. They did it after deciding that an apartment wasn't really the best place to bring up a child, particularly one as active and inquiring as Peter, who, even at such an early age, had consistently demonstrated a fearless tendency toward exploration that had given them cause for alarm on several occasions.

On a late summer day, two weeks after moving into the house, Peter fell out of the window of his parents' bedroom. Marianne Walsh, a devoted and conscientious mother, had briefly left him while she transferred some toilet articles to the bathroom, a journey that took her out of the room for approximately half a minute. Peter was playing on the bedroom floor at the time of her departure, apparently totally absorbed in tracing out the pattern of the carpet with a finger.

As she went through the door, consciously hurrying, his finger moved into a patch of sunlight. He lifted his hand, fascinated by the way the light and shadow changed places on it as he turned it around. The source of the light was plainly the window. He tottered across to it, climbed onto a chair and then the sill, and pushed his hand through the opening. His gesture was too emphatic to enable him to maintain his balance, and he fell just as Marianne Walsh re-entered the room.

She saw him disappear through the window, and fainted. She was unconscious for less than a minute, but she had screamed before collapsing and was heard by the maid. After helping to revive her, the maid accompanied her outside, expecting to find the worst.

The two shaking women found Peter sitting on the lawn, tugging up tufts of grass. He was plainly unhurt, appeared to be emotionally unruffled, and was very obviously enjoying the intriguing sensation of what he was doing. Apart from a minute graze on one arm and a privet leaf caught in his hair, there was no evidence whatever of his recent adventure. He couldn't understand the fuss that was made of him, and would clearly have preferred to have been left to pursue his newfound activity.

Marianne Walsh was an honest person who felt her responsibilities keenly, and she told her husband about the fall and her own part in it when he got home from a business trip two days later. Sidney Walsh was a patient man, not given to recriminations, and he understood what she must have been going through. He talked sensibly about how accidents can happen to or be caused by the most careful of people. He deliberately refrained from checking Peter's physical condition immediately after hearing his wife's admission, and only did so surreptitiously when he had taken him for a walk in the garden while Marianne was preparing the evening meal.

He stood on the lawn, looking up at the bedroom window and marveling at the circumstances of the fall. The single bush on that side of the garden was located directly below the window. It was large, a full six feet tall, and considerably overgrown, a profusion of leaves thoroughly blanketing its branches. On the preceding Sunday he had halfheartedly considered trimming both it and the lawn, but a heavy shower in the morning had cancelled out the gardening that he had planned.

He picked Peter up, held him in one arm, and pointed up to the window. "See that? That's what you fell out of and nearly scared your mother to death. And this here is what you bounced off. Remember?"

"Bounced off," Peter said. He nodded, sagely, and tugged at his father's collar. "Piggyback, now."

Sidney laughed, hugged him, and they played piggyback until Marianne called them inside.

14

Walter Hurley sat by the front window, looking out onto the street, waiting for Joe Cassidy and Phil Cross to appear. He wondered if he dared go outside when they did. There had been some rain overnight, but it had soon evaporated and everything was bone dry again now. He knew that his mother wouldn't have let him go out if she had been there, even though he seemed to have been a bit better the last few days, but she was out at work and wouldn't know anything about it.

He wondered what they had done at school that day, not the lessons, but other things, like at lunchtime and the fooling around that went on in class, Phil Cross making his faces and that kind of thing. On the increasingly rare occasions that he was fit enough to go to school he was always too scared to actually join in these activities, but he was a willing audience and found himself tolerated by his peers because of that.

He saw Joe and Phil come around the corner, dodging in and out of the roadway, periodically attacking one another. He hesitated, and then decided to chance it. He didn't feel too bad, and it was Friday, so he probably wouldn't see them again for a couple of days. . . .

He went out into the garden and walked down to the sidewalk. The air was dustier than he had hoped it would be, but he didn't want to go straight back because he had been getting really bored inside the house.

"Hi, Joe," he said. "Hi, Phil."

"Lay off, will you?" Joe Cassidy said to Phil Cross. He pushed him away with one hand while protecting his fly with the other. "Hi, Walter. How you doing?"

"Not bad, I guess," Walter said. Actually, he wasn't too sure. His breathing had still been a little restricted when he had been inside the house, and now he could feel it tightening rapidly. He cleared his throat. "How was school?"

"Oh, the same old crap," Joe said. "When you coming back?" He made a sudden counterattack, half-undoing Phil's fly. Phil swore and laughed and walked a little way down the road, pulling it up again.

"I don't know for sure," Walter said. He knew now that he had made a mistake in coming outside. He was having trouble getting the air down into his lungs, and he was sweating badly. "Gotta go," he said hoarsely. He turned and walked back toward the house, his chest heaving and his shoulders high.

"Sure," Joe said. "See you, Walter." He sneaked up on Phil and hit the back of his head with his book bag. They ran off, swinging their bags at each other and laughing.

Walter shut the front door and leaned against it. He wondered if he'd be able to get his breathing back to normal before his mother came home. Even if he did, though, Mrs. Adamczewski next door would probably tell her he had been outside, because he had seen her looking out her front window as he had turned to come back to the house.

He lay on the sofa, his mouth open, breathing in shallow, shuddering gasps, and thinking what a dumb thing that had been for him to do, going outside the house on a day like this when he had only been out of the hospital for a couple of weeks and when Dr. McCready had warned him so definitely not to.

15

In a shamefaced, guilt-ridden kind of way, John George had gradually taught himself to turn a blind eye to a lot of things that happened at Cousin Martin's restaurant.

He knew that he shouldn't, that his apathy was bound to get him in bad with the Lord, maybe even with the law eventually, but whenever his conscience really troubled him he quickly reminded himself of his responsibilities to Sarah and John George Junior. After all, he had to feed and clothe them decently, provide a good home. They were used to a certain standard of living now, and it would be selfish and cruel to take it from them.

So he stayed at the restaurant while the years slipped by, keeping to himself as much as possible and repeatedly promising atonement, just as soon as John George Junior was old enough to look out for himself and had made some sort of start in a life of his own. Thinking about John George Junior and his future, so much brighter in prospect than the life he had managed to make for himself, helped a lot. The boy was a happy child, deft and clever, who very early on had demonstrated that he possessed a genuinely precocious talent for music. He had single-fingered tunes on a neighbor's piano before he was two years old, and was augmenting them with simple harmonies by the time he was three.

John George took enormous pride in this evidence of creative ability entering a family line that had never to his knowledge been much inclined that way before. He bought a decent upright for him to practice on, and the elderly woman in the next apartment, who'd had piano lessons when she was young and still played occasionally, agreed to teach him what she could. John George Junior outstripped her just about the time that he was due to start school, but the school had a good music teacher who agreed to give him special lessons outside school hours for eight dollars a month.

It was money well spent. He loved the piano, practiced religiously, read music with a fluency that belied his age, performed regularly at school concerts, and by the time he entered his early teens was playing occasionally at the gospel hall. Despite his natural caution, John George was seriously entertaining thoughts of a real musical career for his son, most probably in the church, when he came home unexpectedly one day to find this dream dragged down from the ecclesiastical heights that he had envisioned to what, to him, constituted the level of the gutter and all the filth that it contained.

The boy was playing jazz — rocking, insinuating music, with a degree of polish that clearly demonstrated his familiarity with it. An appalling scene followed. Sarah screamed defiantly, telling John George that what the boy had been playing was the music of their real world as opposed to the pie-in-the-sky fantasies offered by hymns and the classics, that he had the right to play what he wanted.

The boy cowered at first but, bolstered by his mother's defense, said that she was right, that his father had no right to tell him he couldn't do something that he had a feeling for.

Filled with a boiling mixture of rage, disgust, guilt, and frustration, John George dragged the boy to a cupboard, opened it, and tried to push him inside. It was an old, heavy cupboard, a fixture that had been painted over before they moved into the apartment. The boy was hanging onto the outer frame with both hands when John George slammed the door.

16

Less than a month after giving birth to her baby in the department-store bathroom, the girl had her wish to die fulfilled, largely due to the hospital's failure to detect an internal injury caused during her fall and the infection that resulted from it. If she had wanted to live, she might have done so, but the truth was that she didn't really care any more.

Attempts were made to find anybody who might have been concerned about her death, but she had managed to put a fair amount of distance between herself and her parents by then, and she had been living and working under a false name. She had lied copiously about her background, too, so who she actually was remained a mystery. The owner of the store grudgingly parted with ten dollars toward funeral expenses, but the best that could be managed was a pauper's grave and a few flowers.

Thanks to the efforts of the young intern, the baby's head had been massaged into some sort of acceptable symmetry, but his other physical deficiencies defeated the doctors. He was badly underweight, a condition for which no real solution was ever found, and he turned out to be subject to seizures that invariably concluded with incontinence. He was also totally deaf in his right ear.

During the time of her employment at the store the girl had been using the name Margaret Pierce, so the baby was called Michael Pierce. He was eventually sent to the local orphanage, an underfunded establishment where some of the staff members did their best in fairly hopeless conditions and the rest of them simply treated their jobs as a regrettable means of livelihood. As a result, Michael Pierce's formative years were spent in an atmosphere where affection from adults was the exception rather than the rule.

If he had been less ugly he might have fared a little better in this respect, but the comments of the intern at the time of his birth had been justified, and apart from the remolding of his head nothing occurred to improve his looks. He had a small forehead and tufted, straw-colored hair, and his eyes stayed directly adjacent to his small, beaklike nose. To all intents and purposes he was chinless, and he also had the widely spaced teeth that were a frequent result of the circumstances in which he had been conceived, a flaw that was amplified by their uneven protrusion from his jaw.

He did badly at lessons, finding it hard to concentrate on words and figures, and was rapidly classified as educationally subnormal. He had no real friends. Some of the kinder children tolerated him to the extent of talking to him occasionally, but they soon tired of the one-sidedness of the conversation and transferred their attentions to people from whom they could reasonably anticipate a response.

Shortly after his fifteenth birthday, Michael Pierce was released from the orphanage. He hadn't been happy there, but it had been the only home he had known, and his forced departure to live in hostel accommodations terrified him. His total lack of aptitude was something of a problem as far as finding employment was concerned, and it was some time before he found a job as a cleaner in a small local print shop. It was dirty, unrewarding work, its unpleasantness compounded by the indifference and frequent irritation of his colleagues. His employer was a decent but preoccupied man who called him Michael, but the boy had only been there a few months when the owner died and the place was taken over by the people next door who wanted to extend their motor-repair business and who had no place for him in their scheme of things.

He tentatively looked for other work, but openings at all levels were scarce and were quickly filled when they did occur. He realized that the people who ran the hostel wouldn't go on accommodating him forever, so he left the town and went on the road, carrying his few belongings in a rucksack. He took some food from the hostel kitchen before he left, but it wasn't much and he knew that soon he would have to find some more — from where, he wasn't sure.

17

Peter Franklin Walsh fell out of no more bedroom windows and suffered no other notable mishaps during the years preceding his attendance at high school. Despite Sidney's steadily increasing affluence, the Walshes continued to live in the same relatively modest Cleveland house, partly because they saw no real need to move elsewhere and partly because although neither Sidney nor Marianne was notably superstitious, each independently nursed a secret belief that the house was lucky for them.

They thought this way partly because of Sidney's smoothly burgeoning progress in the highly competitive world of light engineering, and because the incident of Peter and the bedroom window was never really far from their minds. After all, his survival had been something of a minor miracle, and the odds on a solitary, suitably cushioned bush being adjacent to an uncut lawn at exactly the right point to have broken his fall must have been astronomically high.

So they stayed at the house, and Peter grew to look more and more like his father, but with his mother's eyes and mouth. He was a well-built, amiable boy; athletic, with a very good sense of balance, and he did well at school. He read a lot, and shared Marianne Walsh's interest in drawing and painting.

Sidney and Marianne, understandably, were enormously proud of him. Their son was fit, talented, handsome, and well-mannered, and had a pleasant, open personality. He made friends easily, was curious about all aspects of existence, and clearly enjoyed the simple fact of being alive. By the time he reached his middle teens he was filling out a little and was only an inch or so short of Sidney's five feet eleven and a half. He was also very good-looking and had a nice, dry, unmalicious wit that amused both his peers and the less sober-minded members of the high-school staff. He got along equally well with both the scholastic and athletic elements because it was plain that he genuinely derived pleasure from both kinds of activity. The female students who were his contemporaries adored him, and he was secretly admired by quite a few of the older girls as well.

Very few of his less fortunately endowed or gifted fellows — which meant, on balance, the remainder of the student body — begrudged him his unreasonably profuse share of good fortune for long. He was friendly and open in his attitudes, and the few people who initially resented him were soon won over by his amiable refusal to accept that there was any really sensible basis for their antagonism.

He was astute enough to recognize that in some respects this was a fallacious attitude on his own part, and that in terms of hard reality quite a few of them had perfectly understandable reasons for feeling jealous of him. He came from a stable, well-to-do home, and without being overtly vain knew that he was both good-looking and intelligent. Conversely, quite a high proportion of his associates were neither, and came from backgrounds that were unstable or poor, frequently both.

Until he was nine he had remained an only child, despite valiant efforts on the part of his parents to remedy this, but Sidney and Marianne had conscientiously seen to it that he wasn't spoiled. He had a sister now, Margaret, a belated and rather unexpected arrival whose advent had been marred by the fact that her left leg was marginally shorter than her right. In all other respects she was perfectly normal, but this deficiency made him very conscious of his own excessive luck. As a result, he was unpatronizingly and unselectively kind to people, so that even the most truculent were shamed and charmed into liking him.

18

"The 'a' tends to be broad," Corma said. "As in 'mark.'" He stressed the vowel sound. "A word for you to perhaps consider rather more seriously than your present class position would indicate has been the case this term." The student concerned affected indifference, and one or two of the others smiled dutiful and slightly bored smiles.

Corma didn't blame them. The concluding pre-vacation assessment was traditionally a difficult time to stimulate genuine interest. He dismissed the class a little early, attended a brief meeting with the other members of the languages department staff, then retired to his residence and packed. By noon on the following day he was several hundred miles away in the familiar desert resort that he visited three times a year. He carefully checked his cabin, belongings, and apparel for tracers, then ate a leisurely lunch and went to the bazaar in the town center. It was crowded, as usual. Fifteen minutes after his arrival he was three hundred feet below ground, being told by M'doi of the satisfactory completion of 8069.

"You are to be congratulated," M'doi told him. "Your record of success is now such that I have arranged for your future activities to be concerned with Class 1 targets only." He gestured acknowledgment of Corma's thanks, produced a recording bead, and pushed it across the desk. "Your first exercise at this rank is at an interesting stage of development, a textbook example of Nyleve's Law of Progressive Revendication emerging in Group 7 culture. All relevant preliminary information is here. I am sure you will find it a rewarding assignment."

Corma restrained his elation. It was inevitable that he would have reached this level in due time, but it had happened sooner than he expected.

"This is very pleasing," he said.

M'doi smiled briefly. "It is deserved. Too, your philological background will be of particular value in this context. There is no great urgency, in the sense that hostilities are unlikely to commence for some little while, so you will have ample time for preparation and individual emergency procedure study. Even so, I feel it prudent that you familiarize yourself with the general structure of the situation now. As you would expect, it is complex and of considerable interest. I think you will find it an excellent opportunity to make use of your academic specialty."

Corma thanked him again and retired to study the information already gleaned. M'doi's reference to his philological expertise promised an operation that would at least

stretch his capabilities and initiative to new limits, a chal-
lenge that fired him with renewed enthusiasm.

In the privacy of his allocated cubicle, he activated the
bead, carefully memorizing what it contained.

19

When John George had slammed the cupboard door on the
boy's hands, it had struck directly on the knuckles. All the
joints had fractured, none of them cleanly. It had taken
months for them to mend again, and the inadequate treatment they received at the time ensured that they ended up
as lumpy travesties of what they had been before. What
had originally been ten slim, smoothly functional pieces of
mechanism, ideally suited to the purpose for which they
had surely been intended, had become ten stiff, inflexible,
clumsy digital extensions with strictly limited use. The
nerves of several of the boy's fingers had also been affected, and he frequently cut or grazed them without being
immediately aware of the fact.

Shortly after the accident the police had caught up with
Martin Bush, and it turned out that all the suspicious acts
that John George had been guiltily turning a blind eye to
were unlawful. Cousin Martin wasn't only tied in with
gambling and liquor rackets; he had actually been hiding
out two wanted people in the upstairs part of the building,
an area that John George rarely visited. The trial got a lot of

publicity, and when it was over Cousin Martin went to jail, the restaurant closed down, and John George had to look for other work, never with any real success.

He worked at several jobs, none of them having any likelihood of promotion or permanency. For a while he had thought about going back to Greenwood, but a mixture of shame and apathy and the realization that they'd probably be no better off, maybe even worse, made him decide to stay in New York. He and Sarah and the boy moved to a smaller, shabbier apartment where they had to share a bathroom and toilet. They had been there a little more than three years when John George was killed by a car while he crossed the street, abruptly ending what for him had become an endless purgatory of guilt and remorse.

Sarah and the boy stayed on in the apartment, but Sarah had to work now, and the only regular job she could find was night cleaning in an office building, because Martin Bush was still in jail and couldn't help and cleaning was the only kind of work she had ever done. The money wasn't very good and she had to work long hours, from six in the evening until four the next morning, which meant that the boy was left to his own devices a good deal of the time. He took to wandering around the streets after she had gone to work, always on his own, his hands bunched awkwardly in his pockets. Harlem at night had its dangers, but he managed to avoid them most of the time, quickly becoming adept at scenting the approach of trouble and melting into the refuge offered by doorways and alleys until the threat passed or subsided.

He was in one such alley when he first heard the pianist. The music came from high up, at a point somewhere along the wall of the large building that flanked the alleyway. He was separated from it by a wall and a gap beyond the wall that he assumed must be some kind of small yard. The music was faint, but it touched something inside him that made him hungry to hear it at closer quarters.

There was no one else in the alley that he could see or hear. He tried to climb the wall, but the darkness and his now ineffectual hands combined to foil him. The next day, he stole a small grappling hook from a hardware store, took it home, padded it with strips of rag, and tied a length of strong cord to it.

That night, wearing his darkest clothes and his sneakers, he went back to the alleyway, praying that the pianist would be there again, that what he had heard hadn't simply been rent-party music, a one-night affair only. The music floated down to him again, a rippling siren-song. He threw the hook over the top of the wall until it caught, then scrambled up the cord and dropped into the open area between the wall and the building.

It was a small yard, as he had surmised, with bins lined against the side of the building. A single-story projection with a peaked roof, an area that could have been a storeroom or passageway, was located directly below the point where the music was coming from. He saw an air vent of some kind that identified itself by faint slats of light. He carefully moved the lightest of the bins against the side of the projection, stood on the bin, and gently lobbed the hook up toward the peak of the roof.

The hook caught, and he scrambled up the cord, his ears cocked for any sound of movement in the alleyway. He reached the crest and eased himself up to a standing position, excitedly finding that this placed his face directly in front of the air vent.

Despite the tilted slats of the vent, he had a reasonably clear view of the scene beyond it. It was a fairly large room, the only unmasked lighting being a naked bulb suspended over the shabby grand piano that was located just below his viewing point. The rest of the room was shadowed, but in the dim light provided by several shielded wall-lamps he could detect groups of people, some seated at tables, others moving around. There was a steady drone of voices, punctuated by frequent laughter.

The pianist wasn't playing just then. He was a bulky man in a crumpled, light suit, and as the boy caught his first glimpse of him he was drinking, rather delicately, from a small glass, and softly fingering bass notes at the bottom end of the keyboard with his free hand.

Somebody came up to the pianist, talked to him for a few moments, then took his empty glass away, leaving a full one on a table beside the piano. The pianist pulled a handkerchief from his jacket pocket, wiped his lips, and put the handkerchief away again. He lowered his head and began to play.

The talking and laughter gradually dwindled, and then stopped. The pianist played a slow blues melody, following a simple path at the start, but gradually inserting right-hand progressions that danced down the keyboard like flashes of light, unfailingly finding a note or chord to lead him in new directions, his exploration sustained by the broken pulse provided by his left hand. It was virtuoso music, beautifully played, and it finished to yells of approval and a lot of clapping. A girl came up to the pianist, draped her arm across his shoulder, and kissed him.

The pianist laughed, drank his drink, and played again. He played at widely differing tempos, occasionally at near-breakneck speed, but the music never faltered or blurred. The boy watched and listened, spellbound, losing all track of time, conscious only of the movement of the pianist's hands and the brilliant sounds they evoked from the shabby, out-of-tune piano. It was only when the pianist at last stood up and another man, infinitely less skilled, took his place, that the boy realized that his legs were shaking with exhaustion.

How long had it been? Two hours? Three? He was suddenly aware that he was very cold. Exhausted and bemused, he lowered himself into the yard, climbed back over the wall, and trotted tiredly down the alleyway toward the lighted street, with images of what he had seen and the patterns of the sounds that he had heard clogging his brain.

A figure suddenly appeared in front of him, silhouetted in the alley mouth, and white light dazzled him. He jerked to a halt, the images and patterns abruptly replaced by fear. Without thinking, he turned and ran.

A voice shouted behind him, and he heard running feet. Confused by the weaving light and the erratic movements of his shadow, he misjudged the turn at the end of the stretch of alleyway and crashed into the wall. He fell, dazed. The light and footsteps stopped next to him, and a hand hauled him to his feet and propelled him back toward the alley exit.

Back on the lighted street, still dazed and sick with terror, he looked up and saw that his captor was a policeman.

20

Sidney Walsh weathered the Depression without experiencing any real problems, largely due to his luck in having snared a government contract only months before the crash came. Few of his direct competitors were as fortunate, and by the time the economic situation had begun to stabilize again he was controlling something of a small empire in the light engineering field, with business interests in Pittsburgh and Detroit as well as Cleveland.

The Walshes stuck with their luck and stayed on in the same house, maintaining their modest standard of living. They made a practice of vacationing abroad, but that was their only regular extravagance. Peter graduated from high school, with the honors that had always seemed inevitable, and went on to a midwestern college noted for its excellence in the literary pursuits. Several well-known authors were graduates of the college, and a lot of the major jobs in journalism were occupied by others who had been students there.

Peter had always enjoyed writing and had decided very early in life that that was what he wanted for a career. Sidney, who had always been rather bemused by his own success, had never really thought in dynastic terms, and encouraged his son to follow his own path. His private reasoning was that since Peter was plainly talented, he should have his chance, with this belief cushioned by the knowledge that if for any reason he should fail — which Sidney considered highly unlikely — or change his mind, he could always come into the business.

Peter enjoyed college in the same way that he enjoyed most things. He derived a great satisfaction from the disciplines and craftsmanship of writing, and his natural curiosity meant that he always had an endless supply of raw material with which to practice them. Shortly before his nineteenth birthday he had the distinction of selling a short story to *Cosmopolitan*, which made him the youngest student in the history of the college to be published at that level. He returned home for summer vacation with his check framed and under glass, and hung it in his bedroom. He laughingly dismissed it as the spoils of good fortune rather than good writing — he knew it wasn't a bad story, but he was already conscious of its weaknesses — and got on with the business of enjoying his temporary return to the comforts of home.

Despite his frequent necessary forays away from Cleveland, Sidney Walsh prided himself on being the head of a closely knit family. He had adequate justification for this belief. He and his wife had both retained their good looks, and had mutually practiced a degree of fidelity that was becoming rather uncommon, Peter was a clever, handsome, kind, and level-headed son, and their belated daughter Margaret was turning out to be a creditable echo of her mother. Her physical defect was a source of permanent sorrow to Peter and her parents, but she had never taken it very seriously and refused to be catered to in this respect. Specially made shoes compensated for her differing leg lengths to the extent that the defect became virtually unnoticeable. She, too, was kind, clever, handsome, and level-headed, and because she was female she dared to be more openly affectionate toward the other family members.

"When are you going to write a novel?" Margaret asked. She and Peter were sunning themselves on the front lawn. Summer vacation was almost over and, although they hadn't talked about it, they were both a little sad at the prospect. She tickled his ear with a piece of grass. "You know — a *best-seller*, I mean."

"Give me a chance," Peter protested. He swatted at the piece of grass. "I might never sell anything else." He knew this wasn't true. His head was full of ideas; characters, situations, dialogue. It was a chaotic jumble at the moment, but he had already proved himself capable of handling the fine disciplines demanded by the short story. "Would you really like a boy wonder for a brother?"

"You're too old," Margaret said. At eleven, she was three parts serious. They laughed, and grappled for the piece of grass. A car pulled up at the curb, and a dark, slim youth got out and loped up the driveway.

"Lay off him," the young man called to Margaret. "He's no match for a roughneck like you. Hey, scribe, in case you didn't know, Goodman's in town tonight. Feel like bending an ear?"

"Solid, old man," Peter said. He lifted Margaret off the ground, held her above him, and let her wriggle. The dark youth's name was John Archard, and although he and Peter had been close friends in high school they saw one another only infrequently now. John hadn't gone on to college, and in many respects their tastes had developed in different directions, but they still enjoyed one another's company occasionally. "Who is it, just you and me?"

John Archard squatted on the grass. "There's . . . um . . . a girl who'll be coming along. Nice kid, but not your type. Not exactly literary, if you know what I mean. Would you like me to see if she's got a friend?"

"No, thanks," said Peter. There was someone at college whom he was beginning to take rather seriously. "I'll just stick with the music. What time?"

"Celibate," John Archard said. "Okay, I'll pick you up around seven-thirty." He got up, smacked Margaret's bottom, and left.

"What's sellabit?" Margaret asked, still halfheartedly trying to get out of his grasp. "Is it something rude?"

"Go look it up in the dictionary," Peter said. He laughed and let her collapse on top of him.

John Archard's girl certainly wasn't very literary, but she was quick and funny and didn't flirt with Peter, for which he was grateful. He danced with her a few times, but for most of the evening she danced with John while Peter stationed himself at the front end of the balcony overlooking the band shell and enjoyed the music. They left a little before twelve o'clock and headed back for the north side of town, the girl beside John Archard in the front of the car while Peter lay on the rear seat, humming riffs and beating on the upholstery.

He never knew the exact details of the accident. The only warning he got was a sudden shriek of tires followed by an abrupt, disorienting lurch of the car, and then he was jerked forward. His body struck the back of the front seat and fell to the floor. Above him, glass shattered.

Dazed, Peter pulled himself back onto the seat. The car was stationary; still upright, but tilted to the left and rammed up against a shadowed brick wall. An obstruction partially blocked his view out the broken windshield — a motionless huddle that he realized with numbed disbelief was the girl. John Archard was still behind the wheel, pinned between it and the straining upholstery of the seat cushion. Like the girl, he was totally still.

Peter opened the rear door and climbed out, finding it impossible to keep from shaking. People were converging on the car from both sides of the street. Someone grabbed his arm and said, "You okay?" It was a man in a waiter's jacket. "Hey, what about them other two?"

Peter didn't look back at the car. "They're dead, I think." He looked past the man, listening dully to the sound of an approaching siren.

At the inquest, a passerby reiterated what he had told the police on the night of the accident: the car had swerved to avoid someone who had suddenly stepped out into the road and then vanished immediately after the crash. The coroner's verdict was that the accident and the deaths of Fay Miller and John Phillip Archard had been caused by the carelessness of a person or persons unknown, and that John Phillip Archard had been in no way responsible. Medical evidence showed that the deceased had consumed alcohol a short time before the collision, but the amount in his system had been small and, it was judged, unlikely to impair his ability to drive safely.

Ostensibly, Peter recovered quickly from the accident. He had suffered no physical injury, and was sensible enough to recognize that an open manifestation of mourning would only upset his family, especially in view of his imminent return to college. Their relief at his survival was understandable, and he was grateful for the restraint that they showed during the remaining week of his vacation, but he was glad when it was over. He told his parents that he'd prefer to travel by train, a decision that they interpreted as demonstrating a temporary aversion to cars, but which in fact was largely brought about by his realization that by doing so he'd avoid the risk of unbottling his emotional stress during a long car ride.

They saw him off at the station, sadly but still relieved, eventually turning away after seeing his final wave and the withdrawal of his arm into the receding train.

Sidney Walsh rubbed a hand across his face. "Well," he said. He saw that Marianne and Margaret were both near tears. "Oh, come on, now. We ought to be celebrating, not carrying on like this was a wake." He took Marianne by the arm and held Margaret's hand. "Let's get out of here before somebody gets the impression I've been kicking you around and tries to give me a punch in the nose." He steered them carefully out of the station, silently offering his own prayer of thanks.

21

In many respects the mountains were similar to those where he had found a base in central Germany, Corma noted. They were roughly the same height, and the slopes were wooded in much the same fashion.

He cruised over them for some time before finding the basin, a fairly deep natural refuge not far below one of the

*higher peaks. There was a road half a mile below it and no
detectable habitation for twenty or so miles in any direction.*

*He landed and ran the customary pre-exit check on all
systems. The power was being maintained with no evidence
of deterioration and the emergency recall circuitry seemed
in order, but he patiently adhered to the rulebook and sub-
mitted it to the standard double check. The recall circuitry
was, after all, in many respects the most important mechanism in the ship. He had few qualms regarding his capacity
for survival — his fallibility rating was in single figures, as
it had been for all of his line — but death itself was the only
true certainty. Others had died on distant worlds, most of
their endings still unexplained, but the recall system had
ensured that their deaths had simultaneously triggered
their own programmed dissolution and the ship's un-
manned return to base, removing all conclusive evidence of
their presence there. Above all were secrecy and security.
He repeated the litany to himself as he worked his way
painstakingly through the checking sequence.*

*Satisfied, he closed the circuit cover. Well, he could do
no more, and at least he had the reassurance that all possible precautions had been taken. But he sincerely hoped, as
always, that there would be no necessity for the system's ef-
ficiency to be put to the actual test.*

*He reduced the power to sustaining level and ran a final
check on the contents of his rucksack. It seemed in order:
papers, necessary basic equipment, money. He broke out the
flying pack and went outside to a cold, cloudy evening. Yes,
this basin would serve well. Its walls were almost sheer,
and the likelihood of visitors was remote in the extreme.*

*He drifted up and out of the basin, maintaining mini-
mum altitude. The chances of his being seen were slender,*

but there was no point in taking risks, however small. He found a suitable crevice in some rocks about a hundred fifty yards above the road, concealed the flying pack there, and walked down the wooded slope, noting landmarks as he went.

There was a clearing beside the road at the point where he reached it, with a distinctive cluster of large boulders at its westward end. He memorized its salient features, then continued down the mountain, pacing along the edge of the descending strip of asphalt. He should be able to obtain a ride eventually, but traffic had been light during his period of observation from the ship, and with dusk approaching it would inevitably thin out even more.

He wondered what the Americans were really like. The preliminary survey reports had depicted an interestingly diverse species, an almost total denial of the naive German belief in racial purity. Prejudices abounded, as they did in all mixed cultures, but the records seemed to demonstrate the Americans' ability to survive and prosper. The British had been seriously considered before them, but the relatively advanced level of their research was not matched by their manufacturing capacity. No, the Americans had been the logical choice. They were a wealthy nation, restlessly hovering on the brink of total commitment, in some ways eager to demonstrate their strength, and their direct involvement could not be far in the future.

A proud, self-conscious, in many ways gauche people — that was the informed conclusion. If this was true, Corma reflected, it meant that the combination of ingredients could hardly have been bettered. German arrogance, American pride; a fanatical belief in racial superiority on one hand, a sworn pledge to the concept of equality on the other. It real-

53

ly would have been difficult to have pictured a more suitably inflexible conflict of ideologies.

The language, of course, would test him. Although he had been glad to get away from the oppressively military atmosphere that seemed to permeate almost the whole of Germany, he had felt at ease with the Germans' relatively precise use of words. It would be different here. The polyglot American language was an altogether looser, more slang-filled form, and might prove to be interestingly tricky.

It was almost dark when the truck appeared — an old, wheezing vehicle that betrayed its approach with sound long before it materialized through the half-light. He stepped out into the road and flagged down the vehicle. The driver was middle-aged, lumpily rural, and ostensibly unsuspicious. Corma told his story but did not preface it with the use of mind control, curious to see the man's natural reaction.

During the telling, he was conscious of having retained certain elements of German pronunciation, but this seemed to be accepted without question. One of the advantages of working within a culturally diffuse society, Corma thought.

This was going to be relatively easy, after all. Even his own language would probably be accepted by most as some obscure mid-European tongue. Reassured, he talked easily as the truck lumbered down the mountain toward the darkening plain below.

22

"That'll be seventy-five cents altogether, Walter," Mr. Paxton said. Walter Hurley handed him a dollar, and Mr. Paxton rang up the purchase and gave him his change. "Give my regards to your mother," Mr. Paxton said. "Tell her I hope she's feeling better soon. It's this humid weather, I expect." He smiled, nodded, and moved down the counter to attend to another customer.

Walter pocketed the change, put the aspirin and Band-aids and Vaseline into his shopping bag, and went out into the street and started to walk slowly home.

He had often wondered how it would have turned out if he had been well enough to ask Mr. Paxton for a job in the drugstore. None of the people who worked the soda fountain seemed to stay very long, just used the job to fill in time while they looked around for something better. If he had been well enough and he had been able to persuade Mr. Paxton to take him on, he could have jerked sodas for a while and then maybe worked his way over onto the pharmacy side, actually helped with the making of prescriptions, that kind of thing. It wouldn't have been real doctoring, but it was pretty close because lots of people relied on the advice of druggists rather than going to visit their doctor, unless it was something really serious, of course.

It wasn't likely that it would ever happen, though, Walter thought. His asthma had steadily worsened as he had gotten older. He had attacks almost every day now, and none of the drugs that Dr. McCready kept coming up with ever really helped much. His eyes were pretty bad, too, so he would have had trouble finding the right ingredients and making change as well.

But despite everything, his dream of doctorhood, the ability to heal and mend, lingered on. Dr. McCready was gray and paunchy now, but to Walter he still represented an ideal. He didn't just give people medicine and fix broken bones; he talked to them in a way that made them feel that maybe they weren't so bad after all. Everybody liked and respected him. It must be a wonderful thing, Walter told himself, to really warrant that kind of respect, to know that people . . .

As he turned the corner onto Washington Drive, he saw what looked like Dr. McCready's car parked outside the house. But he wasn't due to call that morning, Walter thought. He walked a bit faster and went down the driveway and in through the back door.

Dr. McCready was in the kitchen with Mrs. Adamczewski from next door. He looked despondent and tired, and Mrs. Adamczewski was crying.

"I'm sorry, Walter," the doctor said. "I got here too late to do anything — not that I could have done much, anyway. Mrs. Adamczewski called me, but she was gone before I arrived." Walter wondered what he meant, and his confusion must have shown on his face. "Your mother," Dr. McCready said kindly. "She died about twenty minutes ago."

Walter's confusion increased. His mother — dead? It didn't make any sense. "But she wasn't really sick," he said. "She just used to get tired lately. . . ." His voice trailed off.

Dr. McCready nodded. "She got tired because of her heart. It didn't seem all that bad, but sometimes these things can happen without any real warning. She wouldn't let me tell you about it, and I guess if you had known she might have gone sooner, what with the tension of worrying about what you were thinking, that kind of thing. . . ."

He carried on talking, but Walter didn't really hear him. It was all he could do at the moment to grapple with the dreadful sense of loss, the knowledge that half his world, the strong half, had suddenly and inexplicably been snatched away from him.

Now he was alone. His mind fumbled with the word, and shrank from it, terrified.

23

After leaving the hostel and going on the road, the boy who had been named Michael Pierce was rapidly exposed to the pressures exerted by necessity. He learned to beg and steal — both acts that were anathema to him at first, but which soon became such natural facets of his existence that he practiced them almost without conscious thought. He found, unexpectedly, that in this situation his physical disabilities had become, if anything, slight assets. He was small and runty and plainly no sort of threat, and people quite often reacted with relative generosity to his near-mute pleas.

During the next four years he crisscrossed countless miles of country. Twice he was jailed, the first time for vagrancy, the second time for theft. In the winter of the third year he broke a leg when jumping from the back of a truck on which he had sneaked a ride. He was found by a passing motorist and taken to the local hospital for a period of recuperation that was virtually a holiday. He was in poor general health by then, and while he was in the hospital he was fed reasonable food and kept in a warm bed. But the respite was soon over, and he moved on again, drifting, existing, crawling off to some quiet, deserted place when the seizures came, as they continued to do with disturbing frequency.

He knew very little about what happened beyond the confines of his own existence. His world was a place of basic, uncomplicated acts of necessity: the procurement of food and drink, the finding of somewhere warm and dry to sleep, the avoidance of trouble. He heard talk and read occasional news placards, so he knew that somewhere a big war had started that some people seemed to think they'd have to join in soon, but thankfully it appeared to have little if any effect on his own circumstances.

24

"All in all," Corma said, "I feel that it has gone well, given the circumstances and limited time available. It is inevitable that a certain imbalance exists at present, but this can easily be redressed at the time of my next visit. Now that they are directly involved, this will provide additional stimulus, of course, but computations indicate that it would be prudent to expedite matters further to ensure that completion is reached within the estimated time span." He unlatched his wristlet, removed the record stone, and laid it on the desk. "Full details are in my report. I trust that you will find it satisfactory."

M'doi inclined his head. "On the basis of what you have told me, I am sure that I shall." He stroked his upper lip thoughtfully. "You made no mention of technical difficulties, so I assume that none were encountered." Corma confirmed this. "The deterioration problem remains unsolved," M'doi continued, "but the researchers believe that they are on the right track. Nevertheless, it is essential that a solution is found as quickly as possible. One quails at the prospect of suspending all operations until a totally satisfactory answer is forthcoming, but such a drastic measure cannot be entirely ruled out."

M'doi nodded in response to Corma's questioning frown. "Yes, there is already a strong feeling in this direction, and it cannot be denied that it would be extremely unwise to place too much reliance on local substitution. Emergency procedures can never offer more than second best, after all." He shrugged and tapped the desktop lightly. "Well. Did your own findings tally with the information supplied?"

"The groundwork was expertly done, as always," Corma said.

"Class 1 preparation leaves little room for error. Preliminary surveying has become a very fine art indeed." M'doi picked up the record-stone and carried it to a filing slot. "I take it that you will be returning to the calm of your academic pastures tomorrow. The opportunity to relax will be very welcome after your recent concentrated activity, I am sure."

Corma nodded. "It makes for a balanced existence. I shall miss the contrast when time dictates that I must be restricted to such harmless grazing." In fact, he knew that the forthcoming term would be a restless period for him. It would have been possible, he supposed, to have completed the exercise during his initial foray, but that would have necessitated cutting a corner or two, perhaps finding a marginally less safe, more conveniently located base, for example, which would have allowed him to dispatch the details that remained.

He chided himself. He must not be impatient. He had established a satisfactorily secure pattern of procedure, and he would adhere to it. After all, he had been entrusted with his first major, and it must be handled with finesse and care. But he would be glad to get back there, to apply the final touches.

25

Sharing with his countrymen the shock and anger that followed Pearl Harbor, Peter Franklin Walsh decided to quit college at the end of the current academic year and volunteer for military service. He abominated the whole concept of war, but felt uncomfortable about the idea of remaining cocooned in academic pursuits while others were fighting and dying to preserve an ideal in which he believed.

Besides, he told himself, look how lucky I've been to get this far unscathed. Johnny Archard didn't get the same kind of breaks, and everybody has to die sometime.

John Archard's death was never far from his mind, but fairly soon after the incident he had recognized the futility of brooding too deeply over it. It had been an accident, pure and simple, and Peter found himself shamefacedly grateful that he and John hadn't really been as close at the finish as they once had been. But he had happy memories of his and John's times together, too, and he had long since arrived at an acceptance of the inescapable risk involved in simply being alive. The war was a daily reminder of vulnerability and impermanence; it was simply a question of when. But he still wished that John and the girl had been given more time.

During his last vacation he had finished the novel that he had been sporadically working on and sent it to a New

York literary agent who had contacted him after his sale to *Cosmopolitan*. The agent had expressed a liking for it but suggested modifications. Peter was pleased by the general response and not altogether surprised by the suggestions. When he had finished college and was waiting for his service papers he returned home for a few days, then went off by himself to the family cabin and spent a solitary, concentrated three weeks there, reworking the manuscript. When he had done what he felt was necessary, he sent it back to the agent and telephoned the family that he was finished. They joined him at the cabin for the weekend, the plan being to spend as much time together as possible before he was called for service.

"What's the book about?" Sidney asked him. He and Peter were strolling by the edge of the lake on the evening of the family's arrival while Marianne and Margaret stayed at the cabin preparing a meal. It was the first time he had asked Peter such a question, because he was normally content to let his son volunteer information about his writing, but recently his normal parental pride had been augmented by a touch of awe. *Cosmopolitan* had been a milestone, but a novel was something else again.

"About me, I guess," Peter said. He laughed. "I've got a feeling I'm going to be one of those writers who specializes in exposing himself in print. I've never thought of myself as being an exhibitionist, but I suppose I must be, really. It's a sobering thought."

"How do you mean, about you? Really autobiographical?"

Peter shook his head. "No, more the way I think about things, the way I feel. The people are made up, but there's a lot of you and me and the girls in it. Johnny Archard, too. I wanted to say something about the preciousness of life, how we should treasure it and not waste it, that kind of thing."

Sidney nodded, faintly embarrassed. Just prior to Pearl Harbor he had taken on a defense contract to manufacture military small arms. He hadn't really liked doing it, but he had known that if war came he would most likely have been given some kind of straight directive. But it's a necessary war, he thought, not like the one I was in. . . .

"I hope you didn't push too many of my bad points," Sidney said, "like my snoring and the way I grab the comics page before anybody else can get hold of it." They laughed and headed back to the cabin.

The accident happened the following afternoon. It was a warm, dry day, and Peter and Margaret had taken the skiff two hundred yards off shore when they struck what later investigation showed to be a submerged tree trunk, diagonally wedged between rocks. The boat tilted, then capsized. Margaret, a moderately good swimmer, was thrown clear, but Peter failed to surface.

She panicked and clung to the overturned boat, screaming. Sidney had seen the boat go over and took the power dinghy out to them as fast as he could. Ignoring Margaret, he dived, immediately finding the unseen tree trunk as it grazed his right arm.

He blinked desperately and tried to gaze through the green gloom, but there was no sign of Peter. When he was at last forced to surface, he saw the gently swaying foot as he passed it on the way up. He took another lungful of air and lowered himself under the capsized boat. Peter was there, apparently unconscious, his head tilted back and somehow wedged under the inverted single seat located at the stern. Sidney freed him and guided him to the surface. Margaret was in the dinghy by then, and between them they manhandled him aboard. Peter's heart was beating strongly, and he expelled very little water. There was a lump on the side of his head, but the skin was unbroken. Within minutes, his eyelids flickered, then slid slowly open.

By the time they reached shore he was fully conscious and able to walk to the cabin, supported by Sidney. He allowed Sidney to towel him, but insisted on dressing himself. Half an hour after the event, he was sitting in the rocking chair, a wet towel around his head, and drinking a mug of tea. His color was returning, and apart from the concealed swelling he showed no other traces of what had happened. Margaret, exhausted emotionally as much as physically, had fallen asleep on one of the bunks. Peter brushed aside suggestions that he, too, should try to sleep for a while, and he joked and chattered, cajoling Sidney and Marianne out of their nervousness.

Sidney sat by the open doorway, half-listening, contributing only occasionally to the conversation. He wondered what the odds would be on a person being knocked unconscious by a capsizing boat and then somehow getting his head wedged in the one available place that ensured that it would stay above water until he regained consciousness. Billions? Whatever it was, it was a number far beyond the range of his imagination. I wasn't even needed, he thought. If it hadn't been for Margaret out there, I could have stayed where I was and simply waited for him to sort it out for himself.

He glanced at Peter, seeing his son's smiling, no-longer-pale face, the patent aliveness of him. How ironic it would be, he thought, if he should experience something like this, only to die in the kind of lunacy that he would soon be involved in. But it had been his decision to go, and it was his life, after all. He wasn't a child any more.

Sidney stared out across the lake, trying not to think about the future.

26

"A reflector shield will be required to encase the plutonium," Corma said. *"Beryllium is the most suitable material for this purpose. The explosives will be grouped symmetrically around the shield, and wired for firing by electrical impulse. Repeat that, please."* He listened carefully as the man in the crumpled brown suit echoed his words in a high, accented monotone.

The room in which they sat was drably anonymous, furnished with nondescript pieces: a dining table, assorted chairs, and a heavy, darkly domineering sideboard. Books and papers were piled and strewn on many of the available horizontal surfaces.

The man facing Corma was pale and gaunt. His hair was plastered flat against his skull, and his eyes were haunted behind heavy-framed glasses. He shifted restlessly as he talked.

Corma said, "That is correct. The information that you have received will be remembered sequentially in the stages

that have been described. The dates on which these will occur are as follows." He listed them, listening carefully as
the man in the brown suit echoed him again, expression-
lessly. "You now have sufficient . . ." He paused and tilted
his head. Beyond the room, he heard the opening of the front
door, followed by footsteps in the hallway, then the sound
of the door closing.

He moved his flattened palm quickly from left to right in
front of the gaunt man's glazed eyes and spread one of the
printed forms on his knee. "Additional coverage for personal belongings costs very little more if . . ." He stopped
as the door to the room opened.

A woman came in. She was small, weathered, and wiry,
about the same age as the man in the brown suit. She
paused in the doorway, looking at Corma, making a swift
appraisal. "I interrupt?"

The man in the brown suit smiled as he levered himself
up out of his chair. "No, no. This gentleman has been telling me about the advantages of changing our present insurance arrangements." To Corma he said, "I am sorry. The
differences are marginal, and as I have told you, we are personal friends of our broker. You understand, I hope."

Corma accepted defeat pleasantly, gathered his litera-
ture, and left. The woman watched him go, her eyes wary.
As he drove away, she said, "Did you tell him that we already had insurance when he first got here?"

The man took a moment to answer, then nodded as he
absently filled his pipe. "Yes."

"Then why did you let him in?"

"What?" the man said. He shook his head slightly, as if
ridding himself of the vestiges of some vague distraction.
"Oh, company, I suppose. Someone to talk to." He smiled

*and put his arm around her shoulders. "With you not here,
my darling, I sometimes get lonely."*

*The woman made a dismissive sound. "I did not like
him. There was something—"*

*The man squeezed her gently. "We are in a free country
now. You must learn to trust people again." He released
her, lit his pipe, sat down, and took a book from the table.
He opened it and began to read, his eyes still haunted behind the heavy-framed glasses.*

27

The boy-turned-man who had been named Michael Pierce
normally traveled on his own; partly through choice, because of the seizures and their aftermath, and partly because he was too shy to purposely seek the company of
others whose circumstances were similar to his own. His
meeting with the man who called himself Charlie was neither sought nor wanted, and mercifully in some ways its
duration was brief, but it was a salutary experience that
both frightened and depressed him.

Whenever possible he kept away from towns. In some
respects they were easier places in which to exist than the
countryside, especially the larger ones, but towns always
carried their special problems: the greater likelihood of en-
counters with authority, the degree of competition for
whatever pickings were to be found there. But they were

warmer in the winter, and the larger ones had hostels and sometimes soup kitchens that he found himself forced to use when things were particularly bad.

The town where he met Charlie was a flat, dull, dusty place, like the surrounding countryside. Although it was early summer he had been driven there by the sheer poverty of the locality. The farms that were to be found were meager places, their few assets jealously guarded, and experience told him that it would be wise to stay away from them. The encounter with the man called Charlie took place at the rear of an eating house that he had earmarked as soon as getting there; a greasy spoon that had an alleyway running alongside it. He kept on the move until after dusk, and then went back to the alley, cautiously entering its shadows.

He found that he was a late arrival. Someone was already there, rummaging furtively in one of the two large bins at the rear of the building. The man snarled at him, but it was a weak, frightened snarl that he decided offered no real threat. He silently moved up to the second bin — an unusually bold move, but he was very hungry.

Fortunately, the collective pickings were enough for both. They ate without talking, eyeing one another guardedly in the dim light. The other man finished first, then said that he knew of a good place to sleep. It was a blunt, take-it-or-leave-it piece of information that the young man who had been named Michael Pierce would in some ways have preferred not to have received, but he was very tired, and although it was summer the recent nights had been cold.

The other man led him to a lean-to at the rear of a small factory. It was warm there; a little heat seeped through the brick wall of the building to which it was attached. There was a pile of sacks, and they shared them before locating themselves in opposite corners of the lean-to. During the night the stranger's coughing kept him awake a good deal of the time, but he was reasonably comfortable and temporarily not hungry, so he counted it a minor inconvenience and ignored it as best he could.

In the morning, when the first traffic was beginning to move in and out of the town, they left the lean-to and headed out into the country. The young man who had been named Michael Pierce didn't particularly want the company of the other man, but the man did seem to know the area, so he decided that it might be to his advantage to stay with him for a little while. Besides, the other man was plainly sick, and he felt that he owed him something for sharing his knowledge of the lean-to. Michael's first clear sight of the man in the morning had revealed a face that was drawn and waxen underneath the stubble. He walked slowly, too, and he coughed a great deal, occasionally spitting out black, varisized clots of coagulated blood. Although nothing was said on the subject, Michael sensed that the man welcomed his company, that he had probably reached a point where he was in fact afraid to be alone.

On the fifth day after their meeting, in the galvanized barn where they had spent the night, Michael Pierce woke to find the man stiff and cold beside him. During the night, sleeping fitfully as he always did, Michael had wondered about the unaccustomed absence of sound, but the weather had turned a little warmer, and he had assumed that the man had slept better because of it.

He crouched beside the body, wondering what to do. He hadn't liked the man very much, because he had been bad-tempered and bullying, irritated much of the time by his own inadequate hearing, but he suspected that it was behavior provoked by fear and ill health rather than an inherent cruel streak. Of course, he hadn't really known him at all. He had been called Charlie, he said, and Michael guessed he had been in early middle-age, but it was hard to tell for sure with sick people.

He went through the corpse's pockets, but the only thing he found worth keeping was a small pocket knife with two blades, one of them broken. He covered the body with straw and slipped out of the barn, this time heading away from the loosely circumscribed area of country and town that seemed to have formed the man's universe. He didn't really imagine that anyone would think that he had been responsible for his death in any way, because Charlie had clearly been very sick, but there was always the risk of having to answer to authority when things like that happened.

He wasn't exactly saddened by the man's death, but it made him gloomy and fearful. After all, he hadn't been so old, maybe forty or forty-five, something like that. Michael thought about his own health; the seizures, his frequent brushes with near-starvation, his growing inability to think clearly or remember things. He didn't actively want to die, but when he really thought about it, there didn't seem to be very much point in his continuing to live, either. He had always existed in shadow, but this permanent cloud was suddenly deeper and more ominous now.

He headed despondently southward, but despite the gradual rise in temperature the darker shadows remained with him, casting a cold pall across his rambling progress toward the sun.

28

John George Fuller Junior saw the lights of the gas station go on as dusk fell.

He was desperately hungry. The last time he had eaten was at midday three days before, only a little while before he had made his break from the work party. There was water where he had been holed up near the thinly wooded crest on the south side of the valley, but the few berries that he had found on his way there and had finally forced himself to eat had made him throw up. His temperature had gone up for a while after that, but now he was cool again and aching for something to eat.

He had to have food. If he didn't find some soon — something that his city-bred knowledge told him he could eat with safety — he'd be too weak to last out until . . .

Until what, he wasn't sure. He tried not to think about that. Life had been a matter of simply existing from one minute to the next for a long time now. He didn't dare hope for specific things any more.

His dream about his hands becoming normal again had drifted away a long time ago. It had started to die in the detention home, where he had surreptitiously tried to play the old piano in the recreation hall. He had been caned for that, because he was fooling around instead of mopping the floor like he was supposed to do.

The caning hadn't hurt too much. What had really hurt, and filled him with horror, was his finding that his finger joints were worse than they had been the last time he had tried to play. His fingers had labored like rusted pistons; slowly, painfully, hopelessly. He had still tried to hang onto the dream after that, but only for a while. The bleak realities of the detention home and the things that had happened after he left it had finally pushed the dream away until it was only the dimmest of memories, almost completely obscured by the sequence of disasters that had dogged him like some coldly inescapable malignancy ever since.

He had often wondered how things would have turned out if the police had believed his story about the padded hook and the cord, but he always ended up deciding that it wouldn't have made any difference, because he had been carrying a knife as well when the policeman had chased and caught him. He had found it in the doorway of an empty shop, a genuine switchblade that looked almost new, and he was only carrying it to protect himself when he walked the streets at night, but they had decided he was in need of care and protection and put him in the detention home.

He had run away three times, but he had always been found and sent back, and the only things he had learned in the home that had really stuck were the kinds of things that he wasn't supposed to know, like how to steal and not get caught. He made good use of that knowledge when they finally did let him go, but not for very long, because he had only been out a couple of months when they jumped him as he was breaking into a grocery store, and he had got two more years.

Because of his hands, he hadn't been able to do any machining or any of the skilled jobs, so they had made him work as a cleaner, and it was while cleaning out the dispensary that he started to sneak stuff out and sell it. He had never allowed himself to get hooked, not even on something mild, because he had seen the way a habit could grow and take somebody over, but he didn't let his own caution stop him from exercising the only fragment of power that he had ever known.

But then they figured out what he was up to, and they searched his cell and found some of the stuff that he had taken and hadn't had a chance to unload yet, and he had another two years tacked onto his sentence. After that he had to endure the beatings; mindless outbursts from the more violent of his previous customers, inflamed by deprivation that they senselessly held him responsible for. He had stood it for as long as he could, but when he couldn't take it any more he had seized his chance while he was outside on a work party — a desperate, suicidal move that had brought him to where he was now, crouching on the silent hillside.

He had seen the gas station that morning, spotting it when a truck that he had been watching trundle along the valley had pulled in off the road. It had stayed there for the better part of an hour before leaving again. Other trucks and cars had done the same during the day, which meant that there had to be some sort of diner attached to the gas station. He had started to imagine that he could actually smell cooking odors: sausages, bacon, coffee. He was shaking with anticipation by the time the traffic seemed to have at last petered out and he was making his way through the near darkness down the side of the hill.

There had been no traffic for at least an hour by the time he reached level ground. He wondered if anybody actually lived at the gas station. Maybe whoever ran it only came there during the day. He prayed that this was true. The last thing he wanted was confrontation and possible violence. He was in bad enough trouble already, and they'd be bound to add more time to his sentence if they caught up with him, especially if something like that happened.

He crouched by the fence at the rear of the building, his eyes fixed on the spill of light from the forecourt, waiting.

After a while, another light went on in a room at the rear of the building. A figure appeared briefly at the window and pulled down a shade. A minute or so later, a radio suddenly blared dance music.

He crouched there, cursing, before reason at last reasserted itself. It could have been worse, he supposed. They'd be switching the forecourt lights off pretty soon, and as long as the radio kept going it would help to hide any noise he might make breaking into the diner. He listened to the music: riffy, run-of-the-mill stuff; not good, but loud. Come on, you mothers, he thought. Make a whole *lot* of noise.

The music finished. There was an announcer's voice, bland and indistinct, and another number started; faster, but more of a novelty thing, with band-chanting and a girl singing. It lacked the brassy cover that the first one had offered, and the forecourt lights were still on, but he slid between the fence rails and drifted toward the building, unable to hold his impatience in check any longer. He was halfway there when he heard the click and scrape of an outside door opening somewhere. There was a sharp bark, and the blurred silhouette of a dog skittered around the front of the building and headed straight toward him.

He moaned, turned, and ran back to the fence. The dog caught him there, and he felt its teeth fasten into his leg just above the ankle. He gave a muffled scream, half-falling and grabbing at the fence. The top rail jerked loose at one end. He dragged it free and flailed it up and down, again and again and again. There were dreadful sounds by his feet, and the dog fell away from him.

The unseen door crashed open, and white torchlight flashed in his face. He stood there, shielding himself from it, remembering another man with a torch who had come after him all those years ago when all the terrible things had started to happen.

"Drop it!" the man's voice said. "Drop it, you damn nigger!" The voice was shaking, but he couldn't tell whether it was from anger or because the man was afraid. "I got you covered," the voice said. The tone changed. "Here, dog. Here, boy." The thing that he had been hitting with the fence rail didn't move. The torchlight drifted nearer, dropping from his face and down to his feet, illuminating the still, huddled remains of the dog.

Without thinking, he threw the rail toward the light and jumped after it. He heard it hit something, making a muffled sound. The light thrashed wildly, then fell and went out, and he saw the falling silhouette against the forecourt lights as the man staggered backward and down. He fell on top of him, his hands grasping blindly for the gun that he still hadn't seen and wasn't even sure was actually there. Something metallic glinted beside him as the man lifted his arm, and he grabbed at it with both hands, tearing it loose.

A leg swung over him. It was hard and heavy, and he felt himself levered sideways and onto his back, and then the man's whole weight was on him, and cigarette breath was panting close to his face. His arms were still free, stretched back above his head. Still holding the gun in both hands, he swung it forward as hard as he could. There was a dull, pulpy, cracking sound, and the cigarette breath faded as the weight on top of him slumped and didn't move again.

He pushed the weight away from him and stood up, still holding the gun in one hand. After a while, when his breathing had quieted a little, he heard the radio again. It had been going all the time, he supposed, but somehow he hadn't heard it. It was quiet, dreamy music now, and a man and a girl were singing alternating lines in caressing voices.

He dropped the gun and shuffled backward into the darkness, almost falling across the broken fence, and then ran and stumbled blindly across the unseen ground, away from the horror of the music and the light and the two still figures in the shadow of the isolated building.

29

It was late morning when Corma drove the rented car up the final stretch of mountain road. The occasional flicker of a bird moving across the bright wash of sky was the only detectable sign of life other than his own in the remote and faintly echoing wilderness of rock and trees.

He was tired, but it was the relaxed tiredness that came

from the knowledge of a job satisfactorily done. The work was finished, the trap sprung. Now the links of logic would snap into place, completing the chain that would lead frightened men to their goal and its deadly aftermath.

He felt no qualms. Despite their physical similarity to his own kind, humans were a complex, maddeningly contradictory species, impossible to understand completely. But perhaps that was as well. And after all, he had done no more than nudge probability a little closer to what in their case was surely inevitable. He had simply speeded the process a bit. Another fifteen, twenty years? That would have been the limit of the extension granted to them if they had been left to their own devices. It was a minutely irrelevant fragment of time.

At the point where the road rose closest to the summit, he drove the car onto the familiar clearing and behind the boulders at the far end, where it would be hidden from passing traffic. He left it and started up the slope, monitoring the surrounding area as he climbed. There was little evidence of life; birds, squirrels, one or two larger creatures, none of them nearby.

The flying pack was undisturbed in the same crevice that he had used on his first journey. He strapped it on and drifted up the mountainside, seeing no evidence of intrusion that might have occurred during his absence. It was only when he reached the edge of the ostensibly unoccupied basin and looked down that the coldness of uncertainty abruptly enveloped him like a moist, invisible cloak.

About twenty feet below him, he saw the ruffled bodies of several birds. They hung in mid-air, motionless, small bundles of feathers that were scattered above the central area of the basin in improbable, deathly still flight.

He landed hurriedly and entered the ship, mutely accepting that their presence was a clear statement as to the power level that was being generated. The shield was still holding, but plainly it was no longer capable of complete disintegration of whatever touched the shell of the ship. He went directly to the power chamber, finding reeking confirmation of his worst fears. One of the four pleem was dead, and two others were at different stages of terminal deterioration, their surrounding fluid already beginning to be clouded with the telltale flakes of tissue.

He disconnected the putrefying body, dissected it, refrigerated the sectioned remains, then spent the next hour rigging the support lines as auxiliaries and adjusting the nutrient supply to provide as much additional help for the weakest of the two ailing ones as he estimated would realistically extend its survival. When this was done, he circled the control area, forcing a semblance of order back into the confused and fear-edged anger that still filled his mind.

Although they were operating at disconcertingly low levels, both the visibility and element shields were holding, and there was no immediate danger of total collapse. But the situation was plagued with uncertainties, and he had no time to waste pointlessly railing at the pleem breeders. Despite M'doi's optimism, the possibility of such failure had plainly increased, and now there were an ominous number of new questions to be asked regarding the wisdom of continuing the present program in light of this new evidence.

It was the scale of what had taken place that truly alarmed him. Could the breeding techniques have somehow induced a basic weakness in the entire species, so that soon they would no longer be capable of participating in the alliance? If this was so, then unless a replacement race was found that could in some way be made to function at a consistently stronger level than had until then proved possible, the eventual result could be disaster. The finding of temporary substitutes had always proved simple enough, but they were invariably short-lived, and there were always unknown dangers in their usage. No, if what he suspected was true, it meant that the virtually impossible task of locating a genuinely durable successor would be the only way to ensure the preservation of their advantage.

But that was for the future. He brushed these speculations aside and grimly considered the present situation.

Very soon, the two afflicted pleem would be dead. The single one that appeared to be relatively unaffected — for now, at least — could continue to generate sufficient power to sustain the shields, but that would be the limit of its capability, and the additional generative demand would be bound to shorten its own period of survival. Without supporting power he would be trapped, and would remain safe only as long as the solitary pleem lived. For the present the creature seemed perfectly stable, but he accepted that the same unknown factor that had brought about the end of those already dead and dying might occur at any time.

So only one course remained. He thought about it, resigned to the knowledge that there were no alternatives, realistic or otherwise. He'd had occasion to make use of the appropriate procedures and techniques on an earlier assignment, but that had involved a single unit and had taken place on a world where the principal life form still existed at a relatively primitive level. This would certainly be more complex, possibly more difficult in unforeseeable ways. Finding suitable subjects should be the least of his worries; the large urban areas in particular teemed with potential material, and he had confidence in both his technical skills and his initiative in conditions of emergency. Time had become the real cause for concern. He must not waste it.

He made a final check of the remaining pleem, decided that the additional support being received by the ailing one was at its limit, organized the necessary equipment, and left the ship. Before stepping back into the car, he glanced up, cursing the warm clarity of the sky and recalling the weather of the past few days. The high pressure seemed settled, and there was no detectable wind. But he had no choice; elevation would be necessary to speed up the trace. He dared not wait until dark before using the scanner, he decided; several hours would be lost by such a delay. When the time came, he would simply have to project it to its limit and keep the mask to the minimum possible size and density.

Now, which way? He studied the map that he took from the glove compartment. The nearest sizable urban area was at least eighty miles to the northeast. He checked the fuel gauge and, finding it uncomfortably low, damned his failure to allow for an emergency such as this. He would go west, then, to the closer scattering of small towns that lay out beyond the fringe of the foothills. Inevitably, the choice of subjects would be more limited, but there should also be less risk and a substantial saving in time.

It would be necessary to get hold of a larger vehicle, too; an anonymous truck of some kind. He directed the car back onto the road and down the mountainside, inescapably conscious of the shadow of disaster but thinking coolly now.

30

It started to get dark outside, and after a little while Walter Hurley had to put aside the shirt he was sewing a button back onto because he couldn't see what he was doing any more and his eyes were aching badly.

He didn't really mind sewing all that much, because it gave him something to do. Threading the needle was the hard part, and sometimes it would take him ten, maybe fifteen minutes before he managed it, but after that it wasn't too bad. He knew his mending wasn't all that neat, nothing like as good as when his mother had done it, but he could handle it all right when he could see what he was doing. He didn't dare switch the light on just yet, though, because electricity was expensive and he only used it when it became absolutely necessary. It was too bad he was on a separate meter, Walter thought; if he hadn't been, he could have had it on at any time, but he supposed Mrs. Segal would have to raise the rent a bit to cover that kind of thing, and he couldn't afford to pay any more than he was already.

He sat on the edge of the bed, watching the room slowly darken. He hadn't been out of the house for three days now; it had been very dry and he could tell that there was a lot of pollen around, so he hadn't dared.

The house on Washington Drive had only been rented,

and when Walter's mother had died he'd had to move out almost right away. Mr. Perry, the landlord, had been sympathetic, but he didn't bring the rent down, and Walter had decided that the only thing to do was to move somewhere cheaper so that he could stretch the money he had as much as possible.

His mother had somehow managed to keep up the payments on a life insurance policy that had resulted in his being the recipient of eight hundred fifty totally unanticipated dollars, but he'd had the sense to recognize that even that wasn't going to last forever. He was embarrassed by the idea of going on relief, and certainly didn't intend to apply before it became unavoidable, so he knew he was going to have to budget very carefully. The furniture wasn't worth much, and there had been very little else to sell. He had kept his mother's easy chair and hairbrush, and her sewing and darning equipment, and sold everything else and moved into the attic bedroom in Mrs. Segal's rooming house, hoping that he could make the money last for a couple of years at least. He tried not to think too much about what would happen when it was gone.

Walter found that the pattern of his life was very different from when he had lived on Washington Drive. Then, he'd had his mother to guide and protect and nurse him. Apart from his attempts to attend school, which had become more and more infrequent as he grew older and his health gradually worsened, he had never ventured very far from home. His shopping excursions had been limited and usually only occasioned by his mother's own progressively variable health, but he had no opportunity now to follow such a cosseted existence. There was no one to shop and wash and clean and mend for him any more. His life had become a carefully worked out, cautiously performed sequence of expeditions: to the corner grocery, the library, Paxton's drugstore. He washed his clothes, a few at a time, in the hand basin in the second-floor bathroom, and hung them to dry in his room.

He didn't really believe any more that anyone would ever find a proper cure for his asthma. He had tried all kinds of things, but even the one or two medicines that had made a little difference never worked for long, so it didn't look as though he'd ever be able to seriously look for a job, and the last of the insurance money was almost gone by now. He was down to just a little more than a hundred dollars, and on his last visit Dr. McCready had told him that he'd have to take a test very soon to prove that he really did qualify for relief on medical grounds.

Walter didn't like the idea at all, but he knew that if he didn't have any money, then he'd have to give up the attic bedroom, and what would happen then was something that he still tried not to think about too much. But even if he did get enough to enable him to stay at Mrs. Segal's, it still meant that he'd most likely have to spend the rest of his life there, eating and sleeping and washing and mending his clothes and hiding from conditions that might provoke his asthma and hoping that his eyes didn't get so bad that he couldn't read at all any more. He tried to be optimistic about it, reminded himself that there were people a lot worse off than he was, but that didn't really cheer him up the way he knew it should have done.

When he wasn't reading his library book, carefully limiting himself to the few pages a day that was all his worsening eyesight permitted now, or listening to the radio, he thought a lot, about the war quite a bit of the time and about the people that he had known at school who had gone into the services. If he had been fit, he'd have had to go, too, he supposed, although he wouldn't have liked that because he might have ended up having to kill people, and he wanted to make them well, not kill them.

He wished he could do something useful, though; help out in some way. He tried to lend a hand at the refugee center a couple of times, sorting clothes, but he had to quit because the dust had made his asthma start up, and he had a really bad attack the last time that had put him in bed for four days. But even though that hadn't worked out, there must have been something he could do to help, Walter thought. He didn't mind what it was, really, as long as it didn't mean hurting people.

He'd have to go out next morning, he reminded himself. He was almost out of food, and whatever else happened he had to eat, even though going outside could really be asking for trouble. He got off the bed and wandered over to the skylight, wondering if there'd be any sign that they were going to have some rain so that things would get damped down a little, enough to allow him to make a quick trip to the corner grocery the next morning.

He peered up through the skylight, and as he did he saw a small white cloud slide into view. It didn't really look like a rain cloud, he thought, but it was the first cloud he had seen in a week, and maybe there'd be others coming along behind it. He stood on a chair and pushed the skylight open a bit, but he didn't see any more clouds anywhere — just the small white one, hovering almost directly overhead.

31

When dawn came, John George Fuller Junior found that he was in open country, with the hills and trees far behind him.

In the darkness he had been relieved to find that he was no longer blundering into trees and that the ground had flattened, making running easier. But he still hadn't realized just how far he had moved away from any real cover. All around him the land stretched flat and open, unfenced clay fields, each separated from the other only by a network of dusty, weed-filled ditches. As light rose in the sky and he fell for perhaps the twentieth or thirtieth or fortieth time, he found that he was lying beside one of these ditches. He rolled into it, exhausted, and was asleep within seconds. When he woke, the sun had crossed the sky and it was growing cool again.

He found that his leg had swollen badly by now and that the puffy flesh around the punctures caused by the dog's teeth had a purplish cast to it. He tried to get up, but as soon as he put weight on his bad leg a jolting pain shot through it and on up his side, and he felt violently sick.

During the night he became feverish and delirious. He slept more, but it was restless sleep, full of dark dreams; incidents of pursuit and horror in which he was maimed and helpless, and some unimaginable power drew nearer

85

and nearer to him. He couldn't make out what kind of power it was, whether it was good or bad, but he didn't understand it and he became very frightened because it had a vague scent of death about it.

It was quite warm when he woke again. The pain had gone, but now his leg was numb, and when he pinched it he didn't feel anything. He knew then that he wasn't going to be able to leave the ditch, and that death wasn't simply an ingredient of his dreams. He really was going to die, probably quite soon.

He lay among the dusty weeds as the sun rose slowly in the sky, thinking about death and wondering what it would actually mean. Occasionally he drowsed and dreamed again, but now the dreams were memories that were blessedly undistorted; bad memories, most of them, but somehow comforting because they were in the past and over and done with and couldn't hurt him any more.

He dreamed about his mother and father and the time that his hands had been broken by the cupboard door, and the night that he had stood on the roof listening to the pianist, and later, when the policeman had caught him and everybody had imagined the worst, and all the terrible things that had happened after that, culminating with the savage assaults of his frustrated former customers that had rapidly reduced him to a state of permanent dread, afraid of his own shadow and the slightest unexpected sound. He had grabbed his chance to escape when somebody else in the work party went for one of the guards with his spade because the guard had been needling the man all week. He quickly ducked behind the truck and kept it between himself and the two men responsible for the distraction. Then, while the ensuing uproar continued, he was gone, across the road and through the wheat field until he had reached the trees and the shallow river.

He dreamed about that, too; the rustling of the wheat that was like thunder for all the world to hear as he crashed, crouching, through it, the seemingly endless struggle through the waist-high water, and then the days of hiding and slow starvation.

His last dream was about the man at the gas station and the dog, and when he woke after that he realized there wouldn't be any point in going on living, anyway, because he was lame and poisoned and couldn't run if anybody did find him. They'd put him in the hospital and try to make him better, and if they succeeded it would only be so that they could put him on trial and then kill him later.

Although the sun was hot now, the lower half of his body was cold, and his head swam all the time and he felt very sick and terribly thirsty. He wanted water badly, but the ditch was dry and dusty, and the only cloud he could see was a small white one that didn't appear to be doing anything. It didn't look like a rain cloud anyway, he decided.

He stared up at the sky with glazing eyes, waiting.

Somewhere close by, he heard sounds, a scuffling noise. The sounds stopped, and dust drifted across his face. A shadow fell over him, and he saw a blurred figure standing above him on the edge of the ditch. The figure bent down, and he heard a voice making sounds that he didn't understand.

He wept and cursed as he felt himself lifted out into the light and then carried, very gently and smoothly, away from the shelter of the ditch and toward the hospital and the prison cell and the courtroom and the execution place.

He prayed for death, and after a little while, not knowing that it had happened when it did, he slid away into darkness.

32

The young man who had been named Michael Pierce was walking in sunshine beside a road that curved up a green, sparsely wooded hill when he felt the warning internal wrench and the first slight numbness that told him that another seizure was about to start.

Whenever possible he took himself to a place of privacy at such times, but quite often now the attacks came virtually without warning, leaving him no time to practice such social niceties. This was plainly one of those occasions. Resignedly following his accepted routine at such times, he sank carefully onto his knees and then slid, rather less carefully because he was rapidly losing consciousness, down onto his side.

As the numbness swallowed him, he began to fight for breath while he dimly hoped that no one would come upon him before it was over.

33

Peter Franklin Walsh had two weeks of overseas training to complete when he heard from the New York literary agent that a well-known publishing house was showing interest in his novel. The people at that company were enthusiastic, the agent said, but despite the rewriting that Peter had already done there were still one or two points that they felt might bear amendment. Would it be possible for him to get to New York for a couple of days to enable him to meet the publishers and discuss the matter in detail? It would also give the two of them a chance to meet personally, the agent said in his letter, because he felt that the manuscript had a future beyond straight book publication and he would like to discuss one or two possibilities in that direction.

Peter was astonished but gratified. Stage dramatization? Film script? He remembered Margaret's query about his writing a best-seller, and laughed. Maybe it hadn't been such a crazy question after all, he thought excitedly. He was due for leave at the end of training, a week that would precede his departure overseas and that he had planned to spend at home, but he knew his parents would understand if a day or so of it was used to deal with the question of the book. He telephoned them and told them the good news. They shared his excitement, wished him luck, and said that they'd see him at home when he could get there.

Peter had made friends with the man in the next bunk, a philosophy graduate called Henry Chasen. Like him, Chasen had politely declined the suggestion of officer's training at the time of his induction, but he admitted to Peter that his reasons had more to do with an abhorrence of responsibility than the practicing of some democratic principle. Peter, in turn, had confessed that his own reasons had not been altogether egalitarian; that he saw time spent in the ranks as being potentially more fruitful in terms of literary raw material than the relatively sheltered existence of an officer would have been.

He told Chasen, a New Yorker, about the agent's letter, and Chasen suggested that they travel up to New York together. He had the use of his brother's car, which was kept in a garage near the camp, and New York was around four hundred miles away, a reasonable day's drive if one followed a cross-country route that he knew. There was no point in messing with trains, Chasen said; they weren't really very reliable in that neck of the woods, and this way Peter could stay with him and his parents while he attended to his business.

Peter was grateful, and he accepted the offer. Then, the night before they were due to go, Chasen came down with a virus that pushed his temperature well over one hundred.

"You take the car," Chasen said when Peter visited him in the infirmary. He brushed aside Peter's protests. "No, really, you'd be doing me a favor. If this thing doesn't clear up in a few days, I might not make New York at all, and Mick will have to come down and fetch it, which won't please him. They're expecting you anyway." He handed Peter the keys, registration documents, and a note to his parents. "Take it easy when you put it into third. Like the farmer's daughter, she has to be coaxed a little." He grimaced. "Well, good luck, man of letters. I just hope to Christ I haven't passed this foul disease on to you."

Peter left early. The morning was clear and promised to be warm, and the car, a Morgan, gave him no real trouble. He frequently grinned as he drove, thinking about Henry Chasen's farewell. Man of letters rides to fame and glory in English sports car, he thought. Very stylish, the real Scott Fitzgerald touch.

He covered the first sixty miles in good time and was congratulating himself on having quickly mastered the occasionally tricky third gear when it slipped out again as he was rounding an inclining bend on a lightly wooded hillside.

He wrestled with it, braking to give it a better chance of engaging, when he saw the small grey figure of someone lying beside the road.

34

Peter pulled the car over to the side of the road and got out. He went back to the figure, uncomfortably conscious of the smell as he knelt beside it.

It was a small man who might have been almost any age, lying in a disordered way, his arms and legs at a variety of angles and his head twisted sideways. The olfactory evidence of recent incontinence was overwhelming, and there was froth and saliva around his mouth and chin.

Peter took out his handkerchief and wiped the man's face. He didn't know whether or not it had been a fit of some kind, but was relieved to find that the man had not swallowed his tongue. He looked up and down the road, but there was no sight or sound of any other traffic, and he hadn't seen any houses for some time now.

He checked the man's pulse and found it sluggish and a little irregular. He went back to the car and returned with a hand towel and a pair of slacks. He cleaned the man up as well as he was able, put the slacks on him, and threw the man's trousers and the soiled towel into the ditch. He picked him up gingerly and carried him to the car, then went back to get the rucksack that had been lying beside him. He slung it behind the passenger seat and got back in, offering a small prayer of thanks that the car had an open top.

Peter eased the car out into the road again. He wasn't exactly sure where he was, but he figured a main highway shouldn't be too far away. He was pretty certain that the man was a vagrant; his clothes were torn and very dirty, and the rucksack was evidence that the man carried some, if not all, of his belongings with him. He maneuvered into third gear carefully, keeping his head averted from his passenger as best he could. He had to admit that it would be a relief to unload him. In God's name, he thought, what must it be like to exist like that?

They crested the hill and started down the other side toward flatter, more open ground. There were no buildings visible, no signs of habitation except for the ridged fields on either side of the road stretching into the distance like drab, faded corduroy. The only other evidence of life was a black dot near the horizon, drifting toward them on the gently curving road; apparently a vehicle of some kind, although it was too far away to identify properly.

He wondered if he should flag the driver down and get directions. He had only a very basic sketch map that Henry Chasen had provided him on the previous evening. He smiled wryly. If he had started out with a proper map, instead of Henry's scrawl, in all probability he would have stuck to the main roads, would not even have been in this godforsaken backwater at all, in which case he would have been spared . . .

He castigated himself for this idly selfish thought. In an area as thinly populated as this one appeared to be, the man could have lain there for a long time, perhaps long enough for his condition to have considerably worsened. And he was bound to find help somewhere soon; a farm, perhaps even a village or a small town.

He scanned the horizon again, and then he saw the cloud.

It was small and fluffy and rather white, and it seemed that very soon they would pass underneath it, because it was positioned directly above the road, drifting steadily toward them. He glanced away from it momentarily, then frowned, blinked, and looked up again, suddenly oblivious to the problem of his passenger and stiffly conscious of the incongruity of the cloud's presence and behavior.

In all directions the sky had a hard clarity to it — a still, dry emptiness that accurately complemented the flat, dusty ground. The cloud was a bizarre deviation from the pattern; disturbing, oddly hypnotic. It had no right to be there, he thought. And how could it be moving? It was like a solitary piece of a surrealistic jigsaw puzzle; a fragment of advancing dream that had somehow intruded into . . .

He was suddenly conscious of other movement on the periphery of his range of vision. Startled, he jerked his head down, and found himself confronted by the vehicle that he had seen in the distance when they had passed over the top of the hill only a minute or so before.

Now it was close, less than a hundred yards away. It was a medium-sized, nondescript black truck. As he focused on it, the vehicle slowed and swerved, skidding drunkenly as it stopped, completely blocking the narrow road.

35

Corma applied the hand brake as the truck finally shuddered to a halt. On the seat beside him, the tracer chattered furiously, the needle of the location dial flickering uncertainly as it fought to complete its journey.

He stared through the side window at the two figures in the small red sports car that was now stationary a few yards away. As he watched, the driver got out. He was tall, young, and fair-haired, and wearing an army private's uniform. As he approached the truck, the clatter of the machine became even more rapid, as though it was suffering a trace of hysteria in its vain struggle for completion.

Corma reached down and switched it off, absently re-

turning the soldier's stare.

He had picked up the trace several miles back, shortly after leaving the place where he had found the wounded man in the ditch. Even at such a distance the signal had been exceptionally strong, by far the most promising of the disappointingly variable selection that he had encountered up to that point. This one was different; raw power, there for the harnessing, all that would be necessary to complete his requirements.

The interference had begun a short while ago. The steady progress of the readings had been interrupted by the abrupt attendance of what seemed to be an exceptionally strong countering intrusion. He had stopped the truck and checked the machine, suspecting a malfunction, but his inspection had found nothing to confirm this. The readings had remained the same; location, the power of the original signal, the negative overlay.

He damned the uncertainty of the situation and drove on. Almost immediately, the clatter of the tracer increased to a pitch that indicated a conjunction even sooner than he had anticipated. He slowed again, this time without stopping, and glanced quickly at the location dial. It was indicating a steady drift to the northeast, which meant that both the subject of the trace and the cause of the interference were on the move and heading directly toward him.

He stared ahead at the small ridge of low hills in the near distance. As he looked, he saw a flicker of color and movement emerge from the shadows of the thinly wooded slope toward which the road gently curved.

It was a time for decision. He lifted his foot off the gas pedal fractionally, thinking hard.

The choice was at least direct. He could drive on, ignoring the conflicting elements in the approaching vehicle, and hope to find a less risky alternative soon, or he could take his chances with them; an uncertain, probably dangerous course that it was impossible to assess accurately. He considered the implications of both choices with his eyes fixed unwaveringly on the approaching car, now at the foot of the hill and less than a mile away. This was thinly populated country, and the next nearest town was some fifteen miles to the west. The original reading had been a clear indication that he had found what he was looking for: a source of power that would provide the stabilizing base for his needs. His search so far had shown that such a source was a rarity for which it would be difficult, perhaps impossible, to find a substitute in the dangerously diminishing time that was now available to him.

He laughed aloud, oddly elated by this unsought and potentially disastrous development. A gamble, indeed. Fortune, he thought, you test me hard.

He pulled his foot off the gas pedal and braked heavily. From behind him, in the back of the truck, he heard a muffled cry as the truck skidded and swerved sideways before rocking to a halt before the approaching car.

36

There was no way he could get around the truck, Peter decided. The road was fringed with ditches on both sides, making such a maneuver impossible. He pulled over to the verge and switched off the engine, a reflex movement that brought total silence to the tableau of angled vehicles, now both motionless in the still, empty landscape.

He glanced up. The cloud, too, was still; frozen into immobility directly above the impeding truck. He pulled his eyes away, then looked again, numbly conscious of an additional change.

It was pointing a different way, he told himself. Yes, that was it. The cloud, roughly oval in shape, had been approaching him narrow end first. Now it was almost broadside, its profile mirroring the position of the truck, as though steered there by some undetectable link between the two.

He willed himself to climb out of the car, aware that he was shaking very slightly. He walked to the truck, returning the stare of the face visible beyond the reflections in the window glass. As he got there, the truck door opened and the driver climbed out.

He looked ordinary enough, Peter thought, clinging to optimism and lightheartedness. Not sinister, or crazy, or anything like that. "What happened?" Peter asked. "Did you have a blowout?"

The driver was about his own height, fairly stocky, and had dark hair and rather pale blue eyes. He wore new-looking gray coveralls. He didn't look particularly rural, Peter decided. More of a city type; pale-faced, unweathered. He might have been any age between thirty and forty-five.

After a brief pause the man said, "No. Excuse me one moment." He turned away, reached inside the truck, and pulled out a gray metal case. It had several dials and push switches on the top. It looked to Peter like a rather elaborate battery charger. "Will you please step down the road a little way?" the man asked. "It is necessary to run a quick check." He turned and walked away, back in the direction from which the truck had come.

Peter stared after him. He said, "What kind of . . . ?" He decided that the man was probably already out of earshot. He raised his voice and started again. "What kind of check?" The man ignored him and kept walking. About twenty paces from the truck, he stopped and turned. He said nothing, waiting.

Peter walked toward him. As he approached he said, "Look, if you didn't have a blowout, then please move your truck. I've got a sick man back there in the car. If I don't get him—"

"He will recover soon," the dark-haired man said. "Excuse me, please. We do not have much time." He walked around Peter until he had positioned himself between Peter and the truck. He pressed a switch on the gray metal box. The box hummed and gave off a faint, high-pitched clatter. After a moment he nodded and reversed the switch. The sound stopped. "Please step back to the truck. One more check is necessary," the man said. He moved away, back toward the parked vehicles.

Peter watched him go, open-mouthed. He was too surprised to feel resentment at this peremptory, briskly military-style assumption of authority. There was something a little army there, he thought. What the hell was this? Some kind of exercise? Was there a research establishment in the area? That might explain the cloud. . . .

He walked back to the truck. The driver was rummaging inside the vehicle again. As Peter reached him, he turned. He was holding what looked like a small flashlight, with markings on the rim of the glass-holder. He made some kind of adjustment, glanced briefly up and down the empty road, pointed the torch at Peter, and pressed the switch.

Nothing happened. No light, no sound. After a moment the dark-haired man nodded again, reversed the switch, and slid the torch into a pocket of his coveralls. He looked mildly quizzical.

"What's this all about?" Peter asked. He was conscious of his dry mouth and the fact that his hands were suddenly cold and moist. His voice sounded hoarse. He cleared his throat. "What is that cloud thing up there?" My God, he thought, suddenly. Is he a spy? Now, why the hell didn't I think . . . ?

"Security," the man said. He looked appraisingly at Peter. "I am going to need your assistance." He took the gray metal box from the truck again and went past Peter to the car. He stood beside it, studying the crumpled figure in the passenger seat and manipulating the box controls again. The box hummed strongly, the overlay of clatter now only faintly heard. He returned to the truck. "He will recover soon. His infirmity is something that occurs quite often."

"Are you a doctor, too?" Peter asked, frowning.

The man smiled briefly. "My duties require a certain versatility." He glanced in both directions again. "It would be preferable that we discuss this inside." He turned to re-enter the truck.

"Wait a minute," Peter said. His confusion was increasing by the second. He raised his hands. "Now, wait just a minute." The man paused and turned to face him again, his expression patiently inquiring. It was a strong face, Peter decided. It was innocuous in its way, but there was a discipline about it that he somehow found impressive. "What's this about security? And just what is that thing up there?"

"Thank you," the man said. "An oversight." He pressed a switch on the gray metal box, looking up as he did so. Peter followed his gaze. As he watched, the cloud dropped rapidly toward them, dispersing as it came. It reached the ground beside the truck, where it completed its evaporation. Where it had been there now lay a perforated, pale gray metal cylinder, about two feet long and a foot in diameter. The dark-haired man pressed the switch again, and it began to roll slowly toward the grass where they stood.

He bent down and picked it up with one hand, inserting his fingers into some of the perforations. From the way he lifted it, the thing seemed to be quite heavy. He glanced at Peter again and nodded toward the truck.

"What is that thing?" Peter asked slowly.

"A scanner," the man said. "It is how I found you and your companion. And the others." He gestured briefly toward the truck. "Please. Time is getting short, and we must talk."

The world is a crazy place, Peter told himself. Crazier

right now than perhaps it had ever been in its history of seemingly interminable lunacy. It was full of strange and terrible and wonderful things that he badly wanted to understand so that he could distill their oblique and shadowed truths into words. And there was something unique about what was happening just now, a special element of strangeness.

Maybe there's another book in it, he thought; a wild adventure story. Security permitting, of course. He went past the man and climbed into the truck, suppressing what he knew would have been an hysterically nervous laugh.

37

Corma walked around the front of the truck, placed the cylinder behind the seat, and got back in. He put the tracer between himself and the soldier, activating the local cutout and carefully adjusting the readings to a low-level scan that would warn of approaching traffic.

He started the truck, maneuvered it to face the sports car at the edge of the road, braked, and turned off the engine again. He leaned back in his seat and looked at the soldier searchingly.

The events of the past two or three minutes had decided his course of action for him. It was no longer a matter of real choice. His individual scan of the intruder and his subsequent abortive attempt to neutralize the threat that the man posed had confirmed the level of risk that faced him.

He wondered what the odds were against the likelihood of such a meeting, but then dismissed the thought peremptorily. It was impossible to say, pointless to waste valuable time regretting the fact of its occurrence and seeking other ways of quick termination. It had happened, inescapably, and would have to be played with delicacy and ingenuity until an answer could be found.

How conscious was this man of his power? Corma wondered. It was an interesting face; symmetrically pleasing, firmly contoured, with intelligent eyes. Naive? Yes, that seemed likely. He was young; twenty or so, Corma judged.

"Are you a person with imagination?" Corma asked.

The soldier's expression of wary curiosity blurred. He looked confused again. "Imagination? Yes, I guess so." He smiled, rather nervously. "Why?"

"If I were to tell you that the 'security' I spoke of was universal rather than national, would you be prepared to believe that?"

"I don't follow you," the soldier said after a moment.

"My name is Corma. I am a guardian." Despite the circumstances, he found it necessary to smother a sudden desire to laugh at this irony. He watched the soldier carefully. "Prepare to exercise your imagination now. Do you know how many suns there are in your galaxy?"

The soldier shook his head uncertainly.

"One hundred billion," Corma said. "An approximate figure, you understand. Many of them have planetary systems, a fair percentage partially inhabited, as is yours. In many cases this has resulted in the development of intelligent life, the formation of societies. Do you find this feasible?"

The soldier said, after a pause, "Yes, I guess so."

"Yours is a planet at war," Corma said. "It is a war that will shortly lead to the development of means of destruction far beyond those now used. However, this will not be achieved solely by your own efforts. The information that will instigate the necessary research and experimentation will shortly be directed into the hands of those people in a position to utilize it. What follows if this happens will be unavoidable. However, at this stage it can be prevented."

The soldier's expression changed. He thinks I am mad, Corma thought. It was the natural, expected reaction. He waited, carefully concealing his tension, glancing casually at the scanner dial, which was still mercifully inactive.

"You said something just now about my planet," the soldier said awkwardly. "Does that mean that you're telling me that you're from somewhere else? Some other world?"

"Yes," Corma said evenly. This was a critical moment, requiring fine judgment. He nodded. "Yes, I am. Do not be alarmed by what you understandably think of as my obvious lunacy. I am not mad, nor is it my intention to harm you in any way." He looked at the soldier squarely. "I need your help. Are you prepared to listen to what I wish to tell you?"

There was a long moment of silence. The soldier shifted slightly in his seat and said, "You called yourself a guardian. What exactly is it you're guarding, and why?"

"The history of intelligent life is a complex one," Corma said. He felt a cautious surge of relief. Imagination and curiosity; they were linking now. The soldier was afraid, but his curiosity was blanketing his fear. "You must accept that your species is one of many, and that many of the others have developed technologies that far surpass your own. The

103

actual figure is irrelevant, but it amounts to several thousand in this sector of the known universe alone. Although individual species follow their own local evolutionary requirements, certain traits are universal. The desire for conquest, for whatever reason, is one." He glanced at the scan readings again. He stiffened imperceptibly. The needle was moving now. Whatever the machine was detecting was five or six miles to the south and heading directly toward them.

The soldier said, *"Are you saying that we're due to be attacked by . . . well . . . ?"* He made a vague upward gesture. He looked patently embarrassed.

Corma shook his head. *"There is no necessity for extravagance of that kind."* He fought back the urge to talk faster. *"You must understand that yours is not a universal time scale in the broader sense. The passage of a century here means little to many races. My own racial history predates your own by many billions of years, and our individual life expectancy is considerably greater."* He checked himself. *"You must excuse what could be interpreted as a claim of superiority. It was not intended as such. Longevity is not in itself a virtue."*

"Let me try and get this straight," the soldier said. *"If we don't actually get attacked, what does happen? Do you mean that we're given this information about weapons so that we have the means of committing genocide, and after we do that they take over?"* He was polite, but his face and voice were wary again. *"Even if that was what was intended, what kind of weapon could possibly guarantee that we actually would run the risk of wiping ourselves out?"*

Corma sensed the possibility of a serious loss of ground. *"Have you any knowledge of theoretical physics?"* he asked. He gestured dismissively as the soldier frowned quizzically.

"No matter. You must believe me when I tell you that the fissioning of atomic structure is a perfectly achievable and quite simple process, given the knowledge and necessary materials. Explosive weapons based on this principle have been used elsewhere, many, many times."

He looked at the scanner dial, the steady upward drift of the needle, then back at the soldier. "Your initial supposition is correct. Both factions in the present conflict are to be given the necessary information. The simple fact that you are at war, both sides believing fervently in the rightness of their respective causes, will ensure that the weapons, once made, are used. The result will be a scale of devastation beyond your imagining. Naturally, you question the irrationality on the part of your species that this implies, but logic and reason are relegated to secondary roles in such a situation. In the event, I assure you that the existence of one guarantees the occurrence of the other."

There was a pause. The soldier was studying him, a mixture of emotions playing subtly across his face. Quickly, Corma thought, quickly now. He said simply, "You must believe that what I describe can happen, and also that it can be prevented. But to do this, I must have your help."

"I'm not saying that I believe any of this, or that I don't," the soldier said slowly. "But if it is going to happen, why would you or any other outside agency be interested in doing anything to prevent it?"

"We are the guardians," Corma said. "We are an old race, one of the oldest known. We have survived these things while many have fallen. We see it as our duty to protect others from them." He tried to listen objectively to his own voice, to picture his facial expression. He repressed a slight flutter of panic. There was so little time. . . . "You must understand that evil and greed and cunning are not matters exclusive to your own race. They breed and proliferate in all corners of the universe, and must be fought wherever they occur. We have done this for a very long time now. It is an endless task, but one that we see as necessary." Dignified resolution? Yes, the balance felt right now. But a seasoning of pure fiction would be helpful at this point.

"We do not always succeed, you understand," Corma continued, "and the level of personal risk is frequently high. There were four of us when this assignment commenced. We obtained confirmation of what is to happen, but at a cost. I alone survive." He looked away briefly, then back at the soldier. "The sources and methods of infiltration are many and not always detected, but we maintain a balance of a kind. Your world can be saved, but only if immediate action is taken. We have, at most, a day and a night."

He looked down at the scan reading. "A vehicle is approaching from the south. At this moment, it is approximately two miles away. It is a matter of three or four minutes before it reaches us." He switched off the machine. "Bearing in mind our isolated location and the natural curiosity of the rural mind, it is highly probable that we will soon be questioned as to the reason for our presence here, the assumption being that some kind of assistance will be welcomed. You must decide now whether you believe what I have told you, and whether or not you are prepared to help. Others are already with us for this purpose, but both you and your passenger are vital to any realistic possibility of success. If you decide against it, you are free to go."

He looked at the soldier bleakly. "Remember what you have seen so far — an example of technology well beyond *your own race's capability in such things. If you still doubt me, think of that and all that it implies. The choice is yours."*

38

What in God's name is this all about? Peter thought.

He stared at the dark-haired man, now waiting with controlled patience for his reply. He searched the pale, serious face, trying to find some clue there, something that would help direct him to a decision, some indefinable key to the truth of what had been said.

He means it, he thought. So help me, I think he means every word. But a belief isn't a fact. It needs solid evidence to become that. He looked down unseeingly at the now silent machine on the seat beside him, thinking blurred thoughts; about people, events, the current madness afflicting the world and his own voluntary involvement in it.

Why me? he thought. And the man he had found? The difference between them could hardly have been more extreme. He had said something about others being already with them, too, presumably back inside the truck. What kind of people were they, and what kind of help could any of them give? Why didn't he simply go to the authorities and . . .

He mentally shook his head. No, if what he had been told was the truth, if time really was a vital factor, he could see the utter impossibility of attempting to involve official-dom of any kind. And maybe I'm due to die, anyway, Peter thought. People were being killed in the thousands, hun-dreds of thousands; meaningless deaths, most of them. So even if it did mean that I'd be putting myself at risk, as long as there was even a slim chance . . . He focused on the machine, remembering the cloud.

"If this works," Peter said, "you figure it will take up to twenty-four hours. Is that right?"

The dark-haired man nodded. "Yes."

"All right," Peter said. He tried to check his sudden flush of excitement. Crazy, crazy world, he thought. Crazy me, maybe. "What do we have to do?"

"We must get the other one out of sight," the dark-haired man said. He swung himself out of the truck and went to the car. He lifted the still-unconscious figure from the passenger seat, gently, and came back carrying him in his arms. "The doors. Open them, please."

Peter slid outside, ran to the back of the truck, and un-latched one of the back doors. As it swung open, he caught a shadowed glimpse of movement in the dark interior.

Someone approached the open door — a pale, thin, high-shouldered man with an anxious face, wearing thick glasses.

"These two are with us," the dark-haired man said. "Take him." He slid the small man inside the truck. The pale man knelt down and steered the new arrival clear of the entrance. "We are complete now," the dark-haired man said. "We shall be going soon." He closed the door and turned. He smiled a humorless smile. "Our timing has been very precise. An omen, I hope."

Peter followed his gaze. A car was visible, still some

distance away, but approaching steadily, raising dust as it came.

"We cannot risk the possibility of protracted conversation," the dark-haired man said. "Delay must be avoided at all costs." He glanced at the truck. "We must agree on a suitable fabrication as to our reasons for being here."

"You've had a blowout," Peter suggested, "and I've been lending you a hand. Let's make it look good." He knelt beside the truck and ran his palms over the film of dust-coated grease on the rear wheel. He stood up and held out his right hand. "My name's Peter Walsh. Glad to have been able to help."

The dark-haired man looked down at the proffered hand. He smiled again. It was a coolly approving smile, touched with something else that Peter couldn't quite define. Maybe they don't like getting their hands dirty, he thought.

The dark-haired man reached out and shook hands. He relinquished his grip as the car clattered to a halt on the far side of the road.

Peter turned and looked at it, seeing it clearly for the first time. It was a dented, buff-colored sedan, with a siren on the roof and red spotlights projecting above the corners of the windshield. As he stared at it, stiff with sudden, disbelieving shock, the driver's door opened and a man climbed out.

39

He wore a low-crowned Stetson with a pronounced sweat mark extending above the band, and a badge was pinned to the left pocket of his faded khaki shirt. Beneath the Stetson, his face was pinched and inquisitive. He wandered across the road, his left thumb hooked in his belt, his right hand dangling by his side. Seen at close quarters, he had small, brightly curious eyes that seemed unable to fix directly on anything for more than a second or so at a time.

"You got trouble?" he said. He looked at the dark-haired man, then Peter, finally the truck. His tongue rummaged in his cheek, and he turned his head away and spat.

The dark-haired man took a cloth from a pocket in his coveralls and began to wipe his hands. "All fixed now. I had a blowout." He cocked his head at Peter. "This gentleman gave me a hand." To Peter he said, "Thanks again. Much obliged."

"That's all right," Peter said, startled but hoping his discomfiture didn't show. He had been taken completely by surprise at this abrupt change in the dark-haired man's persona. It was an almost perfect assumption of rural diffidence; the leisurely terseness, the relaxed affability, all in total contrast to his previous formally measured way of talking. The accent, he decided, had been flawless.

"Well," the dark-haired man said. He studied his hands

and passed the cloth to Peter. "I guess that does it, then." He nodded to Peter and the other man and turned toward the truck.

"Sam Coulter'll sure be glad to hear you didn't end up in a ditch," the man in the Stetson said. "He does a lot of business with that there truck." He smiled a parched, sly smile. "Wouldn't want him to have to put it in the repair shop when he gets it back."

The dark-haired man turned, unhurriedly. "How's that?"

"That there's Sam Coulter's truck," the other man said. "You'd be the feller that's fetchin' some furniture down from Allentown. Booked it out just as he was closin' up yesterday, y' did." He looked mildly triumphant.

The dark-haired man smiled. "That's right."

"I knowed Sammy Coulter the better part of twenty years," the man in the Stetson said. "Knowed him afore he took the place over from Perce Whaley. Perce died five years ago last fall." He nodded. "He weren't no business-man, that's for sure. Could've made a mint back there just after the war if he'd played his cards right and got hisself an automobile agency." He looked at Peter. "Last war, I mean, o' course. You'll be goin' off to this one, then."

Peter had been awkwardly manipulating the cloth, prolonging the process of cleaning his hands. "Yes, pretty soon now," he said. He smiled, feeling the stiffness of his reluctant facial muscles. God in heaven, he thought, I need a few lessons at this kind of game. "I just got through training."

The man in the Stetson nodded. "My boy's in the army too." He jutted his lower lip. "Sure miss him around the place." Then he looked toward the dark-haired man again and said, "Why didn't you hire a truck up in Allentown?"

Peter's insides abruptly chilled. "Woulda saved yourself an extra trip."

"Cheaper to do it this way," the dark-haired man said. "They charge pretty high up in Allentown. Saved myself fifteen dollars hiring down here."

The man in the Stetson shook his head slowly. "Still don't make sense," he said, affably persistent. "How about your cost of gettin' down here and pickin' it up?" To Peter he said, "I guess he done his sums wrong." He smiled his parched smile again, briefly.

"Rode down with someone I know," the dark-haired man said. "He had some business in town, so we fixed up to come down on the same day."

The man in the Stetson said, "Oh, yeah. I guess that'd be his car you left at Sammy Coulter's."

"That's right. I dropped him off before I picked up the truck. He asked me to get the car serviced while he was tending to his business. I'll be riding back with him on Sunday."

The man in the Stetson nodded again. "Yeah, Sammy said somethin' about doin' a grease job." He wedged his tongue behind his bottom lip, worked it around a little, then removed it again. "You carryin' anything now?"

Peter felt his insides compress to a tight, cold ball. The dark-haired man shook his head. "Nope. I'm only fetching, not taking."

The man in the Stetson picked at the side of his nose. "Reason I'm askin', there's been a killin' out on the Beaumont road. Feller that ran the gas station there had his head stove in night before last." He glanced quickly at them, first the dark-haired man, then Peter, then looked away again. "We was told on Monday there's a feller on the run from Maxted. Took off when he was out on a work party. Looks like there's a tie-up there, so they tell me." His eyes flickered across them again.

The dark-haired man frowned with concern. "You figure he might be trying to sneak a ride?" He looked thoughtfully at the truck, then shook his head. "Don't see how he could've done that, but I guess you never can tell. Take a look in back, if you want." He walked toward the rear of the truck, fumbling in his coveralls as he went. He got to the corner, clucked his tongue, and started back for the front of the truck again. "Keys," he said as he leaned in through the door.

"Ah, it don't matter," the man in the Stetson said. He picked at the side of his nose again, looking suddenly disinterested. "If you got her locked, nobody ain't goin' to be able to sneak in. Just take my tip and don't pick up no hitchhikers. Never know what you're gettin' these days."

So that was it, Peter thought. There had been a little more to his stopping than just rural curiosity, after all. "You're out looking for this fellow who's on the run, then," Peter said.

"Kind of," the man answered. "Not really my territory, though. Happened over in the next county." He sucked at a tooth and spat again. "Still, wouldn't do me no harm if I did pick him up. We got elections next month, and people sure got short memories. I been chief for two terms and I got a good record, but you'd never know it the way some folks talk." His face and voice were sour.

There was a brief, awkward silence.

"Well," said the man in the Stetson, resignedly. He started across the road, then turned. To Peter he said, "Good luck, young feller. Hope you don't get yourself shot up or nothin' like that. War's a bad business." He went to the car and got in, slamming the door hard. He started up the car and moved off without acknowledging them further. The sedan lurched down the road, clattering, trailing smoke and dust as it went.

40

"It will be prudent to let him get a little way before we follow on this road," the dark-haired man said. "The turn that we have to take is some twenty miles from here." He spoke in his previous, measured way. His mouth was tight, but otherwise he was apparently relaxed. "It would be unwise for us to aggravate any suspicions that he may have already formed."

"Why should he suspect us of anything?" Peter asked. He was suddenly conscious of the moistness of his hands. He wondered, briefly, to what lengths the dark-haired man would have been prepared to go if the policeman had insisted on seeing the truck's interior. "I thought you handled that perfectly."

"A question remained unasked," the dark-haired man said. "Several, possibly. Such people have a natural mistrust of strangers, and his country is at war. Perhaps he shares the suspicions you had initially." Peter felt himself color slightly. "To such a person, the likelihood of criminal activity or some form of espionage would be altogether more credible than the facts."

Peter nodded. "Yes, I guess that's so. But he still wasn't all that suspi—"

"The evidence would indicate that we were traveling in opposite directions when we met," the dark-haired man said. He nodded toward the truck and car, facing one another along the side of the road. "If we were shortly to be seen traveling in the same direction, and in tandem, it would be natural to suspect some form of alliance. Our story indicated that we were passing strangers, brought together by an emergency that prompted your offer of assistance. If he has suspicions, they would be considerably strengthened by evidence to the contrary." He glanced at his wristlet. "Another five minutes, and then we will proceed. In the meantime, it provides us with an opportunity for you to meet the others." He looked at Peter. "Do not be surprised at what you will no doubt regard as a strangely arbitrary choice of allies. Each of them has a quality that is needed in this situation." He turned, and walked to the front of the truck, returning with the gray metal box. He went around the truck to the rear.

Peter followed him. He wondered what was going through the dark-haired man's mind. Was the man frightened in any way? There was no doubting the presence of the tension that lay beneath his cool exterior. It was controlled, but unmistakably there; a shielded urgency that he sensed was totally genuine.

The dark-haired man unlatched one of the back doors and opened it, then gestured inside.

Peter climbed past him into the gloom.

The air inside the truck was heavy, tainted with an assortment of smells. The principal source was plainly the man he had found lying beside the road, but there were other odors as well, one of them vaguely antiseptic. In the shadows at the front end of the cargo area he saw three figures, two of them stretched out on the floor, the other one crouching between them. Someone was moaning, a soft exhalation of distress that faded to silence as the dark-haired man climbed inside and pulled the door closed behind him.

A light clicked on, and for the first time Peter saw the truck's occupants clearly.

41

As he brushed past the soldier, Corma glanced briefly at his face, acknowledging the sudden reversion to doubt and disbelief that he saw there.

It had been inevitable, he supposed. Despite the warning he had given the soldier, he had known that the reality of what the truck contained would strain the credibility of the situation to a dangerously fragile point. To the soldier's youthfully expectant imagination, it must have seemed more like an introduction to a segment of muted bedlam than the start of a glorious adventure with the preservation of his own species as the goal.

Corma knelt beside the young Negro, laid a hand gently on his forehead, and placed the tracer on the floor beside him. The Negro's eyes were closed. His face was still the color of shadowed putty, but his temperature was nearly down to normal now. Occasionally he pawed at the sacking on which he lay.

"Is everything all right, Mr. Corma?" asked Walter Hurley. "Have they gone?" He was breathing in short, labored gasps, and his forehead was creased in an anxious frown. "What was it they wanted?"

"There is no cause for alarm," Corma said. He made his voice placatory now, relaxed. He looked up at Hurley and smiled reassuringly. "It was just someone who thought that there had been some kind of mishap and wanted to lend a hand. We thought it wise not to attempt to hurry him away and possibly arouse suspicion." He glanced at the figure lying on the other pile of sacks. The small man was stirring now, his head rolling from side to side. Corma looked at the Negro again and lifted his hand from the young man's forehead. "He is cooler now," Corma said. "The worst is over, but I think it might be good if the dressing was changed. Would you take care of that, please, Mr. Hurley?"

The bespectacled man muttered assent. He looked suddenly purposeful and eager. "The other one will be conscious soon, but he must continue to rest," Corma continued. "Explain to him that he is being taken to a place where he will be fed and cared for." He stood up. "It will not be long now. I am sorry about the discomfort and the delay, but I am sure that you appreciate that a situation of this urgency leaves very little time to make satisfactory arrangements." Corma gestured to the soldier. "This is Mr. Walsh, who is helping to complete our party. Without him and this other gentleman, it is very possible that our mission might have ended in failure. Now I have every hope of success."

Walter Hurley, already engaged in the careful removal of a coil of bandage from the Negro's exposed leg, paused briefly. He looked up at the soldier, nodded, and smiled.

"What happened to him?" the soldier asked. "Is he wounded?" His voice was tense.

"Dog bite," answered Walter Hurley as he finished unwinding the bandage. "He was pretty bad when we picked him up, but he's a whole lot better now. You can see he was bit pretty . . ." He fell silent, staring in disbelief at the exposed wound. He bent closer, his jaw slack. "Why, he's only had that on there for . . . about an hour, I guess. It's almost down to . . ." He broke off again and stared up at Corma, his face awed.

"Use a little more of the salve," Corma said. "About half the previous amount." He picked up the tracer, which was still emitting its low, unbroken hum. He glanced at the soldier, seeing in his face now a partial rebirth of his earlier guarded conviction. Enough proof? he wondered. It had to be. . . . "We must move on," he said to Walter Hurley. "If everything goes as it should, we shall be at our destination in approximately two hours. Make yourself as comfortable as you can." He smiled, turned, and motioned for the soldier to follow him out of the truck.

42

Peter joined the dark-haired man outside and latched the door behind him. The day was still bright, the air blessedly untainted. The fetid interior of the truck and its bizarre selection of occupants seemed suddenly to belong to another, darker world, far removed from the one in which Peter now stood.

"Look, you've got to tell me more than you have," he said slowly. He gestured awkwardly toward the truck. "Those people . . ." He hesitated, not knowing what to say.

The dark-haired man glanced down at the metal box, then said, "They possess certain latent powers of which they have remained unaware until now. If this present emergency had not arisen, it seems probable that they would have gone through their lives never knowing what they carry within them and what it can achieve. They have not yet been told what is involved, but this will be done as soon as time and circumstances permit."

"What kind of power?"

"Here, it is called psychokinesis," the dark-haired man said. "Do you understand the term?" Peter nodded, uncertainly. He thought he remembered the term, used to refer to . . . the moving of physical objects by some kind of mind control? Yes, that was it. "In your own world," the man continued, "this ability and other similar ones are generally viewed as improbable phenomena and taken seriously by relatively few people. They exist, nevertheless, usually as a kind of compensatory factor. The chemistry and mechanics that they involve are at least partly understood by my own people, which has led to our ability to activate them and influence their usage. I have that knowledge, and the situation demands that it is applied now."

The man paused and looked at Peter steadily. "I understand your continued doubts and reservations, but consider what you have seen so far. A few moments ago, you witnessed further evidence of a science more advanced than your own, its effectiveness corroborated by the unsolicited reaction of one of your own kind. You have the intelligence to know that such things cannot be brought about by trickery or sleight of hand. You must accept the evidence of your own eyes and all that these things imply. Also, you must believe me when I tell you that time is running out and that there will be no second chance. You have my word that you will know the full details when we reach our destination. There is still urgent work to be done there, for both of us. As we work, I shall tell you everything that you wish to know. Remember, finally, that this is for yourself and your kind. May we go now?"

Peter took a deep breath. "All right. You'll have to lead, I guess."

The dark-haired man nodded. "Yes. Do you have sufficient fuel for a distance of approximately seventy miles? During the latter stages it will be necessary to drive in lower gears for most of the time."

The mountains? Peter thought. Somehow that seemed appropriate. "Yes, I think so," he said.

"It will be necessary to refuel my own vehicle shortly,"

the dark-haired man said. "When I do, drive on for a distance and then wait for me. In the event of any kind of emergency, sound your horn twice." He nodded. "May good fortune go with us." He walked around the side of the truck and climbed inside, slamming the door after him. The engine whirred, then caught.

Amen, Peter thought. He ran to his car and slid into the driver's seat. For a fleeting moment he thought of his father and mother and sister, the sanity and stability that they represented, experiencing a last flicker of uncertainty as their faces drifted past his mind's eye. Did he believe what was happening — really believe it? Or was he immersed in some mock-heroic dream, where the complex ethical minutiae of real existence had coalesced into clearly defined patterns, issues that it was now possible to . . .

The truck lurched past him, gradually picking up speed as it went along. He caught a glimpse of the dark-haired man's pale, intent face, and then it was gone. Dust filled the air around him.

A dream? He was suddenly acutely conscious of his immediate surroundings; he felt them where they made contact with his body, smelled the dust and oil and leather, sensed their unmistakable tangibility.

"No dream," he said aloud. He coaxed the engine into life and began to make a U-turn in the road. Seconds later he was speeding after the truck as it headed toward the low hills that edged the horizon.

43

For the first time since his return to the ship and the finding of the dead and ailing pleem, Corma experienced the luxury of an easing of pressure. He sensed that a turning point had been reached and successfully passed.

Serious problems remained, of course. The presence of the soldier and the danger that the young man unwittingly presented were factors that he must continue to handle with extreme caution. But, all in all, the situation had gone as well as he could reasonably have expected. His distortion of the facts had been accomplished with a touch of inspiration, enabling him to simulate a fluent conviction that must have been a conclusive factor in gaining the man's belief, however intrinsically flimsy that belief and trust might still be.

He considered their meeting, and his attempt to apply the power of will and mind when facing the soldier for the first time; the frightening absence of reaction that confirmed the threat that he posed and which automatically limited the use of the power in his presence; then, the subsequent unprecedented failure of the blade. It had been a terrifying episode, a clear invitation to panic and disaster that he had forced himself to endure until equanimity of a kind had returned.

He had relied on cunning, then, to achieve what he

could not obtain through externally induced controls. And he could continue to do so. It had worked this far, more than adequately. Yes, he had coped satisfactorily with a potentially highly dangerous set of circumstances. But the threat remained, and would remain as long as the soldier was involved. On the available evidence, a physical solution seemed highly improbable. But there were other ways. . . .

He drove mechanically, thinking, the tracer at last silent and unwanted beside him.

44

The motion of the truck combined with the inescapable smells to make Walter Hurley feel nauseous, but in a way he didn't mind because it was helping to keep his mind off his asthma, and he always found the asthma easier to control when he didn't think about it too much. I hope I don't get sick, though, he thought anxiously. It would be terrible to make the truck smell worse than it already does.

He supposed that this was what war was really like, very different from the way it was in books and comics, and the movies, too, most likely, although he didn't know for sure because he had only been to a movie once and he'd had to leave halfway through the picture because his asthma had started up. But he could imagine what it would be like in a movie, all fighting and shooting and running, and none of the real smells and that kind of thing.

He wondered if the soldier had been to war yet. He looked very young, and it was only a few months since they had gotten involved, so maybe he hadn't actually been in any fighting. He wasn't at all like the rest of them, but in a way it was a comfort to have somebody like that along, because it made everything seem a bit more normal.

Walter looked at the small man and wondered if he was all right. The man had acted as though he was coming around a while ago, but now he seemed to be just sleeping. A trickle of saliva was coming from one corner of his open mouth. Walter leaned across and gently wiped it off, feeling protective and useful, just like when he had bandaged the Negro's leg. That's how I'd feel all the time if I could ever be a doctor like Dr. McCready, he thought.

The Negro was asleep, too, snoring slightly. Walter sat back in a corner, trying not to think about his asthma and the bad air and the steadily growing heat inside the truck, wondering just what it was they were going to have to do when they got to wherever it was they were being taken.

45

The low hills were behind them now. In the far distance, beyond the thinning trees, the mountains showed clearly against the flat blue of the sky.

Corma glanced at the truck's fuel gauge. The needle was very low, indicating a little more than two gallons left in the tank. Even allowing for the normal emergency margin, he had barely enough to take him another forty miles, and there were still at least fifty to go. He must stop at the first gas station they came to, before they reached the turnoff. Refueling points were virtually nonexistent in the mountains, and it would be foolish to run the risk of finding himself stranded, even with the soldier there to act as a runner.

Several minutes later he rounded a tight bend in the road and saw two pumps and a corrugated building just ahead. He put his arm through the open window, signaled the soldier to keep going, and turned off the road into the station's graveled forecourt. As he braked, he noticed the car at the far end and the figure that was about to climb into it. With a shock, he recognized the man in the faded khaki shirt and the Stetson hat.

Another minute, he thought. Another minute, and we would have missed him. He pulled up beside the nearest pump, parking as far from the policeman's car as he could, and switched off the engine.

Had he seen the soldier's car? Corma wondered. He must have. It had gone by seconds after he had turned into the station, an unignorable flash of bright red.

A man appeared from inside the corrugated building and came over to the truck. "Fill 'er up?"

"Yes," Corma said. He watched the man in khaki at the far end of the station. He was standing beside his car now, looking back in Corma's direction. Despite the shadow thrown over it by the Stetson, Corma could see that his face was puckered and thoughtful.

He must not leave here before I do, Corma thought. He wondered if the soldier had seen the policeman's car, and if so what the young man would do. If the policeman got on the road before Corma did, and if the soldier had parked only a short distance away as he had been told to do, then what he had hoped to avoid would happen inescapably. The policeman's suspicions, clearly visible now on his shadowed face, would be stimulated to a point where there was a danger of his taking some form of direct action, involving himself in the situation and necessitating counteraction on Corma's part.

But what would he actually do? Would he insist on inspecting the truck's interior after all? For the moment at least he appeared reluctant to approach the truck. Perhaps he intends to follow me first, Corma thought, checking to see whether the soldier and I do rejoin forces before deciding that such a move is justified.

He heard the clank of the hose nozzle as it was replaced on the pump. The garage man appeared beside the window, wiping his hands on a rag. "That'll be two eighty. How about oil and water?"

Corma said, "They're fine." He searched his pockets for sufficient change, but only found a quarter and a few cents. He gave the man three dollars.

"Right with you," the man said. He returned to the corrugated building. Corma waited, grimly, watching as the policeman climbed into his car. No, he thought. There must be no sign of panic. To leave now, before receiving my change, would be a bad move. Slowly, slowly. . . . He restarted the engine, still waiting.

The garage man reappeared beside him. "Much obliged," he said. Corma took the change, nodded, and slipped it into a pocket. At the far end of the forecourt, he saw the man in the Stetson hat lean forward in his seat. A puff of exhaust smoke came from the rear of the buff-colored sedan.

Steadily, still unhurriedly, Corma engaged the gear lever and released the hand brake. He drove to the far end of the court and slowed slightly, lifting a hand as he passed close to the police car. There was no response from the man inside.

He pressed his foot down on the accelerator and gripped the wheel tightly as he steered the truck back out onto the road.

46

As the truck turned into the station entrance and drifted out of his line of vision, Peter saw the familiar car and the man standing beside it at the far end of the forecourt.

He swore under his breath, reflexively let up on the gas pedal, then immediately depressed it again as he realized there was no possibility of his going unnoticed or unrecognized, no place to hide. Split-second reasoning told him that the only practical move under the circumstances was to foster the impression, however unconvincing it might be, that he was simply in the process of going about his business; that the truck had simply preceded him to a point where he could get past it and then go on his way.

As he left the gas station behind Peter shook his head, appalled at the thinness of this lie. Since coming out of the hills, the road had offered numerous open stretches where he could have passed the truck with complete safety. Well, okay, then; let's say I simply hadn't followed it immediately when it left the scene of the blowout, and I just now came up behind it as it reached the station. And after all, despite the truck and the car having been pointed in opposite directions when they were parked, he had made no actual reference to a destination. As far as the policeman knew, he could have passed the truck at the time of their meeting, then turned around and come back when he had decided that the driver could possibly use some help.

He frowned. Well, those were possible explanations; slim ones, admittedly, but there was at least a chance that the policeman might reason in this way. He thought of the face under the sweat-marked Stetson, the pinched inquisitiveness and the curious eyes, and shook his head. No, he guessed not. All that was certain was that he couldn't simply stop now and wait for the truck as they'd arranged.

A hundred and fifty yards ahead, on the far side of the road, there was a last isolated clump of trees before the progressively thinning woods petered out into open country again. There were bushes, too, a moderately heavy cluster of them. Just beyond them, a one-lane track led away from the road. He glanced in the rear-view mirror and, seeing no vehicle in the distance behind him, swung the car to the left across the road and onto the track. He pulled up behind the bushes and trees, putting them between himself and the road, nudging the car against the thickest area of concealment that they offered.

He switched off the engine, breathing hard. He felt rather foolish. Hide and seek, he thought. Cops and robbers. Well, not exactly. The issues involved were on a rather different scale. He peered through the bushes, wondering how effective a screen they would be. The car's color would be no help if there were any inconvenient openings. And what about traffic coming the other way? He would be clearly visible from that side, open to further suspicion from some other naturally curious local. He peered down the road in the direction he had been headed, but there was no traffic on the stretch of road visible to him, no sound to signal the approach of a vehicle.

The surroundings were silent, windless. A minute passed, then another. A bird chirped somewhere overhead, provoking an answering call from some distance away. He heard the flutter of a takeoff above him and saw the bird briefly as it flew back in the direction he had come. There was still no sign of either the policeman's car or the truck.

For God's sake, he thought edgily, let's get this crazy business moving. It was absurd to be crouching here, hiding behind bushes like some overgrown Boy Scout. Despite the evidence that the dark-haired man was telling the truth, the convincing things that he had witnessed, there was still an element of unreality about what was happening. Being on the move, having to concentrate on driving, had helped to blunt these last vestiges of uncertainty, but now that he was not moving and had time to think . . .

From behind him, from the direction he had been headed, Peter heard the sound of an approaching engine. He twisted in his seat and looked back toward the road. A few seconds later a car went past, an old Chevy, with a man and woman inside it. They looked more like town people than locals, he thought. As they passed, the woman looked in his direction. She must have seen me, Peter thought. But her expression was a blank, neutral look that didn't really question his right to be where he was.

Maybe she thinks I've stopped to lift a leg, he thought.

Well, when you've gotta go, you've gotta go. . . . He smiled humorlessly, his head cocked in the direction of the road, straining to hear beyond the murmur of the retreating car.

The sound of the Chevy's engine faded — only to be replaced by the noise of another vehicle, this time coming from the direction of the gas station. Seconds later, the truck came into view.

Peter darted a hand toward the horn button, then paused as the truck chugged past his hiding spot. Wait a minute, now, he said to himself. Why no police car? The man in the Stetson had looked as though he was just about set to climb back into his car when Peter had seen him. Did this mean that all this fooling around was for nothing? That his fears had been, in fact, groundless? That the policeman had headed back the other way and was not seriously concerned about them and their activities?

The sound of another engine rose in the distance. Peter sank a little lower in his seat as the buff-colored police car came along the road and went past him. He caught a glimpse of the man behind the wheel, saw the eager, searching crouch, before it pulled away down the road.

"*Hell*," he said. That was it. What they had hoped to avoid had happened, and the policeman had become an active participant in the situation. It remained for them to find out just how far he was prepared to go to pursue his curiosity, but for the time being at least he had become part of the pattern of events, drawn into them by a simple piece of fortuitously bad timing.

Peter started the engine and backed away from the bushes, braking at the edge of the road. In the distance, the sedan dwindled as it moved toward the horizon; beyond it, minute now, he saw the dark rectangle of the truck.

Give it a little longer, he thought. He watched them go, for the second time in minutes damning Henry Chasen's brother for his color choice in cars.

The police car was about three quarters of a mile away when he edged the car back onto the road and started after it, carefully trying to maintain that same distance between himself and the sedan.

47

At least he had the wit to keep moving, Corma thought. He viewed the continuing empty road ahead of him with relief, glancing occasionally in the truck's side mirror.

The police car was visible now, pacing him with what he saw as a kind of dogged perversity. He cursed the curiosity of the man in the Stetson hat and the seemingly endless dips and swoops of fortune that had followed him since his return to the ship. He had no means of knowing how long this interest would be sustained, of course; just how far in both the literal and figurative senses the policeman was prepared to go. But for now, he was there, as though the truck and car were physically connected by some invisible tow line. The line would be severed in time, he was certain of that; would ensure that it did, if necessary.

Corma wondered what had happened to the soldier. Was he still ahead of them, or had he found someplace where it had been possible to hide until the truck and sedan had passed? He looked in the mirror again. Now there was an-other vehicle beyond the sedan in the far distance, too far away to identify visually. He reached down and switched on the tracer.

He glanced at the readings. Yes — he was there, just over a mile away. He stifled another flicker of frustration. Since leaving the gas station, Corma had nurtured a frail hope that the soldier had panicked, enough so that he would keep going, put as much distance as he could between him-self and a situation that was beyond his full understanding, and which now promised to develop further unwelcome complications.

But that had been a tenuous hope at best. The soldier had already given indication of qualities that in other cir-cumstances would have made him a genuinely useful and welcome ally, instead of the potentially deadly threat that his continued presence posed. No, there was little chance of him relinquishing his commitment. His belief in what he had been told had linked him firmly to the situation, a link-age that would not be easily broken.

A dual threat, then, Corma thought, although hardly of equal quality. Now that the initial shock had diminished, Corma was not unduly concerned about the policeman. The tracer readings had registered nothing ominous at the man's location, no innate resistance similar to that of the soldier, so if the policeman's removal from the situation should eventually require extreme action on his own part, that was unlikely to present genuine difficulties. Of course, the soldier would almost certainly oppose such drastic measures, but a seeming accident would not be hard to manufacture, particularly if the policeman decided to con-tinue his pursuit into the mountains.

He studied what lay ahead of him. The land was flat and open for another mile or so. Beyond that, it became lightly wooded again, a gradually thickening selection of spruce and birch. The road had veered so that the mountains proper lay to his left now. The turnoff that would take him up into the mountains was a short distance beyond the wooded area, at a point where the road began to curve over the flanking foothills.

He thought hard, recalling the broad, looping S-shape of the road where it cut through the center of the woods. There was a village there, surely; a few houses, some kind of shop, two larger buildings that might have been grain-storage places. He dredged more details from his memory: a high, weathered fence, double gates leading into a yard that served the two large buildings.

A possible way, he thought, to rid myself of two problems at the same time. . . . He glanced in the mirror again. The police car was still there, maintaining its naggingly precise distance.

He nodded. Yes, it could work. There was little to lose, a great deal to gain. He restrained his impatience, keeping an even pressure on the gas pedal as he drew nearer to the trees.

The road began to bend again as he reached them. He looked in the mirror again, caught a last fleeting glimpse of the sedan as it vanished behind the curving screen of trees, then pushed his foot down hard. The truck gathered speed. Thirty seconds later the buildings were beside him; two, three houses, and then the fence and gates. The gates were open. He braked and swerved into the yard, wrenching the truck into a U-turn that took him back behind the fence.

He switched off the engine and glanced quickly around.

There was a tractor parked a few yards away. Apart from that, the yard was empty.

A minute later, he heard the sedan go by. He restarted the engine, made another U-turn, drove out through the gates into the road, and eased the truck toward the far end of the village. As he reached the last of the houses, the soldier's car appeared in view behind him.

Fortune, he thought, stay with me now. It will not be long. He accelerated gently going into the final curve before the foothills, his eyes fixed on the ribbon of road as it unwound in front of him.

The trees thinned again, and he was back in the open, with the turnoff just ahead. Beyond it, a quarter of a mile away on the road that they were following, he saw the police car disappear over a low rise. He grinned, tautly, exhilarated by this fortuitous timing, the outwitting of his pursuer and the resulting removal of one impediment to what must be done.

"And now the other," he said aloud. "Death, too, I pray you serve me at this time."

He accelerated, one eye on the mirror, carefully gauging the distance between himself and the soldier. The red car had briefly lost ground, but now it was gaining on him again, closing steadily.

And then the turn was upon them. He raised his foot from the gas pedal, touching the brake glancingly at the last possible second and throwing the wheel sharply to the left. The truck lurched as it turned, gained purchase on the road, and steadied. He heard the squeal of brakes behind him and flicked a glance at the mirror, hoping against hope that the tactic had worked, that he would see the red car swerving out of control before tilting and rolling to destruction. But

*no . . . the car was still behind him, rocking slightly on its
suspension but already picking up speed again after negoti-
ating the tight turn.*

*He smiled mirthlessly. Of course. It had been too much
to hope, a pointlessly flailing grasp at opportunity. At least
he had divested himself of one threat. But once again the soldier had demonstrated the futility of what he had attempted,
his survival reaffirming what Corma had already known.*

*Then it must be the other way, Corma thought. If death
was no ally, then it must be mind against mind. And with
deception as his weapon he would triumph.*

*He jammed his foot down on the accelerator, staring
through the windshield at the grayly looming mountains
that filled the skyline ahead of him.*

48

Peter settled in behind the truck again, silently compli-
menting Henry Chasen's brother on his standards of automobile maintenance and simultaneously reproving the
dark-haired man for his failure to signal before turning.

The man could hardly have forgotten the location of the
turnoff, Peter thought. It was the only route to the left that
he had seen for some time, distinctively sandwiched between the woods and the foothills, and with the mountains
its only possible goal. Well, he'd had the police car to consider, had probably kept his eye on it just a shade too long.

But it had been a tricky moment.

After a while, the road began to twist and rise. Peter checked behind him at regular intervals, but the sedan didn't reappear. He wondered how far the policeman would go before deciding that he had been tricked in some way. Either he would think that, or, Peter mused optimistically, he might suppose the truck had actually been capable of a prolonged burst of speed that his own plainly out-of-condition vehicle simply couldn't match. Peter wondered, too, just how the dark-haired man had pulled the switch and wound up behind the police car. The harrowing episode at the turnoff notwithstanding, the whole maneuver had been beautifully timed. It was impossible to estimate just how dangerous the policeman's continued interest could have proved, but it was a relief to have apparently lost him.

Gradually, the grades became steeper, the curves and bends more frequent. Fir trees began to dominate the wooded area beside the road, and the air became progressively cooler although the day was still young. Peter would have liked to stop and put a sweater on over his shirt, but he knew it wasn't strictly necessary and would have just meant more delay. He supposed there was at least a possibility that the policeman had eventually made a correct deduction about the disappearance of the truck; that he was, in fact, still stubbornly tailing them, his curiosity further fueled by their contradictory change of direction.

But even if that was so, as long as they kept moving at the same general speed and there were no genuine breakdowns, there was very little chance of his catching up with them, Peter decided. On the occasions when it was possible to catch a glimpse of the road's lower stretches, they always appeared empty. Oncoming traffic was very light: a car and three trucks in the first hour, and after that nothing.

They continued to climb, the empty hills steadily closing in around them.

49

The sun reached its zenith and began the slow drop toward the western skyline. They were high now, approaching the summit of one of the larger mountains. The trees were sparser, and there was impressive evidence of past rockfalls.

For Peter, driving had become a tiring business, an interminable series of bouts with the increasingly balky third gear. He hoped no permanent damage was being done to the car. He eased the gearshift into third yet again and glanced at his watch. Almost one-thirty. That made it roughly two and a half hours that they had been on the road. He looked up toward the truck, in time to see it slow down and drift off the road to the right, toward an upper slope.

There was a clear, generally flat area that extended almost ten yards away from the road before the land inclined gradually upward toward the peak. The slope above the clearing was wooded, but the trees and occasional bushes were fairly scattered. At the far end of the flat area, a cluster of large boulders fringed the road.

The truck lurched into the clearing, tilting slightly as the tires rolled over various swells and dips in the ground, skirted the ring of boulders, and parked behind the rocks so that it could not be seen from the road. Peter followed to the base of the incline and braked. From where he was he could see the truck, but it didn't look as though there was enough room for him to hide the car in the same area.

So this is it, he thought. He waited, idling the engine, gazing out across the valley that bordered the far side of the road. In the distance he saw more trees and rocks on the slope of another peak, their images minute but sharp in the bright, clear air. How far away was that other slope? Two miles? Three? More? It was a big, lonely place, he decided, a long way from anywhere. He suppressed an involuntary shiver.

A metallic slam echoed across the valley. The dark-haired man walked to the rear of the truck and opened the doors. He spoke briefly to the people inside, then walked toward the road. He stood there for a moment, studying the car and the rocks, then came back and addressed Peter.

"Traffic is infrequent, but it would be foolish to risk arousing curiosity at this stage. There is insufficient space for you to be able to conceal your vehicle entirely behind the rocks, but there is nowhere else in the immediate vicinity that will suffice. A certain amount of camouflage will be necessary. Drive as close to the rocks as you can." He turned and began to climb the slope.

Peter put the car into gear and steered it carefully behind the rocks, edging it forward until he heard and felt a slight impact. He braked and switched off the engine, then looked toward the open back doors of the truck, wondering how the Negro and the small man were doing. It wasn't possible for Peter to see them inside the shadowed interior, but they were sitting up now, watching him.

As Peter got out of his car, the dark-haired man came back down the slope pulling a large bush behind him, its passage creating a minor avalanche of twigs and pebbles that slid and bounced around his feet.

He leaned the bush against the rear of the car, changing its position several times before stepping back to survey the result. "It will suffice." He looked at the people inside the truck, who were still watching silently from the shadows. "It is much steeper where we have to go," he announced to everyone. "Wait here, and stay hidden. I shall bring transportation." He nodded to Peter and began to climb the slope again.

50

The sounds of his departure gradually faded. There was a brief period of silence, during which Peter became increasingly conscious of the members of the mute audience inside the truck.

Talk to them, you dummy, he thought. They're at least as nervous as you are. He went to the rear of the truck and said, "How are you making out? Anything I can do?"

The bespectacled man, Hurley, came forward into the light. His breathing was painfully short, and his face had an unhealthy sheen as he stood, bent over, close to the edge of the truck bed. "Sure glad we got here," he said haltingly. "I don't think . . ." He broke off, unable to continue.

"You'd be better off outside," Peter said. "Here." He reached up and held Hurley's arm, supporting the bespectacled man while he slowly lowered himself to the floor and then to the ground.

He said, with an effort, "Much obliged." He leaned against the truck, his mouth open, weakly fighting for breath.

Even out in the open, it was still possible to smell the lingering remnants of the truck's rancid interior. Peter took a deep breath and climbed inside. He was not surprised to find both of the men conscious and apparently in reasonably good health. "It's clear out there," he said to them. "There's nobody around, and the air will do you good."

He helped the small man to his feet and took him by the shoulders, steering him toward the doors. The small man tripped over the cuffs of his pants and nearly fell. "I'm sorry about the trousers," Peter said. "I had to loan you a pair of mine."

He regretted the apology and the explanation as soon as he had uttered them. The poor guy won't appreciate being reminded of what that means, he thought. Peter knelt down and rolled the cuffs until they were above the small man's ankles.

The small man stood, shaking slightly, mutely accepting what was happening. He looked dazed. Peter got out of the truck and helped him to the ground, where he stayed silently in the shadows thrown by the rocks. The only sound outside now was the continuing struggle of the pale man, still laboring to fill his lungs with sufficient air.

The Negro had dropped into a half-prone position

propped on one elbow and was watching Peter cautiously with city-wise eyes. Peter climbed back into the truck and crouched down beside him. "How are you doing?" he asked.

"Who wants to know?" the Negro said. His voice was like his eyes: wary and guardedly aggressive. He seemed to be fully recovered.

"My name's Walsh. Peter Walsh. Glad to know you." Peter held out his hand.

The Negro ignored it. "What's the uniform?" he asked. "Is this some kind of army outfit?" He looked around him, wrinkling his nose. "Jesus, what a stink." He stared outside at the trees, and his mouth twitched. "Hey, where is this?"

"I don't know exactly," Peter said. "It's where we had to come to . . ." He shrugged weakly. "Well, whatever it is we have to do."

"What are you talkin' about, man?" The Negro paused. His tongue darted out of the corner of his mouth briefly, as though he was thinking. Then he said, "You didn't say what you was. And who was that other guy?"

"I'm in the army," Peter said, "but that has nothing to do with this." He stared at the Negro. "Haven't you been told what's happening?"

"Look, man," the Negro said irritably, "I was layin' in this ditch, and somebody comes along . . ." He stared at Peter with a sudden mixture of horror and rage. "Was that you?"

Peter shook his head. "No, it wasn't." He could feel himself drifting steadily out of his depth. Laying in a ditch? He grabbed at a conversational straw. "Did you get bitten by a dog?" he asked awkwardly.

The Negro's face froze. After a moment he lay slowly

141

back on the floor, closed his eyes, and laid his forearm across them. "Oh, Jesus," he said. He repeated it, over and over, in a soft, despairing voice.

"Look . . ." Peter said, then stopped. He was totally at a loss now, genuinely frightened by his obvious inability to handle this situation or even make sense of it. What the hell was he doing here? Was this the way that worlds were saved; crouching in a stinking truck in the middle of nowhere, blindly treading on sensibilities and fears that he couldn't possibly anticipate? He remembered the cloud and the perforated metal cylinder, and the salve that had probably saved the Negro from madness or death.

Yes, he thought, it seemed that's exactly how it was. "I'm sorry," he said. "How is your leg?"

After a few moments the Negro lifted his arm from his face. His tongue appeared at the corner of his mouth again, and the city-wise look was back in his eyes. "Ain't so great."

"Does it hurt?" Peter asked.

"It's . . . kind of numb," the Negro said. "No feeling." His face was blankly watchful.

"Do you think you could stand on it?"

"Don't be dumb, man," the Negro said. "I told you, it ain't . . ." He stopped, his eyes widening slightly.

Peter made himself smile. "I'll bet you could stand on it. It isn't swollen any more."

The Negro stared at him. The city-wise look was diluted with something else now, something childlike. "How'd you fix it? You a doctor?"

Peter shook his head. "Not me. That was the other fellow. Of course, he hasn't had a chance to talk to you yet, has he?"

The man was surreptitiously moving his injured leg. "No. I been sick. I guess I had a fever." He winced slightly, and disappointment crossed his face. He said tiredly, "What's he want to talk about?"

"About why you're here," Peter said. "And the rest of us. He brought us here because he needs our help." Hold on, he thought. I could really louse this up. He said, rather lamely, "I think he'd better tell you about it himself."

"We're goin' to help him? What are you talkin' about, man?" The man looked away from Peter, through the open doors to where Hurley and the small man were now huddled against the rocks. He suddenly shuddered. "Hey, what is this? Help me up, will you?" He extended a hand.

Peter took it and pulled him to his feet. The Negro's hand was long and hard, with bulging finger joints. He stood, supporting himself against the truck wall. His eyes took in the scene outside. "Where is he? What are we hangin' around here for?"

"He's fetching transport," Peter said. What could he have possibly meant by that? he wondered. The slope was littered with trees and bushes, and there were no visible pathways. "We have to go higher. The road starts to go down again from here."

"Where is here?"

"I don't know. In the mountains, somewhere."

The Negro's eyes widened again. "Mountains? Why the hell are we up in the mountains?" He hobbled to the opening and stared past the rocks and trees toward the horizon. "Jesus," he said. His voice was full of awe.

Outside, the small man suddenly whimpered. Through the open doors, Peter saw that he was staring up at the sky. He continued to whimper as the shadow in which Hurley

143

and he stood abruptly darkened.

Peter moved to the opening quickly and looked up. Overhead, twenty feet or so above them and steadily descending, was a dull grey rectangle. It drifted down and past them and landed gently on the slight incline a few yards away.

51

The only sound it had made was a slight rustling bump as it settled among the debris of twigs and pine needles. It was about ten feet long by six feet wide and slightly less than a foot thick. The dark-haired man, Corma, was sitting on it. He reached down and manipulated some protrusions on a low console in front of him, then rose to his feet.

A god, Peter thought light-headedly, come down from the heavens to bring salvation to all-too-mortal man. He swung himself out of the truck as Corma stepped down and came toward them.

He said, "The road remains clear. The raft will accommodate three people, which will necessitate two journeys." He looked around the group. "Mr. Hurley, I should like you to come now, please, and this other gentleman." He nodded at the Negro, still standing in the truck doorway, then rested a hand on the shoulder of the small man. He smiled down at him. "Circumstances have made it impossible for proper introductions to be exchanged, but there will be time for that later. For now, I ask you to believe me when I say that your presence here is a matter of great importance, and that the contributions that you are equipped to make are both unique and necessary." He looked at Peter. "Mr. Walsh, I should like you to stay with our friend here" — he indicated the small man — "until I return. This will be a matter of a few minutes, no longer." He stared at the Negro, still standing in the truck doorway. "Please. Time is short."

"What . . . ?" the Negro began, then stopped. To Peter he said, "Help me down, man. I got to go someplace." He laughed uncertainly. His eyes were glazed and rather bright.

Peter helped him to the ground and across the incline to where Corma was seating Hurley at one end of the gray rectangle, positioning him to one side and facing toward the center. He was puzzled by the Negro's lack of protest, his apparent abrupt change of mind. Hypnotism? If it was, it had been achieved with startling ease and speed. He watched as Corma pressed a button on the console. Curved metal bands rose from slots on either side of Hurley's thighs and looped over them. He flinched slightly as they snapped home, clamping him in position.

Corma nodded to Peter, pointing at the space beside Hurley. Peter helped the Negro down into the shallow concavity that he found there. The man's eyes were still glazed, and his face was filmed with sweat. The city-wise look was gone again, now replaced by a kind of wondering elation. He said nothing as another set of metal bands rose and bridged his thighs.

"It will not take long," Corma said to Peter. He nodded to him again, then to the small man, still huddled in the shadow of the rocks. He seated himself and manipulated the controls again. The rectangle lifted silently from the ground and drifted up, alongside the trees and then over them. Within seconds, it had vanished.

52

Peter stared up at the empty sky, conscious of the tension that was stiffening the muscles in his back and legs. Take it easy, he told himself. This isn't any time to tighten up. He forced himself to relax and went across to where the small man stood — a stunted, ludicrously baggy figure, hovering uncertainly by the cluster of boulders.

"Our turn soon, I guess," said Peter. It was a pointless remark, serving only as a means of breaking the silence. The small man responded with a gap-toothed, nervous smile. His face had lost some of its earlier pallor, but he still looked unwell.

Peter smiled back, strolled to the edge of the clearing, and stared out across the valley on the far side of the road again. This was one of the rare occasions in his life when making conversation was proving to be beyond him. He actually felt rather shy, an unusual sensation for him. Maybe he doesn't want to talk anyway, he thought. Maybe he's like me in this situation, trying to think sense into something that was way beyond anything he had ever dreamed or imagined.

The raft had served to further strengthen Peter's belief in the truth of what he had been told. The cloud and the cylinder and the ointment had offered their own justifications for acceptance, but despite their uniqueness, their unearthliness, doubt had still lingered inside Peter, a shadow of uncertainty that had required some final confirming element to disperse it.

The raft is it, he thought. It's like a metal magic carpet, a fantasy become fact, the illusion undisturbed by any hum or drone that would have betrayed the mechanical means of its propulsion. It was solid, tangible; something that was hard and cool to the touch, and yet its silent, dreamlike passage removed it from earthly reality into realms of existence far beyond anything in his experience or knowledge.

Minutes passed. Across the valley, somewhere among the distant trees, a bird cried out. It was a faint, lonely sound that quickly died. The ensuing silence was almost overwhelming in its totality. Peter shivered slightly and fumbled a pack of cigarettes from his pocket. Did the small man smoke? he wondered. It would be a way of establishing contact, perhaps provoking conversation, however minimal its actual content.

As he turned to go back toward the small man, a shadow spread across the center of the clearing again. Seconds later the raft landed a few yards away. He put the cigarettes back in his pocket and walked over to where Corma was waiting.

53

John George Fuller Junior lay on the thinly grassed floor of the rock basin, staring up at the sky. It was cool there, even in the sunshine, but quiet and restful. He flexed his leg, wondering how far he'd be able to get on it, then relaxed. There wasn't really any point in thinking about things like that; where could he go? He was on top of a mountain, so he couldn't go up, and to go down meant that sooner or later they'd be bound to catch up with him.

Take it easy, man, he told himself. He grinned. He felt light-headed again, but not in the same feverish, nauseous way that he had before. He didn't know what was happening, what it was he had somehow got himself mixed up in, but whatever it was, it was better than shriveling up in a ditch with a poisoned leg and no real hope of leaving it alive. Now he felt almost carefree, as though the responsibility for what happened from now on had been lifted from him, so that all he had to do was drift with the pattern of events and let them automatically find him some kind of eventual answer.

That crazy ride, he thought. Hey, that had really been something.

"Man," he said aloud. "That was really *high*." He laughed.

Walter Hurley stood by the rock wall, looking out

across the basin and wondering why they were there. It seemed a pretty godforsaken place, really, he thought. It was private, all right, not the sort of place where people would be likely to go normally, so it was good in that way, but he couldn't see any caves where Mr. Corma could have hidden his spaceship. Even if there was a cave, it would have to be a sizable one to hold something like that. He didn't know what the ship looked like, of course, or how big it was, but he supposed it must have been pretty big to have brought him all this way.

The thinner air was causing him a little trouble with his breathing, but it wasn't as bad as he thought it might be. He told himself he'd better take another pill soon, though, just to be on the safe side. It was a real relief to be out of the truck, away from the smells, to be able to move about freely, stretch his legs when he wanted to.

He took a few tentative steps and stared at the far side of the basin. There was a shadow about three quarters of the way up the opposing rock wall that might have been some sort of cleft, but it was hardly big enough to provide access to a spaceship or anything like that. He couldn't see anywhere else suitable, though, so maybe that was where it was. His gaze drifted upward, wavered, then stopped.

He blinked. What were those small, dark things floating above the center of the basin? They were very still, so they couldn't be birds. And how did they just stay there and not fall down? He felt a tremor of nervousness, then braced himself. This wasn't any sort of time to start getting shaky, imagining things. But when he looked again, they were still there. He wandered cautiously toward the center of the basin, closer to the floating things, squinting uncertainly through his glasses.

He had gone about fifteen paces when he suddenly received a violent blow on the face. It was like being hit by an unseen fist; a totally unanticipated, numbing assault that sent him staggering back as he brought up his hands and cupped them protectively over his nose and mouth. His glasses, miraculously, were still intact.

He stared around him, dizzy and bewildered, trying to clear his clouded vision. He couldn't see anything that might have been responsible for the blow, nothing at all. The small, dark things looked as though they were still where he had first seen them, and apart from them and the Negro, who was somewhere to his right and behind him, the whole area was empty, with no sign of movement or any solid object visible between himself and the opposing rock wall.

He felt blood trickling down over his mouth. He groped for his handkerchief, then remembered he had left it in the truck after using it to clean up the small man a little. He wiped the blood on his shirt sleeve as he stared fearfully around. What could it possibly have been? A bird? A piece of rock?

He looked at the ground around him. There was a stone about the size of his fist a little way to his right, but he didn't see how it could have been that. If it had fallen on him, it would have hit him on the top of his head, anyway, not in the face.

He bent over, picked up the stone, and studied it closely. There was no blood on it, no evidence of any kind that he could see that it might have been responsible. He tossed it away. But instead of completing its arc, the stone went only a few feet, halted in mid-air, then bounced back a short distance and dropped to the ground. Its change of direction was accompanied by a metallic, slightly hollow sound.

He reared back, staring at the empty space in front of him, then at the stone lying innocently still a few feet away. He dragged his eyes from it and peered across the basin again as blood dripped unnoticed from his chin to his shirt front.

So that's where the ship is, he thought numbly. That was how it was hidden. There wasn't any need for caves or anything like that if you could make things invisible.

He was still staring blankly across the seemingly empty basin when he heard a whisper of displaced air, and the gray rectangle landed a few yards away.

54

Peter's first startled impression was that Hurley and the Negro had been fighting. As they drifted the last few feet to the ground, he saw Hurley in profile, one hand to his face, the other held tentatively in front of him. Blood was smeared across his mouth and chin, accentuating his natural lack of color. The Negro was several yards away, bent in a half-crouch and moving cautiously toward Hurley.

Corma pressed a switch on the console and then stood up as the metal loops slid back into the raft. He stepped off and went quickly to Hurley.

"I must apologize for not being absolutely specific in

my instructions," he said. He steered him back to the perimeter of the area, away from the place where the stone and Hurley's face had impacted. "Please wait here. I shall be able to give you treatment in a few moments." He walked back toward the center of the basin, stopping in front of a small rock that projected from the ground a few yards to the left of where Hurley had been standing. He knelt, lifted it to one side, and removed something from beneath it. Peter caught a glimpse of a small gray object in his hand. Corma stood again and did something with what he was holding.

At a little below knee height, a gradually deepening horizontal slit materialized in front of him. Within seconds it was several feet long by two feet high, floating about a foot above the ground. Smooth, shadowed surfaces could be seen beyond it. Corma walked to the raft, operated something on the console, then rose and stepped back. The raft lifted off the ground, drifted forward, and disappeared into the slit.

He manipulated the small gray object again. The slit closed, and another one appeared. This was vertical, somewhat more than six feet high, and located a little to the left of the first one. It widened steadily until it was about three feet across. Beyond it, Peter could see some sort of small room, a facing wall with a door recessed into it.

"Please come with me," Corma said. He led the way inside, and the others trailed hesitantly behind him.

Impossible, Peter thought. Things like this simply didn't happen: doorways that materialized in mid-air on the top of a mountain, offering entrance to other worlds, magic places in which it was possible to take refuge from the terrors of reality. This was a miracle beside which the other wonders he had already witnessed seemed suddenly almost mundane.

He watched the others climb through; the small man, the Negro, Hurley. He saw the shock on their faces, but he saw something else too: the first faint glimmerings of a kind of cautious hopefulness. He thought about their individual realities and nodded slowly. Yes, he could understand the potency of what they were seeing, the irresistible attraction it would have for people like them.

He took a deep breath and went forward. As he did, a gust of wind suddenly disturbed the stillness of the basin, coldly pressing his shirt and trousers against his body. He shivered, and went through the opening. The door-slit closed behind him, and another door opened in front of him. Beyond it, he could see the glint of hard surfaces, reflecting a pale, flat light.

They went through, into the dimly lighted interior of the ship.

55

Peter heard the faint thud of the inner door closing behind him. He stared around, adjusting his eyes to the muted illumination.

The area in which they were standing was circular and flat-ceilinged, about thirty feet across. There were no visible light fixtures. The illumination seemed to come from the ceiling itself, rather than beyond it; a pale, overall luminosity that was broken only by a dark central strip running the full width of the area. Instrument consoles were located around the perimeter to his left, two of them topped by blank screens. The remaining wall space was occupied by recessed panels that might have been doors, or some kind of foldaway equipment. There was a circular dais in the center of the area, about four feet in diameter and three feet high. Everything visible was a soft, semireflective gray.

Corma stood by the dais and removed a small case from a pocket of his coveralls. He opened it and took out a small cylindrical container.

"Mr. Hurley," he said, "may I see the extent of your injury, please?" Hurley went forward, eagerly. Corma gently removed his glasses, then tilted his face up toward the light. He nodded. "Ruptured flesh, bruises. Your nose is a little swollen, I see. This will relieve it. Close your eyes, please." He held the container close to Hurley's face and depressed the top. A fine mist was softly ejected, clouding Hurley's nose, mouth, and chin. "It will only take a minute or so," Corma said. He replaced the spray in the case.

Then he turned to the Negro and said, "Will you come and sit here, please?" He indicated the dais. "I am happy to see that your leg is usable again, but I feel it wise to guard against the possibility of a recurrence of the fever."

"It's okay now," said the Negro. "It don't need any more treatment." His eyes were restless, continually flickering around the room.

"This is a precautionary measure only," Corma assured him. "It is possible that despite your present state of recovery, sufficient bacteria have been retained into your bloodstream to permit the fever to reassert itself." He took a small, squat syringe from the case and removed a protective cap from its end. "Please do not be alarmed. Your leg has already benefitted from the treatment that it has received. This is simply to ensure that your recovery is complete." He held out his hand.

The Negro went to the dais. His limp was noticeable, but only slight now. He turned around and edged himself up onto the raised circle. His face was expressionless, but his eyes were cautious. He watched as Corma rolled up his sleeve and dabbed at his arm with a small, white, spongelike disc. He pressed the syringe home, applied the disc again, then returned it and the syringe to the case. The Negro raised his arm and studied it, frowning in puzzlement. He hadn't flinched or reacted in any way at the time of the injection.

To the group, Corma said, "I regret the present low level of illumination, but the ship is being sustained on minimum power at the present time. This is your reason for being here, of course." The Negro slid down from the dais and wandered back to rejoin the others, still studying his arm, still frowning. "It is some while since you have eaten," Corma continued. "What I have to offer will be unfamiliar, but you will find that it satisfies your needs. First, though, you must clean yourselves."

He walked to the wall and pressed a switch. One of the recessed panels slid aside. He took a round plastic container from a shelf and brought it back to the dais. From it he took what looked to be larger versions of the spongelike disc that he had used on the Negro's arm and distributed them among the group. The discs were cool and moist. "One each will suffice. I shall get food now." He walked to the far end of the area and, went through another panel opening, and closed it behind him.

With Corma's departure, the group seemed to lose some of the cohesiveness that his presence appeared to generate. Power of personality? Peter asked himself. Like a good orator, or maybe a film star? No, it was more than that. He was the factor that bound them together in a set of circumstances that only he understood, to which only he knew the answers and how they should be applied. With him there, they were able to cling blindly to this understanding; without him, they floundered in a situation that they were incapable of comprehending without guidance. The still, uniform grayness of the setting in which they now found themselves was further confirmation of the enigma; a complex of materials and machinery that were totally alien in all that they implied.

There were still traces of grease on the backs of Peter's hands. He experimentally smeared the sponge across one of them, and the smudge vanished, leaving a completely

unmarked area of skin. More miraculously, the sponge itself showed no trace of what it had removed. Did it simply
absorb it, he wondered, or was it a kind of particle neutral-
izer that totally destroyed certain elements? Whatever it
was, he had never come across anything like it before. He
continued cleaning himself, enjoying the experience. After
some initial hesitation, the others did the same, their faces
expressing varying degrees of wonderment and pleasure.

Hurley wandered across to him, swabbing his hands.
He probably wasn't the most intelligent member of the
group, Peter had decided; the Negro's face and eyes
showed an alertness that went considerably beyond the
city-wise veneer, but he could see how his own presence,
the respectable conventionalities that he clearly represented, could be a reassuring factor to someone like Hurley.

"They sure do know some stuff, don't they?" said
Hurley. He looked down at the sponge, marveling at it.
"Heck, a thing like this'd make a million if it was marketed
here."

"I don't think the people who make soap and towels
and cleaning fluids would be any too happy about it," Peter said with a smile. "Then again, I guess they could just
switch to making these things."

"Not if they were patented," Hurley said seriously.
"Heck, you could just about corner the whole market. And
what about that spray thing? My mouth and nose were real
sore a couple of minutes ago, and now I can't feel a thing."
He touched his face, tentatively. "How do they look?"

Peter looked closely at him. There was no distortion
visible, no discoloring. The last traces of blood had been
removed, and it was the same pale, rather apologetic face
that he had first encountered in the truck. "Fine," he said.

"You'd never know there'd been anything wrong with it."
He smiled again. "When we got here, I thought you'd been
in an argument."

"Heck, no," Hurley said. "Nothing like that. I smacked
my face on this thing." His eyes showed awe again. "It sure
is strange, isn't it? I mean, we're here, all solid, but somebody outside wouldn't know anything about it." He ran his
tongue across his lips and touched his face again. "They
must know an awful lot about medicine and doctoring."
His face was hungry.

Peter nodded. "Yes, they certainly seem to."

Hurley said, rather shyly, "That's what I always wanted
to do. I guess it must be . . ." He broke off as Corma came
back into the chamber, carrying a deep-edged plastic panel
that was serving as a tray. There were five round containers on it, each half-filled with something dark that was visible through their translucent sides.

He placed the panel on the dais. "You must understand
that this does not constitute the kind of meal to which I am
accustomed. Normally, my race ingests dietary substances
that are very similar to your own in many ways. We do not
eat meat, but with that exception our staple foods largely
resemble yours." He distributed the containers around the
top of the dais. "Nevertheless, it contains all that is necessary to sustain us for the next twenty-four hours. You will
find it pleasant." He raised one of the containers and
drank.

Peter picked up the container nearest to him. It held a
dark, clear liquid that looked like diluted syrup. He lifted it
to his face cautiously, aware that the others were watching
him, delaying their own moment of commitment.

It smelled faintly tangy, and in no way repellent. He

sipped it, watching Corma over the rim of the container. Not bad, he thought. An unusual taste, midway between the softened acidity of an eating apple and . . . what else? Cheese? Something like that, anyway. He sipped it again and nodded. "Very nice. Is it all chemicals?"

Corma shook his head. "No. It is largely food concentrates, with chemicals acting as calorific intensifiers and preservatives. It was developed specifically for this type of situation. Emergency rations, if you like — a practical solution to the problems that would be posed by perishable foodstuffs." He finished his drink and glanced at the others. They were all drinking now; Hurley and the small man eagerly, the Negro a little more circumspectly.

Corma replaced his container on the tray and went back to the paneled area of the wall. He pressed buttons beside three of the panels. This time, the panels dropped open along bottom hinges, projecting horizontally into the room. Their inner sides were padded and had low, fixed pillows at the ends nearest the wall.

"You must rest," Corma said. "Your strength will be needed shortly." Then, to Peter, "The nature of your own role exempts you from this necessity. I shall need your help now." The rest of the group began to slowly converge on the projecting panels. He addressed them again as they cautiously began seating themselves. "We shall return shortly. Meanwhile, please relax. Sleep, if you can. The full necessity of your presence will be explained in due time. The important thing now is that you conserve your energies." He motioned to Peter to follow him and went toward the wall.

From the far side of the room, the Negro said, "Tell me now." His voice was tight and hostile. He was standing

159

beside his chosen panel, staring after them. "Not later, man. I want to know what I'm doin' here."

Corma hesitated, then went back and stood in front of him. "There has been a breakdown of the energy sources that activate the ship. The only way that these can be replaced is by utilizing other sources capable of generating the same kind of power. You are such a source."

The Negro stared at him. A slightly uncertain grin spread across his face. "You're kidding."

Corma shook his head. "No."

"Look, man, even if I believed that, how would I do it? Pedaling?" He laughed. "I just got over a bum leg, remember?" Then he paused and stared past Corma, in the general direction of where Peter stood. His expression changed. "You're kidding," he said again. This time his voice sounded shocked.

"You are the possessor of a reservoir of psychic energy which can be tapped," Corma said. "I have both the knowledge and means to do this. Those with you possess similar power, in varying quantities. Collectively, you are capable of replacing what has been lost. It is of vital importance that you do so. Believe me when I tell you that what we are engaged in is for the benefit of your kind rather than mine."

"My kind? What do you mean, my kind?" The Negro sounded simultaneously frightened and sullen now. "Who the hell are you, anyhow?"

"I am Corma, a guardian, one of a race of self-appointed protectors. I have conclusive knowledge that you and your planet are at grave risk, and urgent action is necessary to combat this. Only I have access to the resources that are needed to bring this about, and only you have the power to enable me to reach those resources. We are in a situation where we have become interdependent, mutually necessary to each other. Your cooperation is therefore imperative."

The Negro stared at him, his eyes dull and appalled. "Man, you're crazy," he said. His voice was little more than a whisper.

Corma shook his head again. "Think of what you have seen since your recovery. These are not the delusions of fever, or the fictions of a diseased mind. They are reality." He waved his hand. "This ship, the drink that you have just had, the raft that brought you here. Think about your leg. You were dying when we found you. Now you are well." He turned away. "Believe these facts for what they are. I shall explain further in a little while." He nodded, dismissively, and went briskly back to the far wall.

The Negro stared after him, saying nothing, his face gray and dumbfounded. As Peter turned to follow Corma, he saw Hurley get up from where he was sitting and go to the Negro. He stood beside him, talking in a low voice.

Corma pressed another switch. A panel slid back, revealing a dimly lit passage that ran parallel to the rounded perimeter wall. He stepped through the opening and disappeared to the left.

Peter went after him, following his shadowed bulk around the gentle curve.

56

In one respect it had been fortunate that the neutralizing capability of the visibility shield had reached its present low ebb, Corma reflected. If it had been strong enough to kill Hurley, that would have meant an enforced resumption of the search until another replacement had been found — a delay that would in all probability have proved fatal. Even if the shield had simply stunned him, it would still have had a detrimentally unnerving effect on the others, undoing much of what had been achieved so far.

It was the man's basic stupidity that had led to the incident, of course. His instructions to Hurley before leaving to fetch the others had been perfectly clear. But it was over now, with no real harm done, and had in fact provided an opportunity to reinforce Hurley's sense of wonderment and his already strong commitment to what was happening.

He wondered what Peter Walsh's response would be to what was waiting for them in the power chamber. The soldier's positive qualities were not in doubt, but initiative and imagination were not necessarily compatible with what was required now.

Corma paused at the foot of the steps. "Are you squeamish by disposition?" he asked

"What?" The soldier sounded startled. "No, not really." His voice lacked conviction. "Why?"

"What we have to do now cannot be avoided." Corma
took a pack from his coveralls and extracted two nasal fil-
ters. *"Please place these in your nostrils. They will reduce
the odor, although not entirely eliminate it."* The soldier
took them, uncertainly. Corma removed two more from the
pack, inserted them into his own nose, and went up the
stairs. He unlatched the door to the power chamber, then
led the way to the nearest of the four closed tanks.

Before opening it, he glanced at the soldier. In the dim
light it was impossible to accurately assess his color, but he
looked paler than usual. Was he the type to actually faint?
It seemed unlikely. And yet, if he was . . .

He dismissed the thought, impatiently. It was much too
late for that. The soldier had become deeply involved, an integral part of the pattern. And even in the improbable event
of his elimination actually becoming possible, it would only
invite further complications. He had seen the reactions of
Hurley and the small one to his presence, their obvious relief at his participation, and it seemed likely that, despite his
hostility, the Negro shared their feelings. A convincingly
simulated accident would be difficult to manufacture now,
and the doubt that would be invoked by such an event
would result in the instinctive erection of a countering bar-
rier against any subsequent attempt that he might make to
impose full authority. In any event, he had reason to regret
his decision to subject Hurley to only minimal control at
the time of his location, but deep application was a relatively lengthy process, and the finding of subjects had been his
first concern.

There would be no chance of his forcing their cooperation, either; any such move would be doomed to failure as
the negating strength of their fear and mistrust automati-

cally sealed access to the power-generating centers located in the innermost recesses of their psychic mechanisms. And even if the soldier's elimination was not possible but the opportunity to apply deep control still occurred, it would not be wise. Now that he was acquainted with the subjects, the resulting marked behavioral changes would arouse his suspicions, invite his open opposition to what had to be done, and effectively remove any possibility of reaching a successful conclusion in the inexorably dwindling time that remained.

No, it was a situation without certainties, one in which subtlety and cunning must continue to substitute for his normal armory. It was even possible, of course, that the soldier possessed no truly dangerous countering force at all, that the readings had somehow exaggerated what was purely a defensive capacity. Corma experienced a vague, momentary flicker of unease at the periphery of his thinking, but pushed it to one side. After all, there were no actual signs that the young man's power was manifesting itself in any destructive way. The situation seemed under control, and it could be argued that Peter Walsh's presence had its positive aspects. He served as a physical helper — a limited role that was not strictly necessary and would have to be made to appear more important than it was — and as an authenticating link between himself and the others.

Corma felt a surge of reassurance. In some ways, the greatest difficulties lay immediately ahead, and yet he held a growing belief that he could surmount them. He was Corma, one of a strong line. The odds were great, but he would survive.

He unlocked the final clasp and swung back the tank lid as he pivoted to watch the soldier's face.

57

Even with his nose plugs in place, the reek from the lozenge-shaped container hit Peter hard. It was acrid, with overtones of putrefying sweetness. The odor sank deep into his lungs and then plummeted past them into his stomach. He stared with nauseated bewilderment at what the tank contained.

Floating in a particle-clouded but otherwise clear liquid was a chalky grayish green, marrow-shaped object. It was about five feet long and totally featureless. A circular alloy band was clamped around its narrower end, with wires leading from it to connections at the far end of the tank. More wires and flexible tubes projected from it at various points, fanning out to other connections around the tank's perimeter. The thing was passive, making no movement of any kind. As he watched, he realized that the clouding of the liquid was being caused by the slow disintegration of what was suspended in it. Minute flakes of matter sporadically detached themselves from the thing and drifted away, adding to the density of the supporting fluid.

"It is dead, as you can see," Corma said. "Do not be misled by the relatively advanced degree of deterioration. Death was, in fact, recent — within the last few hours. The high percentage of fluid in the body structure and the necessity to maintain it in a liquid environment ensure that decomposition is rapid."

Peter struggled to find his voice. "What is it?" he asked carefully.

"It is a pleem," Corma said. "In my own language, that is a word meaning, broadly, generator. As you have possibly already deduced, it was a source of the motive power that activates the ship, the purpose for which these creatures are specifically bred. Unfortunately, a weakness has developed in the strain. It is unpredictable, and at its worst can lead to what you see here. The breeding program is under constant scrutiny, but a truly satisfactory answer to the problem has yet to be found."

"Was it actually alive?" Peter asked. It looked more like a vegetable than anything else, he thought. "I mean, was it a sentient being?"

"Yes."

"Do they come from your own world?"

Corma shook his head. "No. Their planet of origin is remotely located and of limited interest. It is small, and consists entirely of ocean and saline swamp. Their discovery was purely accidental, the result of a probe satellite's malfunction and subsequent change of direction. In such ways are the patterns of history changed." He looked down into the tank. "As you can see, there is a total absence of visible external organs, and they possess what amounts to little more than rudimentary digestive and respiratory systems. Their brain is the point of interest. It is not large, but it is capable of enormous generative response to the right stimulus. This fact emerged while a specimen was being surgically examined to determine the means by which it achieved instantaneous relocation, an ability that had been noted and was the reason for our interest."

Peter felt a brief intensification of his nausea at this matter-of-factly delivered information. He pulled his eyes away from the tank and looked around the domelike chamber. There were four tanks in all, arranged in a spokelike formation around a central console. "Is this all of them?" he asked.

"This is where the power source is normally located. One of the tanks is empty now."

"How many of them are dead?"

"One lives. It is now the sole means by which the ship can retain its protective shield. Beyond that capability, it is powerless." Corma closed the lid, latched it, and crossed the chamber. "At the time that I discovered that it would be necessary to search for substitutes, it became essential to place almost the entire responsibility for maintaining the ship upon it. It has coped well, but now that the others are dead the likelihood of its surviving without early support is lessening rapidly. If it, too, should fail before this can be provided, component deterioration will take place which may well make repowering impossible." He unfastened the clamps on another tank and opened it.

Peter swallowed hard before approaching it. His sight of the first dead creature and the accompanying, never-to-be-forgotten stench, had totally disproved the claim that he had made at the foot of the stairs, one that he had known to be suspect at the time. Now, all too soon, he was going to be tested again.

He was conscious that what he was doing now was as much an act of mental discipline as physical movement. He looked down into the tank hesitantly.

The differences between the remembered vision and what he saw now were very marked. The liquid was clear, and the pleem itself was darker and altogether more compact, a reassuring version of its disintegrating counterpart. Wires and tubes were attached to it, but there were fewer than had been connected to the first one. The odor generated by the corpse still lingered in the closed confines of the room, but it was clearly not being augmented by what he saw now.

A power source, he thought. Four of them could lift this thing and propel it through the universe. Madness? Why should it be? Invisibility, flying panels, miracle cures — why not this, the final, crowning absurdity?

The realization that had been growing in his mind expanded to inescapable proportions. He said, dry-mouthed, "And you're hoping to use these people as replacements. Is that it?"

Corma nodded. "Yes. It will be necessary to drain and pad the tanks, of course, and other adaptations will have to be made. As you can see, there is sufficient room." He paused. "Their capabilities in this respect vary widely, but between them they will be able to temporarily replace what has been lost. The principal source is the one who was with you at the time of our meeting. The Negro's power is strong but almost totally unrefined, which indicates relatively late emergence. Hurley has less to offer than the others, a fact that has partially to do with his age, but his inclusion is still essential." He closed the lid. "Under normal circumstances, variations of this degree would not be considered tolerable, but I hardly need remind you that these circumstances are far from normal. Necessity is the breeder of the makeshift, and time is dictating what must be done."

A dull ache was beginning to press at Peter's temples. Pictures swam in his mind: the three people from the room below them, naked now, wires and tubes sprouting from them like obscene tendrils. He tried to push the images away, but failed. "And what will happen to them if you can persuade them to do it?" he asked. He stared at Corma, trying to read his face. He gestured around the room. "You breed these things specifically for the power they can supply, but what happens still kills them." He shook his head. "That's barbaric. And if you—"

"You do not understand the nature of our relationship with the pleem. Possibly, too, you have temporarily forgotten the purpose of this employment and the scale of the issues involved." He studied Peter's still-troubled face curiously. After a moment he said, "Tell me, do you eat meat?"

Peter said, "But that's . . ." He stopped and looked at the floor. "That's not really the same thing," he continued lamely.

"I agree," said Corma. "Your relationship with the creatures that you rear, butcher, and ingest could not be described as mutually beneficial." He paused. "It would be fair to state that at the present time our alliance with the pleem has become satisfactory to neither party. Nevertheless, until quite recently it was reciprocal, of true benefit to both. At no time could that be said of—"

"What about these people?" Peter interrupted angrily. "Would it harm them in any way?"

Corma nodded. "Eventually, they will die."

58

It goes well, Corma thought. Watching the soldier, he felt the strength within himself grow, his power of will and mind, firm and unshakable. This was the instant of crisis, and still he sensed no hesitation, no faltering in his steadfast belief in his own ability to survive and triumph.

He had considered this moment very carefully; whether to lie, offer some inevitably thin, implausible reassurance as to the substitutes' well-being and future, or to trust the inherent strength of the argument and his own powers of logical persuasion. It was a question that sheer common sense had resolved very quickly. Indisputably, he had to speak the truth. A lie, however well told, would have disturbed the pattern, confronted the soldier's still vulnerable belief with an element of doubt that could ultimately have provoked the bigger danger.

He studied the soldier's pale, shocked face. He said, gently, "There are many things that must still be explained. They will help you to understand that what is to happen will in no way be an act of barbarism or callous expediency. In return for what they will give, I shall give them life — the realization of their dreams. This same sort of symbiosis has been the foundation of our relationship with the pleem."

Peter Walsh shook his head. He looked distressed and frightened. "I don't know what you're talking about," he

said. He half-turned. "You can't just . . ." His voice tailed
away into silence, and he shook his head again.

Corma said, still gently, "Bear with me. The pleem are
creatures that exist in two worlds. To a lesser degree, we
share this duality, your kind and mine. They are rumi-
nants, sleepers, who have learned through necessity to dis-
guise their true nature, and who now spend their lives in
almost total stillness. It is their day-to-day defense against
the predatory activity which surrounds them in their normal environment and against which they can offer no con-
ventional defense.

"But if, despite their expertise at camouflage, they still
find themselves at risk, they are capable of generating psy-
chokinetic force which removes them from the area of danger. This emanates from the brain, which is also the source
of their internal world. What form this takes, what activities and sensations exist there, we do not know. It is a
world of their imagination, of dreams. By chance, we discovered how to stimulate and vastly intensify this experience, the by-product of which is the generation of the concentrated psychic force that we need."

"I don't see how any of this has any connection with
those people," the soldier said. "They already have
real lives . . ." He stopped, his forehead suddenly creased.

Corma felt it — the flush of absolute certainty. He said,
evenly, "You will find that the prospect of death does not
alarm them as it would you or me. Consider their lives.
Hurley is a sufferer from chronic asthma and rapidly fail-
ing eyesight, an almost certain candidate for early cardiac
deterioration; unemployable, almost destitute, alone. The
Negro . . ." Corma paused, thoughtfully. "He is intelligent,
but crippled both physically and emotionally, pursued by

personal demons that he cannot evade. Last, the small one. There is no need for me to list the disadvantages that he suffers. He is a creature without hope, without an even barely tolerable future." He looked at the soldier curiously. *"Would it surprise you to learn that he is a little younger than yourself?"*

The soldier looked at him, startled. *"It is true,"* Corma said. *"A matter of weeks."* The same faint flicker of unease that had touched him earlier returned. Again, he brushed it to one side, urgently preserving his concentration, the initiative that he knew was his. *"What you see is what his real life has done to him. He is old in bitter experience that he has been incapable of defending himself against. His future is limited, and will inevitably decline as it progresses."* Corma shrugged. *"There are the real lives of which you speak."*

After a moment, the soldier said, slowly, *"Are you saying that they're all hopeless cases, that none of them has a chance of things getting any better?"*

Corma nodded. *"The broad pattern of their existences is set, as it is for the majority of living creatures. Variation will occasionally arise, of course, but in the essential areas of their lives, no major beneficial changes will occur. The readings . . ."* He experienced sudden shock as the peripheral doubt jolted into focus. He saw the soldier looking at him questioningly, and hurried on. *"The readings that led me to select the people who are here did not simply indicate that they are the possessors of the power that is needed. They simultaneously showed their level of fallibility, the factor which dictates the degree of fortune that naturally attends them."*

"Fortune?" the soldier asked. *"You mean luck?"* He

frowned uncertainly. "Are you saying that everybody's born either lucky or unlucky?"

"That is a simplification. The vast majority of beings exist somewhere in the center of the scale of such things." *Is he conscious of his own location within it?* Corma wondered. *Not entirely, perhaps. Not yet.* "The variations that occur in their lives are relatively balanced and rarely touch consistent extremes. The people here, however, follow existences that never will and never can rise above the lower end of such a scale."

The soldier turned and began restlessly wandering about the chamber. Corma watched him, saying nothing. *It is done,* he thought. He suppressed his impatience as he thought about the tracer and scanner that he had left in the truck. The vehicle was well hidden from the road, and traffic had been nonexistent in the later stages of the journey, but there was still the slim possibility of its being found. His carelessness was inexcusable, but the element of danger was small. He would get the equipment in a little while.

The soldier stopped pacing and stood with his back to him, staring at the floor. Corma said, "Their initial reaction when they are told will be one of shock and instinctive dismissal, but there is no doubt as to what their final decision will be." He saw the tiredness of the soldier's pose, sensed the gradual crumbling of his resistance in the face of careful rationalization. "In exchange for these lives, I can offer them the worlds of their dreams."

The soldier turned and faced him again. There was still a residue of disbelief in his expression, but it was faint now. "How long would it last?"

"Time is a relative thing," Corma said. "In terms of your own waking time scale, they will continue to exist for *perhaps eighteen hours, a little more."* He saw dull shock reappear on the soldier's face. *"But remember, the world of dreams travels at vastly different, much more rapid speed, which is accelerated even more during the period of transmission. Even without the stimulation that we can provide, a dream that takes a minute of waking time can encapsulate hours, even days, in the subconscious realms of sleep.*

"In those eighteen hours, they will live lifetimes that fulfill all that they have ever desired which cannot exist for them in reality, ever. The only way that such lives can be realized is in their dreams, and these I can give them."

There was another silence. The soldier's face underwent subtle changes, fleeting visualizations of the struggle that still continued in his mind. Corma said quietly, *"You are a person of intelligence and imagination. If you were not, you would not be here now, fulfilling your present role. You, too, are needed, as someone capable of grasping the full meaning of these circumstances and all that they entail. The issues are not simple, and I understand your hesitation. But I also know that you sense the inevitability of what must happen. If you—"*

"What if you're wrong? What if they refuse?"

Corma shook his head. *"They will not."*

The soldier was agitated now, but his agitation had the desperate quality that signaled an unspoken recognition of impending defeat. *"But how can you be sure? We're talking about their lives, their real lives. What if just one of them refuses? What happens then?"*

Corma shook his head again. *"The question does not arise. It will not happen."*

"It might," the soldier said stubbornly. *"It could, very easily."*

"That is a point that could be debated at length, but time precludes such discussion. There is only one way in which it can be settled beyond dispute. Let them be told, and when they are acquainted with all the facts, let them make the decision for themselves." He stared at the soldier across the intervening tank. The soldier stared back, his eyes haunted now. "As you rightly say, the lives that they live now are theirs. Let the choice of what to do with them also be theirs."

59

Peter was the first to avert his eyes.

"How is it possible to guarantee that they'll dream the right dreams?" he asked tiredly. "Dreams are disordered things, just a lot of fantasies and fragments of memory. What's to stop you from stirring up a lot of nightmares?"

"Do not misunderstand what I am saying," Corma answered. "It is not possible to program their dreams in detail. It is possible, however, to activate the subconscious area that contains the positive elements of their personal fantasies. Among other things, the brain is a filing mechanism, something which requires order and design. This has made it possible to recognize and concentrate on the desired elements and avoid their negative counterparts.

"The actual pattern of what follows is beyond our control, as it should be. Perhaps these are random, totally illogical worlds that are activated, where such things as aging and sickness and cruelty and poverty do not exist, and life enters realms beyond the range of our own imaginings. But whatever form they take, they represent the fulfillment of personal desires, the realization of all that they have ever longed for and could never hope to receive."

"Can you prove that?" Peter asked.

"It is inevitable that a demonstration will be called for," said Corma without hesitation. "It would be unrealistic to expect unquestioning acceptance. Naturally, they will ask for evidence that what they will receive is everything that has been claimed. This will be provided."

Peter stared at Corma for a long moment. He felt numb and desperately tired. I don't want it to be the truth, he thought. That's the real problem. But how is it possible to argue with what he's saying? And I've got to remember what it's being done for — the reason for all this.

"All right," he said at last. He looked down at the tank again. "Do we have to tell them just yet?"

"No. If they rest now, it will help to ensure that they are able to fully realize their potential when the time comes." He went to a bank of small screens located between two of the tanks and pressed a switch beneath one of them.

A picture appeared on the screen. It showed the area where they had left the others; the dais, the rest-panels. Two of the panels were occupied, but one was empty. He pressed another switch, and the picture tracked around the room. Then the screen was suddenly filled with a close-up of the Negro's face.

"He is troubled," Corma said. He adjusted the focus. The Negro's features sharpened, showing clearly his restless eyes and the endless muscular activity of his face as he prowled around the area. "It is not simply what he has been told that is the cause. Something haunts him. His problems go beyond the fact that he is crippled." For a brief moment, Peter thought that Corma meant the miraculously cured leg, but then he remembered the man's hand at the time that he had helped him up in the truck; the ugly bulges that distorted the long, slim fingers. "Something else has happened," Corma said. "Recently, I imagine." He pressed another switch.

Another screen lit up, showing a close-up of the two occupied rest-panels. The small man moved fretfully in his sleep, his mouth wet and slack. Next to him, Walter Hurley lay on his back, looking up at the ceiling, his eyes half-closed and his mouth open.

"Did you drug them?" Peter asked.

"Their drinks contained a sedative element," Corma said. "Its purpose was to relax them, nothing more. As you can see, it was not powerful enough to guarantee their loss of consciousness." He switched off the screens. "The Negro will rest soon. It will be a disturbed rest, but the power that he carries is strong and elemental. Despite his recent fever, he requires less sleep than the others." He went to a cabinet and opened it. "What we have to do now is not pleasant, and I shall spare you as many of its extreme aspects as possible. Wear these." He took coveralls similar to his own from the cabinet and handed them to Peter. Peter climbed into them slowly. Corma reached into the cabinet again and removed several large gray plastic containers.

"These will hold the remains, but first we must drain the tanks. You will find a tap at the far end of each, located at the base. The fluid will be automatically stored for later analysis. I should be grateful if you would drain tanks two

and four, please." He indicated them, then knelt by the
cabinet containing the tools.

60

*Corma began his artificially thoughtful selection of equip-
ment as the soldier went to the rear of the nearest tank. He
knew precisely what was required, but it seemed wise to ag-
grandize the proceedings, to augment them in small, superfluous ways whenever possible, in order that the soldier
would be made to feel that his contribution was a genuinely necessary one. There was less urgency now. The surviving pleem had done well — better than he had dared hope.
There were no indications that deterioration threatened,
and if this equilibrium could be maintained for only a few
more hours, the problem would cease to exist.*

*Peter Walsh came back. "Okay, they're draining," he
said as he hunched down beside Corma. "What do we do
now?" He shuddered slightly.*

*"We must remove the remains and refrigerate them for
later analysis. The various attachments will have to be dis-
engaged, and it will be necessary to segment the bodies in
order to facilitate their extraction from the tanks. You will
appreciate from what you have seen that the rate of decomposition demands this." He handed protective gloves to the
soldier and pulled on his own pair. He picked up the assortment of tools that he had placed beside himself and rose.*

"The immediate problem is marginally less urgent than I had anticipated. There are no symptoms to indicate that the survivor is weakening, and if this continues it means that we have been granted a little more time. This, in turn, will mean that it should be possible to do what has to be done rather more painstakingly than I had imagined would be the case." He led the way to the nearest tank and opened the lid.

The liquid was gone, and the body had settled on the tank bottom. Without the liquid to support it, the corpse had spread obscenely. There were openings appearing in the flesh where it folded under the body, and the stench was now extreme.

"It will be best if we continue to talk while working," Corma said. "What must be done now will not be as demanding in terms of concentration as what will come later. Conversation will to some extent take our minds away from the unpleasantness, and it will provide an opportunity for further explanation."

He worked unhurriedly, inventing small, largely irrelevant tasks to ensure the soldier's more or less continuous involvement. As he worked, he talked, following the same course of almost-truth that he had chosen and which had so far justified his decision more than satisfactorily. It was all that had been required; the one basic lie, the solitary inversion of fact. There was no need for continuous, vulnerable invention now. His recasting of himself in the role of protector and friend had negated any such necessity. At times he found himself obliged to expand and augment the lie a little, but these were simple variations, easily remembered.

"What actually got you started on this?" the soldier asked. "How did you find out about the other . . ." He hesitated. "I mean, how did you know that this information was being supplied?"

"Planets that are approaching your own level of development are kept under constant surveillance. The vessels and field equipment used by the beings concerned contain elements necessary to their function that are unique to their technology. These are easily detectable by our scanning systems when they become unshielded. Their methods of screening are not entirely reliable, and fortunately they proved inefficient in this particular instance." Corma eased a connecting line free as he continued to speak. "They were traced, and their activities investigated. What ensued was costly, but it has bought a little time. I believe it to be sufficient for what must be done."

The soldier nodded. "How did you pick up Hurley and persuade him to come along? I'd have thought somebody like that would have frightened off pretty easily when he was told about something like this."

"The power that he and the others possess is not granted to all disadvantaged beings. The reasons for this are not understood, but it places limitations on the material available for selection in a situation of this kind.

"He comes from a town some twenty miles from where we met. Although he is far from being ideal material in the strict sense of the term, he was the best that could be found. There were a few other possible candidates in the region, but age is a factor that has to be considered, and these others were past a time of possible safe usage. He, too, is in the decline in this respect, but still capable of sufficient generative power to justify his selection." Corma reached for another tool. "You are correct in your assumption that a certain amount of instinctive resistance has to be overcome *when attempting to involve such a person in a situation that he naturally viewed as both bizarre and improbable. In this event, it was necessary to employ the powers of will and mind."*

"Hypnotism?"

Corma nodded. "Yes. Not to any great depth, however. He was already subconsciously receptive to the proposition that he was uniquely positioned to be of service to his country and humankind. He is of a strong patriotic inclination, as well as possessing a naturally compassionate character." He handed the soldier a wrench. "It will be possible to detach the main feed-pipe now." He busied himself with the last of the transmission wires.

"Surely people will be looking for him," the soldier said as he worked.

Corma inclined his head. "Some kind of search will be instigated eventually, I have no doubt. However, he lives alone and is unlikely to be missed for some time. It is doubtful that any serious investigation will be undertaken until long after our departure."

"What about the Negro guy? He said something about lying in a ditch." The soldier spun the connecting nut free. "What was that all about?"

"He was attempting to hide at the time of the location," Corma said. "It seems logical to assume that he has in some way run afoul of the law." He shrugged. "It is no concern of ours, and irrelevant in this situation."

The soldier made no comment while he carried the feed-pipe to where the rest of the connecting equipment was arranged on the floor, put it down, and came back. Then he said, with clearly feigned casualness, "Did you hypnotize me, too?"

Corma smiled, carefully. "Do you believe that I have attempted to influence you in such a way?"

The soldier shook his head. "Not really. I suppose it's impossible to tell when it has actually happened to you, though."

"The limited ability that I possess in this respect is only used to temporarily allay initial fears, and has no deep or lasting effect." Corma searched among the tools, experiencing wryly fervent regret at this temporary truth. "The things that you witnessed at the time of our meeting would in any event have rendered it superfluous. Your own imagination is what motivated your acceptance and involvement." He gave the soldier another tool. "Tighten that end connection, please, and then we shall be ready to commence the removal." He began to select cutting implements.

61

Conversation became desultory as the stench thickened. The removal of the bodies was not easy — an untidy, nauseating business that it was a relief to complete. It took a little more than two hours.

Corma removed the last segment and dropped it into the container that the soldier held. He wiped his hands, studying the young man as he fastened its hinged lid. He had done what was required of him without hesitation or protest, keeping a look of drawn determination on his face *throughout the proceedings. It was still there, despite his obvious emotional exhaustion. He watched him as he carried the container to the refrigeration hatch and pushed it through, then turned.*

"Is that it?"

Corma nodded. "Yes. An unpleasant business, but the worst is done. Now the tanks must be flushed and the necessary adaptations made. This will take some time, several hours." He crossed to the tank containing the surviving pleem and raised the lid. The pleem floated serenely, maintaining its darkly firm evidence of health. He nodded and lowered the lid again. "Our luck continues."

"You mean our level of fallibility is holding out," the soldier said. He smiled a small, wan smile.

Corma echoed the smile approvingly. For the first time he experienced a twinge of regret, almost of apology, toward the soldier. In many respects Peter Walsh had proved himself a worthy ally; an unwitting one, true, but in addition to his natural gifts he had consistently demonstrated rather exceptional qualities.

"I do," said Corma. He glanced at the empty tanks. "When they have been cleaned, I shall make the necessary amendments to only one for the time being. This will enable a demonstration to be carried out. It will then be necessary to inform the others of the precise nature of the situation and the part that they are required to play. They will be sufficiently rested by then, and a break in our own activities will be beneficial." He looked at the soldier thoughtfully. "There will be some initial reluctance to overcome, and your help in this direction would be of great value. Can I count on you for this?"

"To help convince them?" the soldier asked. He shook

his head slightly, frowning again. "You said it would be up to them to make their own decisions."

Corma nodded. "That is true. I do not ask you to persuade them to make a specific final choice. What I do ask is that you assist me in helping them to understand the seriousness of the situation that has resulted in my seeking them out and bringing them here. They have been told the purpose of their presence in broad terms, but have received no details as to either the specific nature of the situation or the part that they are required to play.

"Even without this knowledge, Hurley is willing to cooperate because he is by nature humane and sees this as an opportunity to serve his fellows, something that his health has denied him. The Negro's reluctance is outweighed by his need for refuge. The small one does not question because he is unused to kindness and finds it among us." He looked down at the floor. "The future of their present world is the issue. It is not a world that has treated them charitably or brought them happiness. But it is peopled with their own kind, many millions of them." He looked at the soldier again. "It is an appreciation of this and what the future holds for humankind unless action is taken that I may require your help in obtaining. Are you prepared to do this?"

62

Peter tried to focus his mind, to see through the fog of tiredness that was gradually filling it now. It was a question of belief, he told himself. Believe, and the rest was easy. But despite everything that had happened, the inescapable logic of it all, a doubt remained — a minute, nagging uncertainty, far back in his consciousness, that had been there right from the start, when the truck had barred his way and he had seen the driver's face, white and featureless behind the partial glare of the window.

A thought suddenly formed and expanded rapidly. He explored it, uneasily, watching it take shape; a deformed, darkly threatening inversion of his understanding.

Then another thought came, shocking in its implications.

"Answer me one question," he said slowly. He lifted a hand, almost apologetically. "What is there to stop me from believing that, despite everything I've seen, what you've told me isn't exactly true?" He saw the shadow of a frown appear on Corma's face but he plowed on doggedly. "I mean, what if you've told me the basic facts, but chosen to twist them in some way, so that you're using them to . . ." He hesitated, not knowing how to complete the question.

Corma nodded and finished the statement for him. "Using them to conceal the real truth — that there are no guardians, and that I, in fact, am responsible for disseminating the dangerous knowledge to which I have referred." He smiled. "The answer is simple. If that was truly the case, you would not be here now to threaten my escape. You would be dead."

Of course, Peter thought. It really was as simple as that. . . . The doubt flickered again, a final spasm of curiosity. "But how would you have managed here? I mean, would you have been able to do the things that we're doing without me?" He felt embarrassment. "Look, you mustn't think—"

"The sequence of events may have been changed," Corma said. "It might have been necessary to inform the others earlier and obtain physical assistance from one or more of them, although I hardly need tell you that it would have been of a lesser quality than your own. Your absence would have created difficulties, but they would not have been insurmountable in the technical sense. Your true value is as a link between myself and the others. You are of their world, and your own belief will help to convince them of the necessity of what must be done." He smiled understandingly. "I have already spoken of your intelligence and imagination. You are demonstrating them now. Intelligence always questions, never blindly accepts what is offered. It is right that you should voice these thoughts. Only if you do so is it possible for me to refute them with reason and further explanation."

Peter nodded. He felt foolish, a little ashamed, and very young. He wondered how old Corma actually was. He had talked of different time scales, the longevity of his own race. Perhaps he was a hundred years old, two hundred, three. We must be like children to them, he thought, and not very bright ones, at that.

"The adaptation is not particularly complicated in the technical sense, but precision is vital," Corma said. It was a tactful redirecting of the conversation, for which Peter was grateful. "First, though, the tanks and connecting equipment must be disinfected and sterilized. You will find containers carrying the necessary fluid to the right of the cabinet, at the rear." He collected the instruments he had been using and turned away.

The cleaning of the tanks mercifully succeeded in blanketing most of the smell of what they had contained. The adaptation of the chosen tank was, as Corma had predicted, a touchy task, but reasonably straightforward and well within Peter's fair grasp of technical procedures. During this latter process his principal role was that of observer, memorizing what was required. He restricted his questions to matters of the moment now, glad for the opportunity to put his earlier remarks behind him.

The cleaning and conversion took a little less than three hours to complete. When the work was done, Corma said, "Your questions were the right ones, and you clearly anticipated the various stages of procedure. Is your memory sound?" Peter said that he thought it was. Corma smiled. "You are a rewarding pupil. I feel confident that you will be able to offer direct assistance when it becomes necessary to deal similarly with the others. This will expedite matters considerably." He returned the tools he had been using to their designated places in the cabinet.

"Do we tell them now?" Peter asked reluctantly.

"Yes. The conversions will take a little time, and we must not allow ourselves to be lulled into complacency by the continuing stability of the pleem. Deterioration is rapid once it begins, and on past evidence I know it can happen with relatively little warning. We must maintain a constant check on the pleem, which I will ask you to make your responsibility for now. Any textural or color change will signal the beginning." He closed the cabinet and went to the bank of screens.

The picture of the lower level reappeared. The Negro seemed to be dozing restlessly now, but Hurley and the small man were awake, sitting on the edges of their panels facing one another. Hurley was talking, his normal look of anxiety currently replaced by one of reassurance. The small man nodded repeatedly as he listened, his head tilted to one side and bobbing obligingly at regular intervals. It occurred to Peter that as far as he knew the small man hadn't actually spoken since the time of their meeting. That he was hard of hearing was evident. Was he mute as well? He felt a spurt of pity. Even if he wasn't, he was a pathetic creature, a catalogue of deprivation and inadequacy that made Peter feel irrational shame.

Corma switched off the screen and walked to the stairs. Peter hesitated momentarily, then followed him.

63

Hurley and the small man sat together on the edge of the panels. The Negro had declined to sit, and stood by the dais, his back against it.

Corma studied the faces of the silently waiting group, seeing in them the mixture of anticipatory expressions that he had known would be there.

The small man showed unquestioning devotion, plainly overlaid with acute shyness. Walter Hurley was eager, but the occasional uncertainty of his expression betrayed an undercurrent of fear. The Negro was afraid, too, but his tension was more openly revealed by his ever-changing pose and the restlessness of his eyes.

Corma sat on the end panel, facing the three of them. The soldier stood a short distance behind him, an agreed-upon position from where he could unobtrusively leave the room occasionally to check the condition of the pleem.

"I thank you for your patience," Corma said to them. "Certain tasks have been necessary which have occupied us up to this time. Now I must tell you the full reasons for your presence here, and what it is that you can contribute. It will take a little while, but bear with me." He looked around the group, soothing them with will and mind, preparing them. "You will find much of what I have to tell you strange, but do not be frightened by its lack of familiarity.

The universe is a place of endless diversity and many wonders, most of which remain hidden from us during the time of our existence. Some of them I shall reveal to you now."

He talked steadily and simply, repeating in essence what he had told the soldier, but sequentially this time: his assumed history and role, the supposed incidents that had brought him there, his augmented version of the things that had happened since his arrival. No one interrupted. Lastly, he talked about the pleem, the part that they played and what had now become necessary.

He finished, and waited for their response.

64

Several times during Corma's monologue, Peter had left the area to check on the pleem, on each occasion thankful to find that there had been no discernible change. His periodic visits to the upper level had afforded a bizarre relief from having to look at the faces of the group and witness the gradual changes that appeared thereon, the steady erosion of confidence that he had seen in their expressions, as Corma talked.

He looked at them now. The small man was confused, still desperately clinging to the remnants of his faith, but uncomprehending and visibly afraid. Hurley's already pale face was bleached and ghostlike. The Negro stood like stone, his eyes fixed on Corma in a shocked, rigid stare.

Peter lowered his head, unable to look at them any more. Corma's presentation was good, he thought. Very good, in fact. Simple, straight to the point, no hedging. The facts. But couldn't he have softened them in some way, made them less brutal, less irretrievably final?

Peter wasn't religious, but he found himself praying, although he wasn't quite sure for what; his mind formed vague, agonized generalizations from which he received no comfort or hint of guidance. To him, the facts *were* brutal, *were* irretrievably final. But would the others see them the same way? His life had been cushioned, filled with affection; he had been blessed with good health and an active mind. The prospect of ending his life, exchanging it for another briefly idealized, intangible world, was obscene. He had no desire for a tailor-made existence that would be predictable, confined, without challenge or surprise.

But what about them? They existed in conditions so different from his own that they, like Corma, might have belonged to other worlds; in their case, hard, dark places, where indignity and physical distress were everyday things, to be inescapably borne. For them, the facts might mean salvation, a release from endless torment.

Who am I to say? he thought. He looked at them again, still fighting his own confusion and uncertainty.

"I'm not quite sure that I understand, Mr. Corma," Hurley said hesitantly. "The last bit, I mean." His chest was rising and falling in an exaggerated way again. "Do you mean that we'd actually . . ." He faltered, unable to complete the question.

"In a matter of hours, you would be dead," Corma said quietly. "But that would not be before you had lived the life that you have always wanted — the life you have longed for, but known could never be." He looked at each of the others, briefly, then back to Hurley. "Each of you has a dream. In exchange for the life that you live now, I can give you that dream."

"I'd like to . . ." Hurley began, turning his gaze toward Peter. Oh, God, no, Peter thought. He wanted to scream, to wake up, to run away and hide. Then Hurley said, "Sir, what do you think about this? I mean, does it make sense to you?" He coughed. "I don't mean any disrespect to Mr. Corma, or anything like that, but it's an awful big thing we're talking about. I just want to be sure that what we'd be doing was sensible and right . . ." His voice tailed away in a fit of coughing.

Sensible and right? Peter thought. He had started to pray again while Hurley was talking, but then he had stopped. There was no point in pleading with a deity that he didn't know whether he believed in or not, no sense in asking for words to be put into his mouth to absolve him from the responsibility of decision. He waited until Hurley had recovered, then said, "If you mean, do I believe about the trouble he says we're in, this business of information being provided so that we're in a position to wipe ourselves out, yes, I guess I do." He paused. "The other thing is something that I don't think I should express an opinion on. It's your lives we're talking about, not mine." Again, he felt sudden, unreasoning shame. "You've been told what the issues are, and you've got to decide that for yourselves."

Hurley removed his glasses and wiped his watering eyes. "Yes, I can see that. Thank you very much." He put his glasses back on, glanced furtively around at the others, then at the floor, fighting his reactivated asthma.

"What about these dreams?" asked the Negro. He didn't look frightened any more. His face was alert and cautiously probing. "What are you telling us, man? That you can fix it so we dream the stuff we want to?" He grinned emptily. "That sounds great, but saying don't prove anything, right?"

"Are you willing to be the subject for a demonstration?" asked Corma.

The Negro stared at him, his mouth open. After a moment he said, "Is that a straight offer? I mean, it's a demonstration, right? Just a couple of minutes, something like that?"

"Approximately five minutes would be required. It will take at least two minutes to reach the level of sleep necessary to permit the interchange to take place."

"The what?"

"Until such a level is reached, your dreams will be the kind that you always dream. After that, your generative potential will be ready to respond to the stimulus that will be supplied, simultaneously channeling and magnifying your subconscious wishes."

"Hey, I never knew I had a generative potential," the Negro said with a laugh. "I guess it's time I tried it out." He laughed again, a slightly wild, hollow sound in the hard-walled room.

Peter looked at him, seeing despairing defiance in his humorless, skull-like grin and remembering the speculations of Corma the first time they had watched him on the screen in the power chamber. He was right, he thought. He's running from something, something so bad that he doesn't think he has a future anyway. This is his way out.

Peter heard his voice saying, "Why are you doing it?"

193

He checked himself, horrified. "Look, I have no right—"

"That's okay, man," the Negro said. "I don't mind telling it. I broke prison, and I killed a guy." He looked at the stunned faces of Hurley and the small man and laughed the same slightly wild laugh. "No patriot, me. Uncle wants this boy dead. You can all go to hell in a basket, for all I care. I don't have nothing to lose, so why not?"

There was a long, cold moment of silence.

"I am grateful for your cooperation," Corma said gently. To Hurley and the small man he said, "I feel it desirable that you should witness what takes place. It involves a minimum of physical inconvenience, and there is no discomfort of any kind. Believe me, I fully understand your reluctance to commit yourselves before having been satisfied that all I have claimed is true. That evidence will be forthcoming now." He looked back at the Negro. "Are you ready?"

"Sure. Why not?" The Negro grinned his death's-head grin again, his eyes bright and empty. "Make my dreams come true, man." He flexed his knotted fingers against his thighs.

65

Peter stood a little way from the rest of the group as they ranged around the tank in which the Negro lay.

No one spoke. Corma stood at the far end of the tank, working with expressionless concentration, adjusting connections, checking terminals. The air in the room was clearer now, but there was still a lingering hint of putrefaction beneath the disinfectant overlay. In the dim light, the faces of the others reflected fear, curiosity, reluctance, lingering disbelief.

I don't belong here, Peter thought. I'm an outsider, an observer. He felt enormous relief, touched with an uneasy mixture of embarrassment and something else. What was it? he wondered. A kind of perverse envy? Something like that, anyway. He was the boy who had been shut out of the game that only the older children could play. If only it was a game, he thought; a wild, fanciful recreation that could be ended when they tired of it.

But there was only one ending to what was being played out now. He closed his eyes, then opened them again and looked at the Negro.

He lay on gray padding, his naked body lightly filmed with perspiration. An alloy band — one of the same ones that had been attached to the pleem — was fixed around his forehead, with foam wadding holding it firm where it failed to make direct contact with his skull. He stared at the ceiling, woodenly, saying nothing.

Corma left the tank and positioned himself by the console. "You will sleep now," he said. "Remember, your initial dreams will be similar in mood and content to those that you normally dream. The transition will be sudden, but there will be no discomfort when it happens. It will mean relief, your escape from the world that you have learned to hate and fear." He pressed a switch.

There was the faintest of sounds, a humming that existed on the very edge of audibility and which was almost drowned out by the fluttering rasp of Hurley's breathing. A small white light appeared on the panel above the Negro's head, a dim, flickering point of illumination that looked as if it could wink out at any time.

He's fighting it, Peter thought. He looked at the man's eyes, still staring at the ceiling with a kind of forced intensity. He doesn't want to, really, but it's instinct that's holding him back. As he watched, the eyelids suddenly slackened, drooped, then closed.

The white light steadied and began to brighten. Corma watched it with poker-faced concentration, his hands resting on the console. Hurley and the small man were looking at it with a degree of tension that had now frozen them to almost total stillness. It was as though the light had become a beacon, something that would guide them all to the thing that they sought; Corma to the power that he needed, the others to the resolving of the uncertainty still faintly mirrored in their faces.

The Negro moved and began to make sounds of distress; soft moans, sobs, and then a horrified shout. His body was bright with sweat now, and making violent spastic movements that tugged at the encircling wires and tubes.

There was a sudden jolt. Simultaneously, the sound jumped to a muted roar that vibrated the whole room. Peter could feel it under his feet; a rapid, growing tremor that was moving his entire body. He braced himself and looked at the Negro. The spastic movements had stopped, and his face showed total concentration now. His hands were raised, the fingers dancing in small, sluggish, but oddly graceful movements. . . .

John George liked the piano. It had a few dead notes and it needed tuning, but the action had a balance that spoke of fine, caring origins. He tried it at a wide variety of tempos and degrees of volume, and it responded unfailingly.

He played until three o'clock, then went on to another place where he was again greeted with delighted shouts from the musicians and other people there. He played for another two hours on a small piano that was newer and better cared for than the earlier one, but it was no more than adequate, he decided. A girl who he hadn't seen before brought him drinks, and he took her back to his place afterward and put her in a taxi after breakfast later in the day.

That next afternoon, in the company of musicians of his own choosing, he played a recording session before an invited audience. It went well, and another session was arranged for the following week. The guy who had been pestering him to go out to Los Angeles to play at his club there was still hanging around, increasing his offer and padding out the terms, but he put him off again, told him he'd think about it. The real action was where he was, and he didn't really want to leave it, even though the California sunshine would have been nice. Maybe next year, he thought.

The girl showed up again every night that week. She was cute, but he didn't encourage her, because some of these chicks had eyes for getting married, a real home, that kind of thing. He was free, didn't want to be tied, not yet. He took her back to his place a couple more times and he told her how it would have to be and she didn't complain.

A little while after that he was playing the piano with the nice action again, having fun skirting the dead notes, when the blackness suddenly shut down like a sheet of ebony. He fought against it, terrified, and at last opened his eyes, seeing the faces that peered down at him in the dim, gray room.

Then he remembered.

"Ah, no," he said. "No, man, *no*. . . ."

He began to cry.

66

Corma reversed the switch, masking his elation as he did so. The tracer readings had not lied, at least not in the negative sense. The Negro's power was even fiercer than he had anticipated or dared hope, almost frightening in its intensity. If only it was possible to develop such elemental force, he thought, to direct it into the necessary disciplined pattern.

But that was a contradiction, of course. Its very nature ensured that it would be short-lived, unable to sustain itself for more than a little while. But it would be long enough, more than sufficient for what was needed now. He wondered if, despite the more promising readings he had received from the small man, that one could really match or surpass the power he had just witnessed.

"Do not be distressed," he said to the still-sobbing Negro. "The world that you have left has not been lost to you." He went to the tank and removed the alloy band, gently, then began releasing the other connections. "The process has been suspended simply in order that you may confirm the truth of my promise." He looked down at the Negro's puffed and agonized face. "Was it as I told you?"

The Negro raised his hands again and looked at them. His face showed horror and disgust. He dropped them to his sides, listlessly. "Yeah, it was. Put me back there, man." His voice was thick and pleading. "Please."

"Not yet. In a little while. What you are able to contribute must be preserved." To the others, he said, "You have seen and heard. Do you believe me now?"

"Mr. Corma," Hurley began, "I wouldn't want you to think I ever figured you were trying to fool us, or anything like that. It's just that it's . . . well, it's better to be actually told, by somebody that's really done it." He was patently embarrassed. "If he says it's all right, then I guess I'll go along with it, too."

Corma nodded, satisfied. Hurley's simplistic philosophies had always practically guaranteed his eventual acceptance of the situation. Would the small one follow now? He glanced at him, seeing the confused uncertainty that persisted on his face.

"Your reticence is perfectly understandable," Corma said to Hurley. "There are circumstances that require a radical adjustment of one's view of the nature of existence, something that cannot be easily achieved." He carefully assisted the Negro to a sitting position. "I think that the time has come for you to talk among yourselves. There are other preparations that have to be made, and these will take some time." Corma stepped back as the Negro shrugged his hand away and levered himself out of the tank. He wasn't crying now, but he looked emotionally drained. He began to dress himself again, ignoring the others.

Corma took the soldier to one side as Hurley and the small man went slowly to the stairs.

"It will be necessary for me to leave for a short while. The tracer and the scanner are still in the truck; an oversight, but not a matter of great concern. The chances of them falling into other hands are slight. I shall be no more than a few minutes, and it will be of assistance if you remain here with the others. The small one is still undecided, and while I am not suggesting that you attempt to influence his decision in any way, a moderating presence may be of use in what is inevitably a situation of considerable delicacy."

The Negro finished dressing and went to the stairs. He didn't speak as he left the room with his head lowered and his shoulders hunched.

"Why don't I fetch them instead of you?" Peter offered. "You say there's a lot of work left to do. Wouldn't it save time if you were able to get on with it right away?"

Corma looked at him thoughtfully. Could this be a belated attempt to run? An indication that he lacked the courage to face the closing stages, now that he was fully conscious

*of what they entailed? Corma studied his face but saw no
evidence of fear there.*

He wondered what the situation would have been now
if the soldier had chosen to turn tail after their meeting, taking the small man with him. Would he have invoked the
presence of the authorities to seek out this madman whom
he had encountered, creating additional problems for Corma to overcome? In fact, Peter Walsh's continued presence
here had been generally beneficial, a help rather than the expected hindrance. Perhaps his power was limited to self-
preservation, Corma thought; perhaps it contained no true
countering element, after all. Such variations in the phe-
nomenon were not unknown.

"It will be best if we do as I have proposed," Corma said.
"You are unfamiliar with the workings of the raft, which
are not as simple as you might suppose. Your continued
presence here will serve our purpose better, and I shall be
able to commence the remaining adaptations very shortly.
Even if the pleem should start to fail now, we have a willing replacement to ensure that power continuity is maintained." He smiled. "The degree of urgency is a little less
than it was."

The soldier nodded. His expression was still reluctant,
but he offered no further opposition. It is natural that he is
distressed at the prospect of what he has to do, Corma
thought. A person of conscience and compassion; both of
them admirable qualities in their way, but with dangerous
limitations. He felt a further twinge of amused warmth toward the soldier, almost of affection.

"Fortune has favored us this far," he said reassuringly.
"I feel that the situation will soon be finally resolved." He
led the way to the stairs, his growing tiredness buttressed

by the glow of unfettered optimism that coursed through him now.

67

It was early dusk when Corma stepped outside. A strong wind had risen during the time that they had been inside the ship. It crossed the basin in sharp, cold gusts, rippling the meager grass and making his eyes water as he released the raft from its storage slot.

He paused before stepping onto it. Wind could be dangerous, especially gusty wind like this. A raft could be easily capsized if handled carelessly. He thought briefly of the soldier, of what might have happened if he had agreed to his proposal, permitted him to use it. The signs clearly indicated that he probably would have come to no harm, but what he was doing now could very possibly be of greater use. If he had posed a genuine threat, it would have manifested itself long before this, and there had been no evidence of danger beyond that already inherent in the situation. There was also the raft itself to consider, and if the soldier had failed to return with it for some reason, that may well have disturbed the steady progress toward completion, invoked concern among the others. Hurley at least would have insisted on searching for him, causing further delay.

He clamped himself onto it and then directed the raft up and out of the basin and down the mountain, traveling

slowly and staying close to the tops of the trees. Visibility
from air to ground was becoming limited in the fading light;
while it would be hard for him to detect unwanted pres-
ences, it would be much less difficult for them to see him if
he was to present himself in clear silhouette against the red-
dening sky.

There were no lights on the road, no sign of life that he
could see. He drifted the raft over the last of the trees and
began his descent into the roadside clearing beside the cluster of rocks where the truck and car were located.

He glanced down and froze, automatically jerking the
controls to hovering position.

Directly below him, occupying the center of the clearing,
was a glint of metal, the shadowed outline of a vehicle of
some kind. He looked to the right of the clearing, where the
truck and car had been parked. They were both there, but
the bush that he had placed behind the car had gone.

The wind? It must have been. The wind had moved it,
and the car had been seen. But by whom? He glanced down
again — and saw the twin glimmers of red on the roof of
the vehicle below him.

Surely not? he thought, shocked. Fear was suddenly rising inside him, chilling the optimism that only moments
before had seemed so comfortingly invulnerable. He looked
down at the vehicle again, and this time saw the central projection, recognizing the siren and grimly accepting this further evidence to confirm what he already knew to be the
truth of the situation.

They had failed to lose the policeman after all. Obviously
his initial curiosity had blossomed into dedicated pursuit,
its growth prompted by the contradictory behavior of the
soldier and himself and their ultimately unsuccessful at-

*tempt to throw him off the track. Those vehicles that they
had passed on the mountain road, Corma thought. He must
have stopped them and questioned their occupants, been
told of how they had passed the truck and the unmistakably
distinctive car. Now the policeman was down there somewhere, waiting, the distance that he had been prepared to
travel with no guarantee of success an alarming testament
to his determination.*

*Corma cursed, revolved the raft, and peered down into
the shadows cast by the trees. There was no suspicious
movement, no telltale sound detectable beneath the hissing
of the wind. Was he still in the car? he wondered. That
seemed likely, a logical thing to do; to sit and wait, on the
assumption that sooner or later they would return to their
vehicles. And what about the tracer and the scanner? Had
they been found, appropriated, recognized as unfamiliar
evidence of some inexplicable activity that would justify
this persistent pursuit?*

*He fumbled the light-blade from the pocket of his cover-
alls, remembering its failure the last time he had attempted
to use it. But that had been when confronting the soldier.
The policeman in the sweat-stained hat had registered no
similar protective reading.*

*He adjusted the range dial to minimum distance, aimed
it horizontally above the console of the raft, and pressed the
trigger. A thin, five-foot-long line of white light appeared,
briefly illuminating the raft and lightening the shadowed
sky around him.*

*Corma almost laughed aloud with sheer relief. He was
armed after all — more than a match for any primitive fire-
power that might be used against him. He reset the range
to medium distance and steered the raft gently away from*

the clearing. There was no one visible in the car. He approached it cautiously and peered inside.

There was nobody there, but the tracer and the scanner were on the rear seat. He opened the door quietly and removed them, leaving the door open. He stood for a moment, listening, then carried them back to the raft and clamped them to it.

His optimism was returning now. He had what he had come for, and as far as he could tell he had not been seen. The policeman was probably some distance away, fruitlessly searching the slope for tracks. With luck, he could get back to the ship undetected, but even if he was seen during the journey there would be no problem once he was there. It seemed improbable that the policeman carried climbing equipment with him, and it was unlikely that he would be rash enough to attempt climbing an unfamiliar mountain bare-handed and alone in the dark. He may attempt it when daylight came, of course, but that was a possibility that Corma did not concern himself with.

He could, of course, apprehend the soldier when Peter Walsh returned to his car, Corma reflected. But what would the soldier say? How could he possibly justify his actions? By telling the truth?

Corma smiled as he clamped himself in position. If that was what he chose to do, the episode could conclude with his being classified as mentally unstable and therefore unsuitable for continued army service. Self-preservation, indeed, he thought. There was the truck as supporting evidence, and Corma's disappearance, but both of those factors would be more probably associated in the minds of authority with some unexplained criminal activity.

No, the situation would be a difficult one for the soldier;

*unfortunate in a sense, but not without its possible com-
pensating aspects.* Corma smiled again and directed the
raft up and over the trees.

As he cleared them, something struck the underside of
the raft; a jarring, metallic blow that vibrated and rocked
the craft dangerously. Simultaneously, he heard the sound
of the gunshot.

He fought the controls, steadying the raft and hunching
low as he peered down among the trees, shocked by the
abruptness of the attack. There was another shot. He saw
the small spurt of flame, below him and to his right, and
then the raft tilted again as the bullet struck and whined
away somewhere among the trees. He steadied the raft
again, picking up speed and directing it over the point
where he had seen the flash. He angled it slightly, holding
the controls firm. He saw him now, among the shadows of
the trees: the faded khaki clothing and Stetson hat; the up-
turned, whitely staring face.

There were no more shots. The man began to run, zig-
zagging wildly between the trees, heading across the slope
toward the clearing. Corma took the raft lower, as close to
the trees as he dared, tracking him, the light-blade held
ready. He saw the hat detach itself from the man's head and
tumble down the slope among the bushes there. Seconds
later, the man tripped and fell.

He tried to rise, but with difficulty. Corma tilted the
raft downward, steadied it, aimed carefully, and fired. The
lance of white light struck the writhing figure squarely. In
the same instant, a fierce gust of wind swirled across the
tops of the trees, thudding against the underside of the raft
at an angle and throwing it to one side.

The raft brushed against a projecting treetop, jarring

*Corma's hand from the controls, then toppled. He raised his
arms across his face as it slid jerkingly down the tree, shear-
ing branches as it fell. There was a final unimpeded tum-
bling descent, a briefly felt impact as it struck the ground,
and then painless, empty darkness.*

68

Michael Pierce sat on the edge of a rest-panel, listening
while the others talked. He didn't really understand much
of what was happening, but what he did understand was
frightening, especially now that Corma wasn't there. He
looked around for him, but he wasn't back from wherever
he had gone. When he was there, the place didn't seem so
cold and hard, and even that strange business upstairs with
the Negro hadn't scared him the way it would have done if
Corma hadn't been in charge.

The Negro seemed all right now. He hadn't said anything for a while after he had followed the rest of them
downstairs, but now he was talking to the man called Walter and him, and you could tell from the way his eyes
shone that he was excited. He said that Corma had been
telling the truth and that he really could fix it so that you
went to a place where everything was all right and you
could do everything you had always wanted to, anything
at all.

That wasn't really true, of course. The Negro had been

in the tank all the time, hadn't actually gone anywhere, but he said it was as though he had been there a long time, maybe a couple of weeks, he wasn't really sure. He told them how he had been able to play the piano again like he used to before he hurt his hands, only a lot better now, and how he was famous and how he had met this girl. When he was telling it, he was working his fingers all the time, and you could see how badly he wanted to get back there so that he could see his girl and carry on playing the piano and being a famous musician.

That sounded wonderful, Michael Pierce thought. He wasn't sure what he'd want to do if he went to a place like that, though. He had never wanted much, really, not to be able to play the piano or anything. If he could just have a room of his own somewhere; a bed and a comfortable chair to sit in and enough to eat and some comic books and maybe a radio, that would be nice.

Another thought stirred in his mind, startling him with its audacity. It was a crazy idea, really, but Corma and the Negro both had said that you could have anything you wanted. If that was so, then maybe he could find a cure for whatever it was that made him pass out and make a mess. He thought about that, wonderingly. Maybe he could even have a whole house of his own, too, not just a room. If he could have a house with a garden, he could grow things, potatoes and carrots and stuff like that, and maybe Corma and the rest of them could come by sometime as well. He'd be able to have a dog, too, to kill any rats he might see. Rats frightened him, but he wouldn't be scared if he had a dog to take care of them, he thought.

He wondered if he should check with Corma when he came back to see if it would be all right for him to have things like that. If Corma said it would, then he wouldn't mind being put in one of the tanks, even if it did mean him dying after a while. He thought about the man called Charlie, and decided that dying in a tank having nice dreams would be a whole lot better than going the way Charlie had, all stiff and cold in a barn or somewhere like that.

Walter still felt a bit scared about the dying part, but not too much now. It was why they were doing it that mattered, he told himself. In a funny kind of way they were all going to be heroes, not that anybody in the world except the soldier would know about it. But it was an easy way of being a hero, really. Most heroes had a bad time before they either died or somehow managed to survive whatever it was that made them into one, so this was almost like cheating, somehow. To exchange something you didn't really want for something that you had wanted all your life but had known could never happen — that didn't make you a proper hero.

The thing that he found really disappointing, though, was knowing that the people he was going to cure wouldn't be real people at all, that they'd only be living in his mind. That was a pity, because he would have liked to have helped some real people to get well. He briefly toyed with the thought that he could maybe have the small man and the Negro in his world, fix things so that he could help them in some way, but then he realized that there wouldn't be any point. The Negro already had a world worked out where his fingers were back to normal, and the small man would be sure to arrange things so that wherever it was he went he'd be fixed up, too.

No, it would be okay, but a little bit pointless in a way.

But it was bound to be interesting, and he had to remember the reasons for it all, the millions of lives that they'd be saving by stopping people from building those bombs.

He looked across the room to where the soldier, Peter, was wandering around, looking worried. He hoped nothing happened to him when he went off to fight. He was a really nice person, and it would be an awful shame if he was to get killed or crippled, because it would be a terrible waste, not at all like what he and the other two were going to do.

He wondered where it was Mr. Corma had gone. He seemed to have been away a long time now, Walter thought.

69

Peter glanced at his watch again. It was a little more than forty minutes since he had first looked at it, but it seemed like much longer than that. Corma had said that he'd be back very quickly, and it must have been almost an hour since he had left.

He went to the airlock door and studied it. There was a switch on the wall to its right, and a few inches above that, held vertically in a bracket, a small cylindrical object with a press-switch projecting from its top end. He recognized the cylinder as matching the device that Corma had taken from underneath the rock and used to effect entry into the ship at the time of their arrival. He removed it from the bracket, pushed the wall switch, and the airlock door opened. As he stepped through it, the outer door slid open, too, permitting entry to a gust of cold air; a fraction of a second later, he heard the gentle thud of the inside door closing behind him. He went outside, turned, and pressed the switch at the top of the cylinder, seeing the outer door close in response. He pressed it again, and it opened.

So that's it, he thought, relieved. They open and shut alternately. He closed the door once more, shivering slightly in the sudden coldness that had greeted him outside the protection of the ship, and looked around.

It was dark now. Broken clouds scudded across the top of the basin as he stared up at the sky. The wind, cold and strong, tugged sharply at his clothing. He thought about the raft, picturing it in these flying conditions. An accident, he thought. That has to be it. Oh, God, what now? He went back into the ship as the clouds above him parted to reveal a hard, clear sky, sprinkled with minute points of light.

The others had stopped talking now. They watched silently as Peter closed the entrance and crossed the room to the door leading to the corridor and the stairs. I mustn't overplay this, he thought. I could be wrong. It could be just a mechanical breakdown, but even that would be serious enough.

"Just going to check upstairs," he said. He smiled reassuringly back at them as he went through.

He could see no indication that the pleem had changed in any way. He went back down to the lower room, thinking hard.

"I'm not suggesting that we should do anything right away," he said to the silent group, "but it's beginning to look as though he might be having some kind of trouble." He saw the alarm come over their faces and was quick to qualify that statement. "That doesn't mean to say that he's had an accident. The raft might have broken down, something like that. There's a strong wind blowing now, and it must have made flying difficult. Maybe he's decided to wait until it dies down a bit. I just don't know." That last possibility could be it, he thought, although it wasn't really likely in view of the situation. Corma had repeatedly made it clear that time was important, and he wouldn't waste it waiting for a change in weather.

"Anyway, I'm going to give it another half hour," Peter said, a bit lamely. "If he's not back by then, I think I'd better go out and look for him."

"But it must be dark by now," Hurley said. "How would you get down the mountain?"

Peter smiled, hoping he looked more confident than he felt. "The moon will be up by then. It's almost full right now, so there'll be plenty of light." Child's play, he thought grimly. He pictured the walls of the basin, almost sheer and difficult enough to scale even in daylight, and the cloud-littered sky, and suppressed a shudder. "Look, if I have to do it, I'll be okay. We do climbing as part of our training, so I know enough about it."

"Yes, but in training you have ropes and stuff, and the right kind of boots," Hurley said doubtfully. "And I'll bet they don't make you do it in the dark, do they?"

"Sometimes they do, yes," Peter said. "Anyway, if he doesn't turn up, we can't just sit here." Nobody said anything. "Look, I might not have to do it at all. He could come back at any time. But just in case he doesn't, I'm going to look around and see if I can find a flashlight and some rope. There must be things like that here." He went across to the wall and began checking the recessed cupboards.

There was nothing downstairs, but the cabinet in the power chamber from which the tools had come contained something like a surgeon's lamp, an adjustable headband with a sealed light on the front. There was also a coil of rather thin but extremely strong cord.

He checked the pleem again, then went back below.

The others eyed the lamp and the cord as he reappeared, but gave no sign of approval or encouragement. He glanced at his watch again. They're right, he thought. It'll be a crazy thing to do if it actually comes to it. But what other acceptable choice is there? "We'll give it another ten minutes," he said. He sat on the nearest rest-panel and took out a cigarette.

Hurley wandered across the room and sat down beside him. Peter put the cigarette away. He hadn't really wanted to smoke, and it would probably have aggravated Hurley's asthma. The man's breathing was already ragged again, signaling his anxiety.

"You know, you're going to be taking an awful chance out there," Hurley said in a low voice. "I mean, you could have an accident real easy in the dark." He looked and sounded genuinely concerned. "I'd like to come with you, but I guess I'd only slow you down. I never did any climbing or anything like that."

Peter was touched. "We couldn't risk having the two of us away at the same time, anyway," he said equally softly. "I would like you to come outside with me in a few minutes. If I have to go out looking, maybe you can help me get started. But then you'll have to come back in. If anything happens to the pleem, somebody's going to have to set up the . . . the alternate power system, and you're the only one who could handle it."

Hurley nodded. He's relieved, really, Peter thought. He doesn't mind actually dying, but he doesn't want to risk a broken leg. He forced a smile. "I think it would be just a question of having him" — Peter indicated the Negro with a tilt of his head — "go back in the tank and having somebody else fit the headband and clip the wires back on. Let's hope things don't get to the point where you have to find out, but if anything looks to be going wrong with that thing up there you'll have to try it."

He detailed what was involved as simply as he could, got Hurley to repeat it, then glanced across to where the Negro was sitting. The man's surge of excitement had plainly evaporated now, and he was slumped forward, his elbows on his knees, staring sightlessly at the floor. He's still there, really, Peter thought, in this new reality of his; still playing the piano in some studio or dive while his girl waits on him. This is just an unwelcome break as far as he's concerned. "We'd better tell him," Peter said. "I wouldn't think he's likely to object, anyway."

He went over to the Negro and said, "Walter and I are going to check outside again. He'll be right back inside, and maybe I will, too. But if the wind has gone down and Corma's not back in a few more minutes, I'm going to go and see if I can find him." Then he told him about the possible necessity as far as the power supply was concerned. The Negro had been listless at first, disinterested, but his eyes steadily brightened as Peter talked.

"Yeah, sure," he said. "Okay." He checked himself, suddenly cautious. "Hey, are you sure it would be like last time? I mean, you don't really know how that stuff works, do you?"

Peter admitted that he didn't. "But I helped him when he was setting it up, and I watched everything he did. I can remember it, and I've explained it to Walter. It was really pretty simple after the wiring had been changed around. I don't see how there could be any problems."

The Negro laughed, briefly and without humor. "I seem to have heard that line somewhere before, man." He shrugged and looked up at Peter. "I guess it would be okay." He stared at the floor again, his eyes hungry and his hands restless.

Peter picked up the lamp and the cord. He headed for the outside door with Hurley at his heels, went through, and closed the entrance behind them. The wind had ebbed to a light breeze now. They stood for a while, peering and listening, but there was no sound and no trace of movement against the coldly brightening sky. "That's it, then," said Peter. "Either he's got a mechanical problem, or he's crashed." He thought, appalled, of what this could mean. "There's no point in me hanging around. The sooner I go, the sooner it gets settled."

"What happens if you don't find him?" Walter asked, shivering. "What if he's dead? If he's dead, what do we do then?"

"There's no point in speculating like that until we know what's happened." Peter was chiding Hurley now, reversing their former recent roles. "He could be knocked out, or have a broken leg or something. You shouldn't start thinking the worst. Look, it's natural to be concerned, but try not to let this get to the others too much. We've got to keep our heads, whatever happens now. If anybody panics, we could be in real trouble."

"Yes, I can see that," said Walter. He tried to smile, his breathing ragged and his face wan in the coldly pale light. "I'm sorry. I guess I'm just not as optimistic as I ought to be."

Ought to be? Peter thought. He wondered how optimistic he would have been if his health and circumstances had been similar to Walter Hurley's. "It'll be okay," Peter said, touching Walter's arm in a gesture of reassurance. He gave Walter the entrance operating unit, explained how it worked, and told him to be sure to leave it by the projecting rock when he went back into the ship. Then Peter scouted the adjacent rock wall for a spot where he could begin his climb.

"I think I can handle this by myself," he said to Walter after selecting what looked like a good starting point. "I'll be back as soon as I can."

Walter said, "Good luck." He shivered, hesitated, then moved back toward the ship. Peter watched him open the door, deposit the device as he had been told, and go back inside. Then he turned his full attention to the challenge that lay before him.

It took about thirty minutes for him to climb up approximately the same number of feet along the almost sheer rock wall. He encountered some problems that he hadn't thought of: the effect of the cold on his hands, the moonlight being at his back, so that possible places for his hands and feet were submerged in shadow. He wasn't fearful or even apprehensive about heights, but the almost continuous necessity to direct the lamp toward some small, not very clearly defined fissure or projection, many of them required for footholds, was making him giddy. In the time it took for him to ascend the first leg of the journey, there was no sign of Corma.

He finally reached the top of the basin, then crossed the narrow encircling strip that preceded the slope.

This doesn't look too bad, he thought. Not the first part, anyway. He directed the lamp downward and began to descend.

70

It was dark when Corma returned to consciousness. He opened his eyes, feeling the wind as it drifted against him; a light breeze now, barely stirring the clutter of foliage in which he lay.

The raft was on top of him, angled against the tree. His right arm was underneath his body, pinned there by the combined weight of himself and the raft. He tried to raise his left arm from where it lay beside him, and cried out reflexively in pain. The movement was restricted to his shoulder joint, and the terrible feeling of bone scraping against bone told him that his arm was broken just above the elbow.

He lay there, feeling sick and dizzy. What am I going to do? he wondered. It was physically beyond him to lift the raft without help. He thought of the soldier and the others, waiting for him, the solitary pleem that was maintaining the shields, the ship isolated on top of the mountain.

Was this how it was to end? He tried to close his mind to the inescapable consequences of such a happening. The mechanism implanted beneath his ribcage would ensure his own disintegration and that of the raft, but the ship carried insufficient power to respond to the signal-break. It would remain where it was, undetected until the shields finally collapsed, and then . . .

No, it must not happen. He gritted his teeth and tried to obtain some sort of leverage with his legs. The raft stirred, then slumped on top of him again.

It was impossible. He lay there, panting, cursing this last reversal of fortune and feeling the remorselessly tightening grip of the cold as it struck up at him out of the ground — a numbing hardness that was gradually affecting his whole body.

71

The first stretch of rock was a relatively gentle, adequately illuminated incline, but after a hundred yards or so it gradually steepened and became harder to assess in detail. Peter's progress was a matter of fits and starts in which the lamp and cord repeatedly demonstrated their necessity. After a while he paused to get his breath, staring down the dark, broken surface that stretched below him.

For the first time, the full nightmarishness of what he was doing hit him. At any time, he could find himself stranded, unable to go safely in either direction. And even if he was able to continue downward and eventually locate

Corma, this would result in one of two situations: both distasteful, both bizarre, both with terrifying implications.

If Corma was dead, then the whole business was out of their hands. The bombs would eventually be built, and the holocaust would, it seemed, inevitably follow. If Corma was alive and able to function with a reasonable degree of normality, then everything depended on the raft. If it was broken and irreparable, the first possibility would still apply. The alternative was in no way comparable in terms of scale, but in its own fashion no more attractive; less so, in some respects, because of his personal involvement with the people concerned. If the raft was able to get them back to the ship, then it would be so that the three men inside could be put to death; not needlessly or pointlessly, but it still meant that they would die while he stood by and permitted it to happen.

So that others can live, he thought. But no one except him would ever know that. He thought of his father, mother, and sister; his friends in Cleveland and at college; Henry Chasen. What would happen if I told any of them? he wondered. He saw their faces; uneasily amused at first, then blank or horror-stricken, finally wary and compassionate. No, I won't be able to tell even them. He swore, loudly and violently, and continued his cautious descent.

To his relief, he reached the base of the slope without any more real difficulty. He called out several times as he walked between the trees, but the distant hooting of an owl was the only reply that he received. He wondered if he was going in the right direction. He was bound to reach the road eventually, he told himself, but it might be well away from the point where the clearing and the vehicles were.

He called again and this time heard a faint response,

somewhere to his right. He stopped and repeated his call. The reply came again, still faint but recognizable. He worked his way along the base of the slope until he saw the raft. It was tilted over, partly supported by an adjacent tree and partly by a large, dark object that he decided must be Corma.

He kicked aside the branches that littered the ground beside the man and the raft and knelt down. In the light from the lamp, Corma's face was white and starkly shadowed. Peter decided that some of the shadows were actually bruises. He said, "I was beginning to think I'd wandered off course. Have you broken anything?"

"My left arm." Corma's voice was quiet, but still even and controlled. "My right arm is trapped, and I have been unable to reach the clamp release. It is the third button from your left."

Peter bent lower, reached past him, and pressed the button. The clamps clicked back into their slots. "Lift it now, please," Corma said. "As you will see, it is not particularly heavy."

It was, in fact, heavier than his remark implied. Peter wondered just how strong the man was. He was solidly built, but without in any sense giving an impression of great muscularity. Stronger than he looked, Peter decided, but not able to use his strength very well with a broken arm. He pulled the raft upright and slid it around to the far side of the tree.

Corma sat up carefully. His left arm hung limp, but the right one appeared to be undamaged. "It will be necessary to splint the fracture," he said. "Branches will do."

Peter selected two from the surrounding clutter and broke them to appropriate lengths. Corma continued to talk evenly as Peter positioned them and began to bind them in place with the cord.

"Was there any indication of power deterioration before you left?"

"No." Peter told him what he had arranged with Walter Hurley and the Negro.

Corma nodded. "A sensible precaution. In view of your arrival, it may not be required, but you were correct in your assumption that it would be possible to resume the support without difficulty." He shuddered and fell silent as Peter carefully continued to bind the cord around his arm.

72

He has good hands, Corma thought. They have intelligence and feeling. He watched the soldier as he worked, enormously relieved at his presence, at the conclusion of this terrifying episode.

He thought about the journey that the soldier had just undertaken, the risks to which he must have exposed himself, what would have happened if he had failed to find him. It is very probable, he thought, that I would have slowly frozen to death.

Corma chided himself for not taking the precaution of telling the soldier of the existence of the flying-pack and instructing him in its use. But he hadn't done that, in any event, and at considerable personal risk Peter Walsh had still managed to save his life. He found the inescapable irony of this observation singularly lacking in humor; instead, it was an irritant that aroused conflicting emotions, uncomfortable stirrings of regret. He dismissed these feelings quickly. He must not allow his understandable relief to distort his sense of proportion. The consequence of his failure to survive would have been total disaster. The advantage that had carried him and his kind so far would have disappeared, gone forever, and the triumphs of the past three thousand years shown in their true light, exposed for what they really were.

There would have been penalties invoked, he thought. He wondered about them, briefly, but the possibilities were too grossly horrendous to consider objectively. Then he noticed that the soldier was finished binding the splints into place and said, "That will serve." He used his good arm to lever himself to his feet. "I see that you were able to equip yourself at least adequately. Your journey cannot have been easy."

"Not particularly," said Peter Walsh. "It could have been a lot worse, though. I probably wouldn't have made it without the lamp and the cord."

Corma nodded and looked around. "We must find a more open area to enable us to take off with safety. I cannot guarantee total accuracy of direction at the present time, and a repetition of what happened before must be avoided at all costs."

"How do you know it will fly at all?" the soldier asked.

Corma smiled faintly. "It is not the ability of the raft to function that is in question. Conveyances such as this are built to survive much harder treatment. It is my own condition that concerns me. As well as feeling the effects of ex-

posure, I am concussed to a certain degree, which may affect my coordination."

"I could try—"

Corma lifted a hand as the soldier began to speak, cutting him off. "Raft control is not as simple as it appears. It is in some ways a question of touch, which only comes with experience. You may well have a flair for such things, but I do not consider that further risk would be justified at this time."

The soldier shrugged. "Okay. I came through some open space about fifty yards back. That ought to do, I guess." He went to the front of the raft and hefted it. "Do you think you can manage the other end?"

Corma picked up the rear end and braced it against his hip. "When you are ready."

Corma found the trek very tiring, but the effort was justified. The clearing was about forty feet across, and the surrounding trees were only sparsely branched. They put the raft down in the center of the clearing and positioned themselves on it. As the clamps closed over the soldier's legs, he said, "You can manage with one hand, presumably."

Corma thought of the man in the faded khaki shirt and the Stetson hat, the windblown chase and its conclusion. "Yes," he said. He felt the faint touch of the wind, gently icy against his bruised face. You caress me now, he thought grimly. "Yes, the mechanism is not heavy."

He activated the ascent control, and the raft lifted, drifting steadily up between the shadowed trees.

73

Peter looked down at the mountainside as it slid diagonally below them, an uneven sequence of bulking shadows and grayly lit open ground. Only a little while ago, he thought, I was slithering around down there like a one-legged blind man. He shivered and wrapped his arms around himself, wishing he had on warmer clothing and grateful for the wind's subsidence.

The raft crossed the lip of the basin, descended into the depression, and sank to the ground. For a fleeting moment, Peter had a wild vision of Hurley or one of the others inadvertently pressing a button or pulling a lever that had sent the ship hurtling out into space during their absence, so that the basin really was occupied only by himself and Corma, the raft, a scattering of rocks, and a few tufts of grass.

But that couldn't have happened, he told himself. There isn't enough power yet. He helped Corma to his feet, trying to push the thought of what that meant to the back of his mind.

The raft was dispatched into its now barely visible storage slot, and the shadowy interior of the airlock appeared in front of them. They went inside, the outer door closing behind them and automatically triggering the inner one to open. The small man and the Negro were in the lower chamber, and both rose to their feet as Peter and Corma entered. The small man seemed simultaneously relieved and startled, the Negro edgily nervous. There was no sign of Walter Hurley.

"Jesus," said the Negro. "You did get busted up." He stared at the splinted arm, then at Corma's bruised face, scowling with a kind of angry disapproval.

Corma looked around the room. In the dim lighting of the ship, Peter could see that his unbruised skin had taken on a translucent quality and that he was perspiring heavily. "Where is Mr. Hurley?" Corma asked.

"Upstairs, checking something," answered the Negro. His tongue appeared at the corner of his mouth, and he looked suddenly thoughtful. "I guess he's been up there about five minutes now."

Corma said to him, "Come with me, please." He went to the stairway entrance. Peter followed with the Negro trailing behind. The small man stayed where he was, sensing that he had not been specifically ordered to come along.

Walter Hurley was standing by the tank occupied by the pleem. His worried expression lightened as he saw the group come through the doorway. "Gee, Mr. Corma, it's sure good to see you," he said. He blinked and focused on the splinted arm. "Say, is that really broken? You ought to get it fixed properly if you . . ." His voice trailed away as Corma went past him and stared down into the tank.

"I'm sure glad you're back," Walter said nervously. "I just couldn't make up my mind whether it was changing, or if it was just the light in here." He removed his glasses, shyly, and rubbed them on his shirt sleeve.

Peter went to the tank and looked inside. The last time he had checked the pleem, it had retained its dark compactness. Now this had faded to a chalky, fibrous gray, as though some kind of bleaching agent had been introduced into the liquid. As he watched it, he saw a sluggish tremor disturb the surface, sending shallow ripples to the side of the tank.

"It has begun," Corma said. His voice was still even, but very weary. He lowered the lid. "This will necessitate rather more preparation than I had hoped would be required. It must be kept alive long enough to form the basis of the recharging operation and to ensure that a controllable balance is maintained."

"Does that mean I go back in now?" the Negro asked. His eyes were hungry again.

"No," Corma said. "That was my first thought, but your own power is too elemental and must be reserved for when it will be of most use. A lesser force will do." The Negro's eyes abruptly dulled. Corma glanced at Hurley, paused, then shrugged tiredly. "There is no real choice. The matter has reached a critical stage and must be dealt with immediately. I am sure you understand."

Hurley's face, already pale, lost all color. Momentarily, he appeared to shrink. He swayed slightly, and Peter saw the shaking of his hands as he fumbled his glasses back on.

"Can I handle this?" Peter asked tensely. I must do it, he thought. At least I'm his own kind. He'll know that I'll be suffering, too, in my own way. It may help a little. "You look pretty beat to me, and I don't see how you could cope with only one hand, anyway."

Corma nodded slowly. "It is an offer that I am in no position to refuse. You have become my left arm, and there will be occasions when I shall require you to be both my hands as well. Without you, I should not be here now, and none of this would be possible. I have not yet thanked you formally for your help. I do so now." He bowed gravely. "You are owed a debt that can never be repaid, but service all too frequently constitutes its own and only reward." He turned back to the tank.

74

A strange, wry situation, Corma thought. But at least much of what he had said had been true. His gratitude had been genuine enough, and his recognition of the soldier's having become a truly integral part of what was happening had been no exaggeration. Without him, none of the things that remained to be done could have been realistically attempted. None of the others possessed the manipulative skills that were required. Now it would be his hands that sealed the fate of his world; the ultimate unwitting treachery, made unavoidable by circumstances.

It was in some ways a regrettable development, he thought. His interpretation of the readings had plainly been in error. At no point had the soldier posed a genuine threat. Rather, he had become an ally, without whose support and active assistance the situation could long ago have deteriorated to a point hopelessly beyond salvation.

"We must arrange temporary extensions from an adjacent tank," he said. "Auxiliary nutritional support must be supplied in order to extend the period of survival. I will get

the necessary equipment." He knelt carefully by the cabinet, forcing himself to concentrate, fighting the dizziness that periodically drifted through him. This, and this. . . . His hand shook slightly as he selected tools and arranged them beside him.

75

Peter worked in silence, trying to shut out everything beyond his immediate task and surroundings, focusing his attention on Corma's instructions and doing what he was told without question. There are a lot more things I want to know, he thought, but they'll have to wait until later. Right now, all that matters is saving this thing. It's still hard to think of it as anything other than some impossible kind of vegetable, though, even now. But no vegetable smells like this, emits the same rank acridity of ailing flesh.

The arrangement of the extensions and the preparation of Hurley's tank took the better part of three hours. Peter finished and smeared the sweat from around his eyes with one of the sponge pads, watching tiredly as Corma studied readings on the central console.

He nodded. "It should hold. It will be the first to die, even after the other source is engaged, but by that time the buildup will have passed beyond the minimum requirement." He straightened. Earlier he had allowed Hurley to put a new splint on his arm with plastic strips and bandaging, but this had resulted in only partial restoration of his usual controlled, ordered image. Despite the bulk of his body, since returning to the ship Corma had taken on an almost wraithlike quality. His face was gaunt and deeply shadowed by exhaustion as well as the bruising, and his eyes were brightly feverish. "Will you tell Mr. Hurley that we are ready, please?"

Peter hesitated, but only briefly. There was no more time for agonizing and indecision, he thought. *The life of an individual doesn't really matter any more in a situation of this kind. The issues are too large, the stakes too high. But still I feel guilt, and blessed relief that it isn't me who has to die.*

He nodded and went to the stairs.

76

I'm glad I didn't actually faint, Walter thought, but it had been a near thing. Somehow, though, he had held on, and the dizziness and the sick feeling had gradually subsided. In a way it wasn't as frightening as it had been, because he'd had time to think about it now and remind himself that it wasn't really going to be like dying at all. He was going to know what it was like to be fit and to have good eyesight and live a normal life, and that was actually something to look forward to, not be afraid of. He didn't only have Mr. Corma's word for it, either; the Negro had told him that if that was what he wanted, that was how it would be.

He remembered how the Negro had been after he had been woken up, all upset and then excited and then nervous and irritable, and finally sulky and quiet. It must have meant an awful lot to him, the place that he went to, Walter thought. He had looked at him just before he had left the room with the soldier, and he could see that the Negro almost hated him, just because he was going first. When he had said goodbye to the two of them, the small man had sort of smiled, but the Negro hadn't said anything, just glared and looked away. That was a shame, Walter thought, because he didn't want him to feel badly, even for just a little while.

He got to the top of the stairs, the soldier behind him, and then they went over to where Mr. Corma was doing something to one of the tank connections with his good hand.

77

Naked in the padded tank, Walter Hurley looked frail and bloodless. Clothes had at least served as partial camouflage for him, filling out and hiding the reality of his meagerly fleshed frame. Without them, he was sticklike, a pigeon-chested near-skeleton in the pale light.

Peter concentrated his eyes and hands on what he was

doing, pity and confused anger mixing in his mind as he inserted wadding beneath the metal band encircling Walter's head. He tried very hard to picture the world as it must have been to him, the restrictions that had automatically been imposed by his deficiencies, the remorseless decline of his health over the years. To someone like him, he thought, the situation and what it promised probably wasn't going to be any kind of sacrifice at all; rather, it would be a merciful release from an inexplicably unjust world. And what he and the others were doing would be an achievement unparalleled throughout history, on a scale that defeated the imagination.

He adjusted the final piece of wadding and asked, "How is that?" His eyes pleaded apology.

"Fine, thank you," said Walter. He tried to smile, and failed. His breathing was very agitated. "Try not to feel too bad about this," he added.

Peter closed his eyes briefly. "I hope everything turns out the way you want it." He moved away from the tank, smearing his hands against his coveralls.

Walter's eyes closed quickly, much sooner than the Negro's had. He wants to get it over with, Peter thought. Despite everything, he's still scared. Peter turned away, feeling sick.

"He is asleep," said Corma. As he spoke the humming vibration started, faintly this time. Peter saw him adjust a dial on the console. The vibration stilled, and the sound faded to silence. "He is generating at the required support level now. His dreams will be only fleeting, but they will stabilize and intensify when his power is more deeply tapped. He will serve later as a balancing factor, which could prove to be a critical role." Corma pushed his hand tiredly across his face. He was an incongruous, deathly figure by now, his paleness exaggerating the discoloring bruises. "You may close the lid," he said to Peter, then went to the nearest empty tank.

Despite his relative familiarity with what was required, Peter found the final adaptation to be tedious, exacting work. The basic routine was the same as before, but there were still slight differences to contend with. After a lengthy period during which he lost all track of time, Corma left him to work on his own, relegating himself to a purely supervisory capacity. Corma's active participation had become progressively more clumsy, slowing down the work, in one instance necessitating the dismantling and reassembling of a section of wiring that they had almost completed.

As he discarded one tool and picked up another, Peter glanced across to where Corma leaned heavily against the equipment cabinet, his pose a graphic illustration of fatigue. "Why don't you go down and rest for a while?" Peter suggested. "You're going to need your strength later. I've got the hang of this now, I'm sure."

Corma stirred. "Thank you for your consideration, but it is best that I stay. The possibility of encountering some minor requirement unfamiliar to you still exists, even now. It is a chance that it would be foolish to ignore." He pushed himself away from the cabinet, went slowly to the console, and looked down at it with hooded eyes. "The balance is being maintained. He is providing sufficient output to ensure that the pleem will survive long enough to serve its purpose." He nodded. "I believe now that we are safe."

You and I will be safe, you mean, Peter thought. All those others, too, I guess; as safe as they could ever be. He shook his head, blinking, wishing that he was less tired. He had been wearing the headlamp for much of the time, but despite its help the continuous necessity to focus on what he was doing was making his eyes sore and heavy, occasionally blurring his vision. There's still so much I don't know, he thought, so many questions left unasked.

"How long will it take to get where you're going?" Peter asked.

"In terms of your own time, a little more than sixteen hours."

Peter paused in what he was doing, startled. Sixteen hours? How could that be possible? Surely they were talking about going somewhere that was light-years away. "I don't understand," he said. "How far away is it?"

"Your confusion is caused by your preconception of what is required to travel from one point to another. Telekinetic power has provided us with a new perspective of the universe, a release from the supposed inviolacy of a three-dimensional concept and its inevitable constraints. In a sense, time and distance are compressed, so light-years are traversed in less than seconds in your time scale."

Light-years that were spanned faster than the ticking of a watch? It can't be, Peter thought. It just couldn't happen. But how else could they do what they did, take the enormous leaps that would be necessary?

Something struck him, a graspable straw that surfaced from his confusion. "You just told me sixteen hours," he said cautiously. "But I thought you said they'd have at least eighteen."

"That is correct." Corma walked slowly back to the cabinet and leaned against it. "Before the journey itself is possible, the power must be rebuilt. It is a process similar to the recharging of an electric battery, and will take a

233

minimum of two hours, possibly a little more. When it has reached the required level, the spatial displacement can be performed. By the time we are ready to leave, you will be in your car, returning to the life that you left less than twenty-four hours ago." He paused and looked down. "It has been a momentous time that neither of us is likely to forget."

Was that all it had been? Peter thought. Less than twenty-four hours? Dear God, it felt like a lifetime. He thought of the others, the compressed quasi-lives that they would soon lead, oddly similar to Corma's description of his forthcoming journey.

It dawned on him that the wire he was holding was the last one requiring connection. He positioned it with a mixture of reluctance and gratitude. "When will you be back? You'll have to recuperate first, surely?"

"Very soon," Corma said. "It is medically possible to accelerate the bone-knitting process. There must be a minimum of delay if the information is to be retracted before it is fully understood and put to use." He pushed himself away from the cabinet again and came to the tank. "You have done well, remarkably so. My congratulations and thanks. Without you, failure would have been certain."

"Will I see you again?" Peter decided that it had been a stupid question as soon as he asked it. I'll soon be going off to God knows where, he thought, and he's got his work to do, too.

He wondered what this entire episode really meant. Were Corma's missions always as difficult and involved as this one had been, or had this been a uniquely confused situation? I know nothing about him, really, Peter thought. He's a guardian, a member of a superior race — beings that look remarkably like us and whose natural mode of speech involved a degree of formality that makes modern colloquial English sound like a different language. And that's it. That's really all I know. If only there was more time. . . .

"I guess it's not very likely," Peter continued when Corma did not respond immediately.

Corma shook his head. "I think not. Our first meeting was fortuitous, and our respective responsibilities render it improbable that we will meet again."

"So I'll never know whether or not you managed to trace these people you're chasing and get the information back."

"The passage of time will provide you with your answer," Corma said. "Or, I could arrange for a letter to be sent to your home address at the conclusion of the operation, a brief note worded in a way that only you would understand." He studied Peter curiously. "Are you sure that you wish to know the outcome? If we should fail, it would be tantamount to receiving the death sentence of yourself and your race."

"I don't know," Peter said after a moment. "I see what you mean, but not knowing might be worse. I'd like to think about it."

"As you wish. The decision must be yours." Corma's voice was very tired. "Now we must prepare the others. Again, my thanks." He gathered the tools and replaced them in the cabinet, then went with heavy steps to the stairs.

78

Corma stood by the console, watching Peter Walsh fit the metal band to the small man's head. The small man lay in the tank to Hurley's right, his eyes flickering from side to side, his face working spasmodically. Occasionally he emitted hoarse, muffled gasping sounds. In the opposite tank, the Negro lay still and silent, staring blank-eyed toward the ceiling.

A matter of minutes, Corma thought, that is all. The movement inside his head spiraled unevenly toward a dark, unseen center that he knew it must eventually reach.

But not yet. It must not happen until completion. He willed himself to think and feel, forcing the effort that was necessary to control his body, make it perform the tasks that remained. Not yet, he told himself. You are so very close now. He concentrated, mentally injecting strength and feeling into his numbly quivering legs.

The soldier was working fast, locating and adjusting the wadding with sharp, quick movements. He was pale, and his face was stiffly expressionless, a telltale mask for the revulsion that Corma knew he must feel. He finished and said tautly, "You'll be okay now. Thanks for what you're doing." He turned away from the tank, not looking at the small man again.

Corma depressed the tank switches, then waited, watching the motionless needles on the gauges, willing them to move.

The Negro's reading was the first to register. Again, there was the sudden jolt, the humming vibration, followed by the needle's rapid climb. As that reading leveled off, the needle of the gauge tracking the small man began to move; a slower, less violent surge, but more stable, providing the reservoir that was needed. The humming took on a deeper, steadier note.

Corma began to turn dials lightly, trying to balance the gauges, for the moment oblivious to his growing weakness, the now almost irresistible desire to relax, to fall, to sleep. The needles skittered, danced, then gradually steadied. He took his hand away from the controls and leaned against the console, his head lowered and his eyes closed.

"Is that it?" asked the soldier. "Shall I close the tanks?"

Corma nodded slowly. The dark center of his consciousness was steadily widening, but still he pushed it back, ignoring the refuge it offered. I must wait, he told himself. It is done, but not yet complete. Until he is outside the ship, I cannot rest.

He heard the dull sound of a closing lid, the click of its fastenings. Footsteps passed him, and then he heard the final thud, the final click.

"You've got to rest now." The soldier's voice came from close by. "You're out on your feet." A hand took his arm. "I'll watch the readings. If I see any change, I'll call you."

That was the spur that Corma needed. He opened his eyes and straightened his body, bracing himself against the console. "That will not be necessary," he said. His voice sounded muffled, as though blanketed by a screen or a wall. "The readings are balanced and locked, and they will not change." *Slowly, he warned himself. I must choose my words with care....*

He loosened his hold on the console and turned away from it. "There is nothing more that you can do," he continued. "It is now simply a question of waiting. I shall rest until it is time." He looked at the soldier, at his drawn face and bleak eyes. *He is older,* Corma thought. He said again, "There is nothing more that you can do."

He saw a flicker of relief lighten the bleakness on the soldier's face. "You mean I can go now?"

Corma felt himself smile, an involuntary rictus that was not without humor. "Yes. I regret that my condition means that you must undertake the descent on foot a second time, but it is daylight now." The soldier nodded soberly. "I have already thanked you, but I do so again. You have served your people well, as have the others. All that it has been possible to do at this time has been done. Now we shall do our part."

The soldier nodded again. He shuddered and said, "I wish I could say it had been a pleasure meeting you, but that's not exactly the case. I'm sure you understand."

"Of course. Circumstances and necessity have made ours a joyless encounter." Corma held out his hand. "To wish you good fortune is perhaps unnecessary. I wish it, nevertheless." He felt the firmness of the soldier's grip, his own weak response. *Are you, after all, my enemy?* he thought. *If you are, it is as well that at the end we had no occasion to test one another in more primitive ways.*

Corma led the way to the stairs, making each movement with care.

Two minutes later, they stood by the open airlock entrance. It was early morning, the beginning of a bright, cloudless day. The soldier stared outside, the bleakness of his face somehow less marked now. He is reborn, Corma thought; another dreamer, awakening from his nightmare. Not permanently, or completely, of course. It was a dream that he could never totally escape, but time would slowly blur the clarity of its images. And he had temporary consolation in his belief that in their respective ways, he and the others had saved their race and their world. The soldier would be comforted by that, Corma thought. For now, at least. Again, he felt a flicker of contrition.

"Thank you for all that you're doing for us," Peter Walsh said. "As far as knowing or not knowing, I guess I'd prefer to wait and see how you make out." He grimaced and stepped outside. When he was a few steps from the ship, he turned and lifted a hand, then turned again and walked toward the basin wall without looking back.

Quickly, Corma thought. The weakness flooded through him in a rising, irresistible tide. Quickly! He threw the entrance switch, watching the rectangle of alien landscape containing the walking figure narrow as the airlock door slid closed. It thumped home, and the image was gone. Corma went back into the lower chamber, then crossed the room on legs that he no longer felt and collapsed on the nearest of the rest-panels.

Now, he thought. Now you may claim me. He drifted unresistingly into darkness, exulting as he drowned.

79

The air gradually warmed as Peter went down the mountain. A soft breeze had replaced the cold-edged wind of the night before, and on it he smelled pine and grass, growing things; the scent of life to replace the last lingering traces of disinfected death that still coated his mouth and nostrils.

He felt empty, but somehow not as totally drained as he had anticipated. I should feel like a murderer, he thought, but it's not like that at all, not really. The whole thing already felt like a dream. At the top of the basin he had turned, half expecting to see some trace of the ship, some tiny piece of evidence to confirm its hidden presence, but there had been nothing; no sign of the oddly suspended birds that he had seen on his first arrival on the raft, no indication that they or the ship had ever existed beyond the confines of his imagination. What only a short while before had been hard, manufactured substance had become transformed into rock and grass and earth and air.

Daylight was revealing just how much time and effort he had wasted during his journey through the dark. There were still places where it was safer to employ the line, but it was a relatively easy climb. It took him about forty minutes from the start of his actual descent to reach the wide band of trees and bushes that bordered the road.

A hundred yards or so into that area, he found himself

in a clearing that he recognized. Yes, this had been where they had carried the raft for its takeoff. He saw its imprint in the debris of twigs and half-rotted leaves, evidence to confirm his expedition of the night before. The tree Corma had crashed into must be below me, a little to my left, he thought. He veered across the slope in that general direction, idly curious to see the setting of the accident.

He walked more or less directly to the site, identifying it easily by the scattered, broken branches at the base of a partly denuded pine. The tree was a little taller than those around it. Peter decided that it must have been a relatively easy thing for Corma to do — misjudge the height of the tree in bad light and with a strong wind blowing.

He saw something glinting among the debris a few feet away. Something of Corma's? he wondered. Something I can use to prove that all this happened? He went to it, lifting a partially obstructing branch to one side. It was a tubular metal object that looked like a flashlight, with markings around the rim of the sleeve that held the glass in place.

He picked it up, studied it, and frowned slightly.

He had seen it before, once, and only briefly then. The picture formed in his mind; Corma rummaging inside the truck, then turning with this object in his hand; the quick look in both directions, the flashlight pointing toward him, the click of a switch, the apparent lack of response. He saw Corma's face, the wryness there, and remembered his own brief spurt of alarm, the feeling that he had been somehow momentarily threatened.

He held it away from himself, angling it in the general direction of the sky, and pressed the switch.

A beam of light, whitely brilliant among the shadows of

the trees, speared upward. Its diameter was consistent throughout the whole of its length; it was an absurdly long, magically produced fluorescent tube that terminated sixty or seventy feet away, just beyond the tops of the trees.

His hand wavered, and the beam struck the top of the nearest tree. There was a faint concussion, and then the top of the tree collapsed, as though it had been severed by an enormous axe. It landed twenty feet away, a collection of snapped and torn branches that scattered pieces of itself as it struck the ground.

He had snatched his thumb away from the button as the beam hit the tree; an instinctive, startled reflex. He stood for a moment, staring numbly at the small fragments that had come to rest near his feet, then went to the main section of trunk. Its bottom end confirmed his impression of how it had been removed; a clean, angled cut that showed no trace of the wood having been burned.

He cautiously studied the metal sleeve. There were small, closely grouped symbols around it that he decided must be numbers. He counted to the mark that was positioned in line with a shallow groove that ran from the switch to the front end of the casing. Fourteen. . . . and the beam had been about seventy feet long.

He aligned the mark on the casing with the smallest of the symbols on the sleeve, a single vertical line. He directed the cylinder upward and pressed the switch again. This time the beam was short, no more than five feet long. He could see the end clearly now; a clean, abrupt termination, as though its continuation was being inhibited by an unseen roof or ceiling.

He released the switch and looked around. The nearest tree was about twenty feet away. He stepped back several paces, lowered the flashlight until it pointed directly toward the tree, then pressed the switch again. The beam reappeared, but stopped the same distance away as it had after he had made the adjustment. He took his thumb off the switch again. So it works in increments of five, he thought. He wondered what total distance it could cover and how effective it was at long range.

He was cold — and he knew the feeling had nothing to do with the elevation, or the fact that he was in partial shadow. It was an internal cold, the chill of sudden unease, uncertainty. He looked around again, then slowly began to circle the area in the vicinity of the broken tree.

He found the hat lying against a bush a short distance away. It was a low-crowned Stetson, with a pronounced sweat mark showing above the band. He picked it up and stared at it, his mouth slightly open and an odd tightness stirring at the base of his skull.

It couldn't be, he told himself. He had been at least forty or fifty miles away, and he had been headed away from them. And in any case, how could he possibly . . . ?

Peter turned his head and looked down through the trees. He caught a glimpse of the road, only a short distance away now. He saw something else adjacent to it, partially concealed by intervening trees and foliage; a dust-shadowed metallic shape, with a glint of red visible at one corner.

He looked back up the slope. An occasional bird call cracked the stillness, but that was all. He walked slowly back in the direction that he had come, the hat held tightly in one hand, looking at the surrounding ground and conscious of the dull hammering that had started inside him.

He found the body a short distance below the far side of

the clearing. It lay sprawled at a distorted angle, the pinched and previously weathered face bleached now, the eyes wide and blank. The khaki shirt and the top of the trousers were dark with blood, and the shirt was ripped on the right side. He could see the wound through the tattered fabric: an enormous, raw-edged gash that had penetrated more than half way through the body, severing the spinal column and thus causing the tortured pose.

He turned away, fighting nausea and an almost over-whelming sense of horror. There's no point in going any closer anyway, he thought, fighting back hysteria. He's dead, and there's nothing I can possibly do to help him now.

After a while, Peter found that dully growing anger was burning his reluctance away, replacing it with a bleak self-disgust. You'll probably see much worse than this before long, he told himself. You might as well get used to such things. He turned, moved close to the body, and looked down at it.

He remembered their brief meeting with the policeman, the conversation that had taken place, and then he thought about Corma and all the things that he had been told; eve-rything that had happened since the truck had blocked his way on the previous day, all of it suddenly distorted into something very different from what he had accepted and believed.

He tried to kill me, Peter thought. He tried to kill me, and the only thing that stopped him was a temporary me-chanical failure. Appalled, he pictured what would have happened if the flashlight-weapon had worked on that oc-casion. He suddenly remembered something else: the abrupt, unsignaled turn of the truck onto the road that had brought them there. If the car's brakes and steering hadn't worked as well as they did, he thought, I could have gone over. No protective roof, nothing to hold me in the car. I could have been squashed flat, or had my neck broken.

He wondered how much of what he and the others had been told was actually true. It hadn't all been lies, he thought. There had been a consistency about it, a kind of lunatic logic. The Negro had found his promised land, so that part of it, at least, had been a bizarre fact. But what was the real truth? The whole truth?

Something nudged itself into the forefront of his mind — a remembered fragment of earlier speculation, his hesitantly voiced suspicion as to Corma's real role and purpose and the answer that he had received. He said that if my suspicions had been true, he would have killed me, Peter thought. But he tried to, at least once, probably twice. And had there been other times, other failures?

He thought about their last conversation. What exactly was it Corma had said? Something about it being unnecessary to wish him good fortune? He saw a pattern now, still incomplete, but rapidly taking firm, definite shape: the Cleveland house and the bush below the bedroom window; the broken bodies of John Archard and the blonde girl whose name he couldn't remember; the boat incident, only a short time before.

Levels of fallibility, Peter thought. He savored the concept, wonderingly. I'm a survivor. Every time in my life when I've been at real risk, something has saved me, so that I've come out of it with barely a scratch. He didn't kill me because he couldn't. He tried, and he failed, because through some freakish working of natural selection or something like that, I'm a protected species. So instead, he used me, bent the facts just enough to make them acceptable, made me a part of what he was really doing.

He looked down at the twisted body at his feet. This guy wasn't so lucky, he thought. His level of fallibility just wasn't low enough, like most people. He suddenly saw the faces of Hurley and the Negro and the small man; each of them willing to accept death as the price to be paid for a brief, inescapably lethal mock existence in exchange for the emptiness and pain that had been their natural allocation. Losers, he thought — all of them at the bottom end of the cruelly selective scale of such things, the natural poverty of their lives now being used with unfeeling expediency to ensure the death of their own kind.

Peter glanced at his watch, then looked back up toward the crest of the slope, coldly gray against the clear morning sky, trying to calculate how long it had been since he left the ship. An hour, maybe longer?

He jammed the weapon deep in his trouser pocket and began to climb.

80

Peter had temporarily forgotten his tiredness. Now it pressed down on him, almost as though some sort of constraint was being brought to bear from the top of the mountain. He wondered, briefly, if that was what it really was; some kind of extension of the protective field around the ship that was now being directed down the slope, a final precaution against his interference that had been made possible by the increased power now available to Corma and his ship.

He decided that it wasn't. There was no obvious need for such added protection. He was bound to find the policeman's car, but Corma's reasoning would have been that his chances of discovering the body were relatively small. It would be much more probable that, after finding the car, Peter would assume the policeman to be off somewhere among the trees looking for them, and that his instinctive reaction would be to drive away as fast as he could.

No, he was not fighting against a protective device. It was his own physical limitations being reached and tested. It dawned on Peter that he hadn't slept for something more than twenty-four hours, and that during that time he had been almost continually involved in some kind of physical activity. For the first time he felt truly grateful for the concentrated training he had received in recent weeks. If it wasn't for that, he thought, I'd probably be still down by the trees, deciding that I couldn't make it back up to the ship and that we were just going to have to take our chances. But not now. He forced himself upward, fighting muscles that felt as though they were being squeezed into stiffened uselessness by large, cruel hands.

He was still two hundred feet from the top when he became conscious of the true location of the steadily growing vibration that he was feeling, movement that until then he had identified as a manifestation of his exhaustion, an internal thing. He paused and placed his hand flat against the rock slope before him. It was there; deep, shuddering tremors that somehow signaled near completion, a terrifying reminder of the power chamber and what had happened in there. He continued to drag himself up the fissured face of the mountain, praying that his memory served him correctly and that this was the last sheer stretch, that from now on all he would have to negotiate was the uneven slope that led to the rim of the basin.

He pulled himself over the edge of the sheer section and looked up. The slope continued to incline away from him; still steep, but blessedly gentle in comparison with what had gone before. He scrambled up it on all fours, desperately conscious of the vibration of the rock beneath him.

He was gasping for breath when he reached the rim of the basin. He looped the line over a projection and flung it down into the basin, then slid down it, repeatedly kicking himself away from the uneven rock face. He dropped the last ten feet, instinctively relaxing as he hit, then rolling away from the wall in a flailing backward somersault.

Nothing was broken, nothing sprained. He shoved himself to his feet and went forward, his arms thrust out in front of him, blindly seeking the solidity of the ship somewhere within the seemingly empty space.

He slowed abruptly. He recognized a familiar projecting rock in front of him, a yard or so away. That was where it began, he told himself. That was where the entrance was. He stepped forward, tugging the flashlight from his pocket. It's an odd thing, he thought. I keep thinking of it as a light, when in fact it's a knife. All right, you son of a bitch, *cut!* He aimed at a point above the rock and pressed the switch.

The beam of white light shot forward. A black hole, the exact diameter of the beam, appeared at the end of it. He directed the beam in a rough circle, watching the lengthening line of the cut, steering it back to its starting point. He heard a thud as the section of hull fell away, and simultaneously he saw the interior of the airlock appear.

He stepped through the hole he had made and circled the beam again, this time pointing it at the inner door. Another section crashed inward, revealing the dim light and gray surfaces of the lower chamber.

He took his thumb off the switch and ducked through the opening. Corma was there, supporting himself against the central dais, his bruised face now frozen in shocked disbelief. He made no sound or movement as Peter ran past him to the stairs.

Peter crossed the power chamber and reversed the console switches. The drumming vibration quieted, then died. In the sudden silence, he went back down to the lower floor. As he reached it, the lights faded and went out. In the ensuing gloom, illuminated only by the daylight that filtered through the openings he had made, he saw shadows of movement near the entrance.

He pointed the weapon horizontally and pressed the switch. The beam of light appeared, illuminating the chamber with a dead-white glare. It is a light after all, he thought. He looked across to where Corma was slowly sliding down the wall to the floor, his labored breathing the only sound in the now otherwise silent ship.

Peter crossed the room, switching off the weapon just before he reached Corma. In the light of the entrance, he saw that his face was ashen and wet with perspiration. He looks harmless now, he thought; pitiful, even. He stood in front of Corma, looking down at him and thinking about what was upstairs in the power chamber.

"You'd better tell me what this is all about," Peter said.

"I think I know, but I want to hear it from you."

Corma's head lifted slightly, then sank down again. He said nothing.

"All right," Peter said disgustedly. "See what you think of this theory. I may not have it all right, but I'm sure about the main part." He took a deep breath and kept talking, watching Corma's face for the guilt that must surely surface, confirming the accuracy of what he was saying.

"Most of what you've told us has been the truth. The only real lie was about your own part in it. You're not a guardian, you're a kind of agent provocateur. You're the one who's been supplying the information that you talked about, and the only reason you brought me and those people upstairs into it was to help you get away. You were going back to tell your people that you had done what was necessary, and then you were going to wait until we had used the knowledge to wipe ourselves out, or something close to it. After we had cleared the way for you, you'd have come back and taken over what was left." He paused. "That's it, isn't it?"

Corma raised his head. He stared up at Peter with eyes that were now deeply sunken and shadowed. Inexplicably, he smiled. It was a haggard travesty of a smile, but still touched with sardonic humor. He said something that Peter didn't understand, a derisive pattern of sound, then lowered his head onto his chest again.

Peter frowned, sensing a momentary loss of authority. Surely he had it right. . . . He thought back over what he had said. It had been concise and to the point, a summary of what had to be the truth. He said slowly, "Something I've said amuses you. What was it?"

Corma made no sound, gave no sign of movement. He's

very still, Peter thought. He began to kneel, then hesitated. "Don't try bluffing me," he said. "You can't hurt me, and I'll use this thing if I have to."

There was still no response. Peter sank cautiously onto his haunches, nursing the weapon. As he completed the movement, Corma's left leg kicked out at him — a sluggish, clumsy assault that he had ample time to evade. He stood and backed away. Corma levered himself to his feet and lurched after him, attempting to attack him with a series of awkward, flailing movements that were like the uncoordinated gesticulations of someone drowning.

He's crazy, Peter thought. He continued to back and dodge, feeling growing panic. It's almost as though he really does want me to kill him.

There was a sound, an oddly muted click. Corma stopped moving, frozen in the position that he had reached when the sound occurred, his body straining forward, his good arm raised.

Simultaneously, Peter found that he, too, had somehow been locked into immobility.

81

There was no feeling of pressure, no evidence of physical restraint. He could see and think and breathe, but that was all. Like Corma, he had been arrested in mid-movement, one foot lifted clear of the floor, when the click had sounded. We should both have fallen over, he thought, but we haven't. It was like being suddenly encased in ice, like the fleeing mammoths, only quicker. There had been no opportunity to struggle, to offer protest of any kind. They had become a tableau, the final frame of a sequence of action that they were now incapable of completing.

Time passed; a strangely out-of-joint period in which thought, forcibly divorced from action, bred its own unique terrors. Was it only inside the ship that this was happening, Peter wondered, or was it total, all-embracing, affecting the world outside as well? He pictured it: people, animals, birds, even machines, all somehow pinioned in mid-action, rendered helpless and impotent by some monstrous force against which they had no defense.

It can't last forever, he thought, and it must have something to do with what's happening here. Don't panic. Think about something else, anything. He forced his mind through a ragbag of memories, mentally shutting out the frozen face of Corma, still confronting him a few feet away.

Eventually, out of the corner of his eye, he saw movement. Something drifted into his line of vision: a dull metal ball, about two feet in diameter. Its surface was punctuated with an assortment of projections; domed light covers, pieces of metal and plastic, something that looked like a camera lens.

It floated until reaching a spot above Corma, and then became stationary. Two jointed rods with small, bright metal discs on the ends emerged from the sphere and positioned themselves on either side of Corma's head, touching the temples. One of the domed light covers began to radiate a pinkish-red glow.

It can move, Peter thought. We're still locked here like

two flies in amber, but that thing can move around freely. He wondered what it was doing to Corma. He saw no change in the alien's facial expression, no indication that his distress was being aggravated in any way. He remained totally unmoving, a cloth-covered, flesh-and-bone statue, depicting crippled desperation.

After a little while, the rods were withdrawn. The ball drifted toward Peter, maintaining its existing height, and disappeared from view behind his head. Peter flinched mentally, expecting at any moment to feel the touch of the discs against his own head.

But nothing happened. There was no detectable contact, no sensation of any kind. It must have gone to the power chamber, he decided. What's up there is more important than my being here. It must be checking the people in the tanks, finding out what's happened to them. He wondered if his switching off the power had harmed them in any way.

After what seemed an interminable time, he felt a lightly cool touch at his temples: the discs. There was no real pressure, no loss of consciousness or concentration. What is it doing? he wondered. Reading my mind? He felt embarrassment at the thought, suddenly deeply conscious of the limits of his understanding.

After a while, the things touching his head withdrew. The ball reappeared, lowering itself until it was positioned opposite his face, with the projection that looked like a camera lens pointing directly toward him.

There was a brief pause. Then a metallic voice said, "You will now be released." As it finished speaking, he felt himself topple slightly. His raised foot dropped to the floor, and he instinctively fought to maintain his balance. Beyond the ball, he saw that Corma was still locked in his flailing pose. "No harm will come to you," the voice went on. "You have been identified as a native of this planet who has inadvertently become involved in this situation. The other being will remain inoperative." Another jointed rod appeared, this one with a three-fingered metal claw at the end. "You will not require the weapon any further. It will now be appropriated." The claw lowered, plucked the weapon from his hand, and withdrew into the ball, taking the weapon with it. There was a brief, still silence.

"Are you a guardian?" Peter asked. He wondered if the ball could hear him, and if it could, whether it was equipped to converse as opposed to merely issuing statements. Perhaps it isn't allowed to, he thought.

After a short pause the ball said, "You may question me if you wish. What you see is an investigatory device employed by the guardians. At the present time it is forming a direct link between yourself and a guardian vessel that is orbiting this planet. It has been sent because a short while ago our detecting equipment registered the existence and location of this ship. Its presence here is a contravention of the rules, and severe penalties must now be imposed."

"Rules?" Peter said, startled. That word makes it all sound like a game, he thought. "What rules?"

"Your planet is a classified factor that forms the basis of a predictive exercise. It is in a relatively advanced category and contains many imponderables that render it virtually impossible for participants to achieve a high level of unaided accuracy. Our role is to see that no external interference takes place, and that your race is permitted to resolve its problems and conflicts by following your natural evolutionary and cultural development. In this instance and many others that until now have remained undetected, such tampering has occurred. It will now be necessary to attempt to correct this matter."

Peter felt the onset of vaguely humiliating uncertainty. "But . . . these people were planning to invade us eventually, weren't they?" he said hesitantly.

"Such an action would not have been permitted. Until this interference occurred, your planet was only endangered by the activities of your own species. Physical aggression, for whatever reason, and the subsequent acquisition of material benefit are the provinces of the immature and are forbidden."

There was no reproof in the voice, but Peter felt his humiliation deepen. "You mean people like us."

"You are a young race," the ball said. "You have not yet reached a true appreciation of the obscenity that violence represents. Nor have this one's kind, it seems, despite their longevity and their token obeisance toward the rules of contest. In view of their disproportionate success, we have suspected for a considerable time that they had discovered a means of masking their presence on selected worlds and influencing evolutionary patterns to their advantage. Now we know this to be true, and we know how it has been done. You are to be thanked for this." There was a click, a pause, then another click. The ball said, formally, "Thank you."

Peter's throat felt clogged. He tried to clear it, with only partial success. He said thickly, "You talk about rules and contests and predictive exercises and participating worlds. Are you saying that what we're involved in is just a game?"

"That is correct. It is a game based on predictability

patterns and applied to worlds where major changes are imminent but no conclusive prediction is possible. These changes are not necessarily the result of social activity and scientific discovery. Worlds can also be eligible because of instabilities within their own structure or that of their parent system. There are also subclassifications of prediction, covering a broad spectrum of possibilities." There was another pause. The ball said, almost apologetically, "It is a game with many variations."

Peter heard himself laughing. It wasn't a pleasant sound. It was high and shrill, very unlike his normal baritone guffaw. So we aren't talking about the possibility of the world being selected for invasion by an alien race after all, he thought. We're talking about something much more important. We're talking about the outcome of a game — and not even that, really, because we're only a tiny part of it. He sobered abruptly. A game? . . .

"If you're too late to do anything about this information that's been planted," he asked angrily, "then what happens if we do blow ourselves up?"

"If this should happen, this planet will no longer be eligible for classification. It will be withdrawn."

"Withdrawn?"

"If we are not totally successful in recovering the information to which you refer, there will no longer be an acceptable pattern. The result would not be a true reflection of what would have happened if this interference had not occurred."

"Look, I didn't mean . . ." Peter swallowed hard. Keep your voice down, he told himself. It thinks we're immature enough already, and shouting won't help. "All right, so you're going to try to stop it. What are the chances?"

"There is no way in which this can be accurately predicted. Every effort will be made in this respect, but there can be no guarantee of even partial success."

Not good, Peter thought, dismayed. Not very good at all. "If you manage to get it back from one side, but not the other, what happens then?"

"Should one of the protagonists involved retain the information and make full use of it, it is inevitable that the faction in question would emerge the victor. It would be impossible for the opponents to combat the effect of such weapons, and their only course would be to surrender."

Peter stared at it, horrified. "But the people we're fighting are aiming at world domination, and they don't seem very concerned about how many people die in the process. If they keep the information and we lose it, that could end in something like universal slavery."

"Even if this information had not been supplied, there is no guarantee that such an outcome would not have occurred. At the present time, we have insufficient data to compute the probable outcome should the information be successfully withdrawn and the conflict permitted to pursue its natural course.

"If it should prove impossible to regain all the information, thereby producing a state of imbalance, additional action may have to be taken. A decision would be made after the necessary predictive details were obtained and studied."

Well, that's something, Peter thought. But what if they lose it and we keep it? Would that mean . . . No, I can't think straight any more. He said, slowly, "If the information hadn't been planted, would we have eventually made the same discoveries for ourselves?"

"Yes. However, although yours is a planet at war, it is unlikely that your present level of scientific knowledge would have enabled you to reach the necessary conclusions within the next decade. The likelihood is that the current hostilities would have terminated before such developments were arrived at and applied. The premature supplying of this information has been an attempt to accelerate the inevitable by encouraging the introduction of such weapons into the present conflict, in order that their employment by both factions would intensify your mutual enmity to a point where they would be utilized regardless of the ultimate cost. If this should occur, it may well lead to the annihilation of your kind."

Peter felt cold. "You used the word 'inevitable' just now," he said. "Do you mean that it's inevitable that we'd use such power in that particular way, whether it was now or some time in the future?"

"The possibility factor is high, but not conclusive. There are many subtleties involved which will decide the answer to your question. It is a level of development which occurs in all technologically based societies. Our own race reached such a period and survived, as have many others. It is a crisis point in the natural order of things, which is in many respects the first step to a mature appreciation of the nature of existence."

"You mean so that we can reach a stage where we've got enough understanding to recognize that it's preferable to play games, rather than spend our time savaging each other." Peter shook his head. "Most people know that already, and existence has to have more meaning to it than that."

"The playing of the game provides no ultimate answer," the ball said. "We do not claim this. It is a solution to a specific problem." It paused. "The true meaning of existence has still to be learned. Much is known of the universe and its workings, but what knowledge we have is still only a fraction of the whole."

"But what's the purpose of the game? Why is it being played at all?"

"We are an old race, one of the oldest known." Peter recognized this opening statement, an unconsciously mocking echo of his first conversation with Corma. "In the now distant past we engaged in the possibility that you feared, pillaging and colonizing other worlds. Eventually we outgrew such barbaric and ultimately pointless activity, but later found that similar practices were taking place in your own galaxy. In the process, two empires had emerged, both jealous of the achievements and gains of the other but neither prepared to engage in direct combat. A point had been reached where they continued their parallel routes of conquest with no real interest in constructive utilization of the worlds that were subjugated, seeing them solely as tokens of superiority. We took it upon ourselves to protect others from such attack."

"So that you could salve your consciences?" Peter shot back. I shouldn't have said that, he thought immediately. As a race, we're in no position to criticize, and at least they've acknowledged their own guilt.

"Our reasons for undertaking a task of this magnitude were not entirely benevolent or unselfish," the ball said after a pause. "We had vast power, far in excess of our needs. We recognized the situation both as a means of compensating for past practices and as a way of constructively utilizing such power. Perhaps it has always been our des-

tiny to eventually fill such a role. In time, we largely succeeded in containing the two factions concerned, but the
competitive instinct is strong and a necessary aspect of existence if stagnation and complacency are to be avoided.
The game was devised to partially combat this."

"How is it played?"

"Its basic format is simple. Worlds that have reached a
stage of development where several alternative futures are
available within a relatively short space of time are selected
and monitored. In cases where they are inhospitable in
terms of atmosphere and environment, wide-ranging scanning devices are employed, both on the surface and as orbiting satellites. The compatible qualities offered by your
own planet and others similar to it have allowed us to de-
ploy strategically located guardian personnel among you at
the time of survey, making more detailed study possible.
The information obtained in either way is passed on to the
competitors to permit them to extrapolate predictions with
regard to future development."

So in the recent past another alien race had temporarily
moved among us, Peter thought. And it seemed at least
possible that they weren't the stuff of nightmares, after all,
not in the accepted sense. Well, why should they be? He
glanced past the ball to where Corma still maintained his
bizarre flailing pose. Whatever he was, he demonstrated
that beings very similar to themselves existed elsewhere,
that the universe wasn't necessarily populated with what
men would instinctively regard as biological monstrosities.

But what about the guardians themselves? Were they
human in form? Nothing the ball had said had actually
implied that, he thought. They could be animals, birds, in-
sects; anything, almost. Was that why they were using the

ball instead of appearing in person? He shook his head dismissively. It didn't matter, anyway, and their return was going to be very necessary in the immediate future.

"When somebody makes a correct prediction, what do they win?" he asked curiously.

"There is a graded system of points. These are awarded on the basis of the level of classification and the degree of accuracy attained."

Peter waited. The ball floated motionlessly in front of him, silent now. He said, dumbfounded, "Is that all?"

"That is all. No material gain is involved. The real reward of the contest is the win itself. Materialism has always been irrelevant to the true purpose of competition. It plays no part in the game."

Peter stared at it, confused, wondering what to say. How absurd, he thought; how naively simplistic. Were the answers really that ingenuous? Why, we learned those things thousands of years ago — not that we had paid much attention to them a great deal of the time. Maybe that was what was wrong with the world. We knew the answers, but we let more primitive instincts override them. And, of course, they weren't complete answers, anyway. The ball had acknowledged that.

Peter looked at Corma again. "What will happen to him?" he asked.

"He and the others responsible will be penalized. There is no precedent for this situation, so it is a matter to be considered."

"What about the worlds that they tampered with before? Is it possible to do anything about them?"

"The penalties will in part consist of enforced redress in instances where this will serve any realistic purpose."

Any realistic purpose, Peter thought. It was a simple enough phrase, but the implications that it contained were horrific beyond the scope of his imagination. He suddenly felt very tired. It's all too much, he thought. I can't take any more of this; the concept of a universe in which worlds and their inhabitants are nothing more than inadequately protected game pieces, childishly engaged in their own self-destructive stratagems under the clinically detached gaze of unbelievably old, unbelievably superior beings.

There's an element of decadence about it, too, he thought. And yet, and yet . . . Wasn't it better to play games, however absurd, rather than engage in the irretrievable lunacies of war and conquest?

"What happens now?" he asked. "What about those people up there? What happens to them?"

"They still live, but there have been changes. In all senses, they are older. Their deficiencies remain, but much time has passed for them. For obvious reasons, it will not be possible to return them to their former places and situations. Their knowledge of what has happened must be erased and false memories implanted. All other evidence of what has occurred will also be removed. Alternative identities will be provided to enable them to pursue new lives."

"Better lives?"

The ball said, "That would involve a disruption of the natural order. Such tampering—"

Sudden fury coursed through Peter. He snapped, "What are you talking about, the natural order? That's been shot to hell already! Look, if you hadn't singled us out for this game of yours, none of this would have happened. Whether you like it or not, the responsibility of what's happened here comes back to you. Can't you see that?"

"If we had not intervened and halted the former activities of this one's kind and those of their rivals, your planet would in all probability have been invaded many centuries ago. The playing of the game has permitted you to find your own answers during that time. We consider that what has happened has been a small price to pay for such an extension to your independence."

"But . . ." Peter began, then stopped. It was a valid, unarguable point. "If you wanted to, could you help them?" he asked. "Medically, I mean."

"It would be technically possible to effect certain improvements, but the implications of such action are much greater than you appreciate."

"But you could do it. And you do owe them something, don't you?"

There was a lengthy pause. Eventually the ball said, "What you have said will be considered."

No guarantees, Peter thought. And if they do decide against it, that'll be it for the three people upstairs. They won't even have their dreams as consoling memories. But that would be only too logical, of course. They were losers, with inescapably high levels of fallibility, and he somehow doubted that alteration of such things came within the scope of technical feasibility, even for beings as advanced as the guardians. He felt a final impotent spurt of anger, coupled now with deep pity. "What about me?" he asked. "If you're erasing their memories, then why are you telling me all these things?"

"Your own memory of what has happened must also be removed. Your questions have been answered because your role in this situation and the importance of what you have inadvertently achieved entitles you to this acknowledgment, but it can only be a temporary understanding. But remember for this moment that many worlds and beings will now be permitted to determine their own destinies because of what you have done. Think on this while you can." The ball fell silent.

Peter stared at it, experiencing blessed relief that was only lightly shadowed with disappointment. I don't want to remember it, really, he thought, because if I did it would be impossible for me to take life seriously. And it is serious in its own way, within its own context. It may be all nothing more than a rather bad joke, or some kind of meaningless creative blunder, or an even more crazy game than the one we've been talking about, but a very large part of it is pain and suffering for a lot of people. And it is a kind of game, anyway. We've made up a rough set of rules to enable us to cope with it, but they're full of holes, a rickety set of defenses. When it comes to a lot of things that matter, they stay well beyond any ability we might have to find acceptable answers.

He thought about Hurley and the Negro and the small man, what their lives had been and what they would be from now on. Even if it was decided that physical improvements were permissible, that would be the limit of the compensation granted them. There weren't any rules or scientific solutions that would enable them ever to share the kind of rewards that he knew were there for someone like himself to take, more or less as and when he wished. Again, he felt embarrassment at the injustice of such inequality, while simultaneously recognizing the pointlessness of his guilt.

I hope I remember them, he thought. I won't, not in the true sense of remembering, because they're going to be rubbed out of my mind, along with all the rest of this. But I hope something sticks, a bit more humility, a bit more understanding. If only . . .

"It must be done now," the ball said. It drifted over him, and he felt the cool touch of the metal discs as they nestled against his head.

82

He was driving.

The surrounding country was flat; plowed land that stretched almost to the horizon on both sides of the road. The day was warm, and the road was devoid of other traffic.

The car seemed fine now. The man who had towed him in and fixed whatever had been wrong with the transmission hadn't looked all that bright, but apparently he had known his stuff. I was lucky to find someone like that, Peter thought. Really knowledgeable motor mechanics couldn't have been all that plentiful in a thinly populated area like the one where the breakdown had occurred on the previous day.

He had the odd feeling that something was missing. Did I leave something at the motel? he wondered. He had already been robbed of a day's leave, but the feeling was naggingly insistent. He pulled off the road, stopped the car, and checked his bag. Those blue trousers, he thought. Now, how . . . ? He didn't remember unpacking them, but he must have. Well, that was that. I could always buy a new pair of pants, he thought, but time wasn't so easily come by.

He reached for the ignition, then took his hand away again. He was tired. He ached, too, all over, as though he had been subjecting his body to a degree of exertion that it simply wasn't accustomed to. All that concentrated training over the past few weeks must have really taken it out of him, after all, he thought. He had seemed okay at the time, but this must be some kind of delayed reaction.

He could have picked up a touch of Henry Chasen's virus, of course. Yes, that was more like it. But whatever it was, he didn't really feel up to driving several hundred miles without some rest first. He put his legs across into the space in front of the passenger seat and slid down until his head touched something firm. He was asleep within a couple of minutes. When he awoke, the sun had crossed into the western side of the sky.

He rubbed the sleep from his eyes, damning the further waste of time. But he did feel better — not completely, but he didn't ache quite as much and he wasn't so tired. He glanced at his watch, yawning. Just after three o'clock. Well, that was that; there was no point in wasting more time sitting there bemoaning the fact, and at least the rest seemed to have done him some good.

He made New York by late evening and found the Chasen house without too much difficulty. Henry's brother wasn't there, but his parents were, a pleasantly grave couple who listened patiently to his tale of the breakdown and the out-of-order telephone. Mrs. Chasen showed him to his room and said that she'd make him a sandwich and a drink while he was unpacking. There was a telephone beside the bed that he was welcome to use if he wanted to call anyone.

Of course, he thought; the book, the agent that he'd had an appointment with that morning. For some reason the purpose of his presence there had hardly entered his mind during the latter stages of the drive. It had to do with the still insistent feeling that something was missing, he decided. Not missing, exactly; perhaps lacking was a better description. What was the matter with him? A touch of the sun? Nerves, at the prospect of what the meeting might lead to? It was possible, but somehow he didn't think so. He thought about the book, experiencing sudden embarrassment.

That was it, he thought. It had to be. What had previously seemed to him to be a literary exercise in some depth was now disconcertingly inadequate, almost trivial. What on Earth had they seen in it? he wondered, appalled.

The next morning he telephoned the agent, apologized for his absence on the previous day, and told him how he felt about the book. The agent was polite but surprised. Did Peter want to withdraw the manuscript completely? He personally felt that it only required a little more work to be perfectly acceptable, but he wouldn't want him to feel that he was being pressured in any way, hurried into an agreement that he wasn't going to be happy about.

Yes, that was it, Peter said, at least for the time being. He was suddenly desperately anxious to get home, to be with his father and his mother and his sister. He had missed them when he was at college, but this was an altogether stronger, more urgent feeling. It must be because I'm going off to where I could get shot or blown up, he thought. I might not see them ever again. Oddly, he found this last mental observation somehow unconvincing, almost irrelevant.

The agent expressed his disappointment and said that he hoped Peter would get in touch with him again when he felt ready. Peter apologized again, put the phone down, thanked the Chasens for their hospitality, and caught the first available train to Cleveland. He got in fairly late that evening and took a cab to the house.

83

His father was in the front hall as Peter let himself in. He seemed unsurprised by the arrival, and restricted his greeting to a smile and a remark about how he looked tired.

Of course, Peter thought. This is when they were expecting me. I'm not really a day early at all. He dumped his bag and followed his father into the lounge.

His mother and Margaret were both there, both demonstrably delighted to see him. His mother repeated his father's greeting, and Margaret made facetious suggestions as to the reason for his rather drawn look. He caught a glimpse of himself in the fireplace mirror. She's right, he thought. I look as if I've been out beating up the town instead of biting my nails in a motel for twenty-four-hours. Still a touch of Chasen's disease, whatever it was, probably. He kidded her back, welcoming the flippant beginning to what he knew would be a sad time for all of them.

His mother asked him how the meeting had gone, whether they had wanted him to make many changes to the book. He said he didn't know, that he had decided to shelve it for the time being. He had thought about it and decided that it wasn't right, that he had been attempting something that he wasn't ready for just yet.

They were startled, but apart from some brief speculation from Margaret about his sanity they didn't press him on it. Maybe she's right, he thought. This may have been my big chance, possibly my only one. But when I do it, if I do it, I want it to be right, and it isn't that, not yet.

For the remainder of the week he let their affection and concern wash over him, soothed by it, yet still puzzled by the feeling of omission that continued to haunt him. It was an oddly perverse sensation, he decided. In some ways it was as though instead of being on the verge of going off to what would in all probability be the greatest adventure of his life, he had already returned from it. Some kind of precognition? he wondered. If it was, it could be interpreted as being a cause for optimism, a reassurance from the future that he would come to no lasting harm.

Dangerous stuff, he thought. That's the kind of thinking that can lead to overconfidence. But he still felt comforted by it.

When his leave had ended, the family went with him to the station, where they engaged in the fragmentary, self-conscious conversation of people who are suddenly unsure how to express deep feeling without causing embarrassment to one another.

I can't tell them that I know for sure that I'll be coming back, Peter thought. Not without scaring them, or making them think I'm trotting out the usual empty reassurances. But I do know it, somehow. It's a solid, unshakable fact, like the constancy of my feelings for them and theirs for me.

And still it was there, the feeling of incompleteness. I was wrong, he thought. It wasn't the book, after all; not just the book, anyway. It's as though I'm waiting for a question to be answered. I don't know what the question is, whether it's simply the confirmation of personal survival that only the war's end can bring about with absolute certainty, or whether it's something larger, more abstract, altogether more important. But whatever it is, somehow the madness that's afflicting the world just now is going to at least partially settle it. Wait and see, he told himself, wait and see. That's all you can do, anyway.

He looked at their faces, caring for him, silently willing his survival.

"Don't worry," he said. "I'll look out for myself." He smiled and hugged them. "I'll be okay, you'll see." Believe me, he silently willed them in return.

He got on the train and went away, to survive a war and wait for his answer.